Loren Lockner

Love
Never Dies

To Sherry!
Thanks for
being the best of
friends!
X-mas 2009
Tyan
, Loren Lockner

Love Never
Dies

It's so true!
Loren Lockner

"Love Never Dies," by Loren Lockner. ISBN 1-58939-905-6.

Published 2006 by Virtualbookworm.com Publishing Inc., P.O. Box 9949, College Station, TX 77842, US. ©2006, Loren Lockner. All rights reserved. No part of this publication may be reproduced, stored in a retrieval system, or transmitted in any form or by any means, electronic, mechanical, recording or otherwise, without the prior written permission of Loren Lockner.

Manufactured in the United States of America.

Love Never Dies

by
Loren Lockner

Prologue

"You don't have to do this," stated Angus O'Leary decisively. No one knew better than he how things could go so terribly wrong within a split second and he feared greatly for his younger companion.

His somber counterpart's hand rested resolutely upon the black sedan's door handle as he turned his lean serious face to the man he'd contacted only six weeks prior and had come to like and respect.

"I know," he said mildly, "but the wheels are turning quicker than expected and time is short. If I don't go in there and make an appearance all our hard work is for naught."

"I'm worried about your safety," said Angus gruffly, finding it difficult to verbalize his heartfelt words.

"There is so much more at stake now than my own personal safety. I trust you Angus with my life, as well as Mandy's, and because of that and your

1

incredible dedication to an often thankless job, I will complete my task. For once I have a chance to do something really right in my life and I can't let your concerns for my well-being derail our mission."

The blustery late afternoon breeze was scattering autumn leaves everywhere around Toronto's Humber Bay on Lake Ontario. The wind over the massive lake promised an early winter and Angus adjusted his wool coat accordingly, even though he wasn't vacating the comfortable warmth of the car's gray leather interior anytime soon. The younger man took a deep breath and his steel gray eyes met Angus' reassuringly.

Unfortunately Angus didn't feel remotely reassured. "It's just that this isn't your field or forte. You're doing this more as a favor for the police. If something happens to you I'll never forgive myself."

"All will come right," the raven-haired man promised softly. "You just wait and see. Besides, we've covered our bases and constructed a surefire backup plan." He straightened his shoulders confidently and firmly opened the car door, his obscuring gray trench coat disguising the tall, well-built man he really was. He turned for a brief moment and smiling, lifted a casual hand to Angus before trudging down the darkened street to fulfill his destiny. Angus suddenly had a horrible premonition of danger, but knew nothing could now halt those measured methodical steps, and he wished, not for the first time,

Love Never Dies

that he'd told the quiet man headed so determinedly down the damp street how much he admired both him and the stand he'd taken. Unfortunately now he might never get the chance.

Chapter One

The first moment Julia Morris laid eyes on Seth Hayes she knew she was in big trouble. She'd been lounging around her twin brother's new condominium watching her brother Paul valiantly move his sparse furniture this way and that, trying unsuccessfully to fill up the huge vacant spaces.

"So what do you think Julia? Does the couch go better here or over there near the fireplace?"

"The love seat," corrected Julia, "looks really nice by the fireplace. Unfortunately you need to have a couple of accompanying chairs to fill up the empty spaces. It doesn't matter what you do Paul, this place is far too big for what little furniture you have."

"I know," grumbled Paul, surveying the enormous, brand-spanking-new condominium he'd moved into only a week ago. His mother had often told him about his eyes being bigger than his stomach in relation to food, but he felt that concept might pertain to his taste in living accommodations as well. The first time he laid eyes on this particular condominium located so close to the zoological gardens; he'd vowed to own the overpriced accommodation. He'd borrowed, begged, and disinvested all of his ready cash to make the down payment, but now that he was in, Paul recognized he could barely meet the monthly house payment, much less eat! Not only did he not have enough furniture, but his position as a computer analyst at Tri-Tek was probably not going to be enough to cover the rent, utilities, and buy enough furniture to even hold a decent party.

His twin sister Julia grinned at him maliciously out of identical dark green eyes and for a moment he hated her. After all she had been the one who'd said, "I told you so." But this time Paul David Morris was one step ahead of his attractive younger sister, if a twin can really be considered younger at four minutes and thirty-eight seconds, and had placed an ad in the Santa Barbara Herald seeking a roommate. So far he'd only received three responses to his advertisement and if somebody didn't follow through soon and come up with some cash, he was going to have to do the most dreaded thing he could possibly think of, and that was to borrow money from his sister.

His twin now lounged on his only other couch, twisting her blonde head in accordance to his restless movements as she watched him pace the large interior of the beautiful and spacious condominium. Paul had no doubt his sister would lend him the money if he asked her; in fact he'd even suggested discreetly that she move out of her small apartment and take up residence with him. After all, the condominium did have three bedrooms, two of which overlooked the lush zoological gardens, as well as a huge kitchen that was a chef's dream, a lovely fireplace, and a beautiful dining room. Too bad there wasn't a dining room table to occupy the empty parquet floor!

Julia languidly removed herself from the brown and red plaid couch and followed her brother into the echoing dining room where he stood with his hands on his hips, surveying the empty chamber. So far one tiny house plant sat forlornly upon the windowsill opposite the beautiful built-in bookcase, which housed only twenty or so volumes. Paul sighed drearily.

"I think cherry wood would go beautifully in here," said Julia, casting an appreciative glance around. It had always been her secret desire to fill a dining room with beautiful antique cherry wood and Paul smiled indulgently at his twin. They were so alike in many ways, each possessing the same steady green eyes and straight nose they'd inherited from their grandfather. While both had rich, luxurious hair, Julia's was blonde and streaked golden and white by the sun, while his was a dark dusty brown, admittedly cut a little too long for his mother's taste, but highly attractive to his girlfriend, Angie Carter, who also happened to be his sister's roommate.

He surveyed his sister now as she strolled around the spacious room, admiring the beautiful timbered ceiling and rough-textured wall that gave the room its Tudor-like ambience. Diamond-cut window panes completed the effect and Julia had to admit the room, even without furniture, was simply stunning. Julia Ann Morris stood five-foot-seven in her stocking feet, and while deceptively slender, was strongly built. In her fourth year as a second grade teacher at the local elementary school, her strong sense of humor and gentle, encouraging ways had made her a favorite at Hyatt Elementary. Parents and students alike loved her and Paul could easily see why; not only was she kind and generous, but beautiful to behold, with high cheekbones, an angelic mouth, and their inherited steady green eyes that on Julia appeared ever so much more exotic and interesting than on him.

Julia's hair was cut three inches below her shoulders in a carefree layered manner and today she'd tied it back in a nonchalant, haphazard braid, causing her to appear windblown and delightfully sexy. Paul had to admit that almost everything about his sister was carefree and windblown, and sometimes wished Julia would take a little more notice of her appearance. Why, just look at her now, dressed in those sloppy old green sweatpants half-covered by an oversized yellow t-shirt with a smiling face upon it. Julia didn't look like the femme fatale he knew she could, but perhaps that was for the best, since he wasn't always around to beat off unwanted suitors like he'd done in high school and college.

Julia had left her sandals on the doorstep and walked around barefoot, enjoying the warmth of the parquet floor beneath her toes. At twenty-eight years of age, she appeared to possess no worries and enjoyed every day to its fullest. She felt no rush to hurry into marriage even though countless men eyed her as she strolled by, remaining exasperatingly unmoved by their intense looks of admiration. Paul's friend, Tim Stevens, had expressed an overt interest in Julia, but Paul's twin remained aloof, seemingly content to accompany Paul and Angie for a movie or dinner instead of finding a boyfriend. She only occasionally dated and Paul often accused Julia of being halfhearted about her love life, to which his carefree sister would simply shrug a nonchalant shoulder. Paul had to admit that his sister's present lack of love life took a backseat to the more serious problem at hand.

"You know Julia, I've had a couple of interested guys call up and ask about the condominium. Unfortunately, two told me flat out that what I want is way too expensive."

"So what are you asking to rent this place?"

Love Never Dies

"Two hundred twenty-five a week and half the utilities, but they get their own garage space, a beautiful en-suite bathroom, a wonderful kitchen, and an incredible view."

"I know, I know, it's indeed lovely Pauli, but I'm just not sure that this was the time in your life to buy, and now I'm afraid you're going to end up in serious financial difficulty."

Paul turned a frustrated eye on his perceptive sister. "Your point is well-taken, but I wanted to have something to offer Angie, when and if I ever ask her to marry me. And don't you go and tell her I'm even considering matrimony."

"My lips are sealed," said Julia, deciding then and there it was high time to help her brother out. Angie was the best thing that ever happened to her brother and she wasn't about to let her beloved twin fail to woo the woman he loved. Julia, however, planned to let him sweat for awhile, not willing to let Paul off the hook so easily, since her brother had proverbially once again 'leapt before he looked' when he'd bought the too-expensive condo.

"Anyway," continued her brother, not realizing his sister was really on his side. "I'm going to try and set up my ornery computer. Do you think I could coax you into making some of that delicious lemonade you always seem to whip up so frightfully fast? I have some fresh lemons. Maybe that will cheer me up."

"No problem," said Julia, and she strolled into the modern kitchen, smiling affectionately after his preoccupied departure into his office.

It had crossed her mind more than once to move in with him and help relieve the burden of the cost of this new condominium, but she was happy living with Angie in their modest two bedroom flat, ten minutes from her brother's condominium. A loan was a much better alternative she decided. Besides, what was she going to use the money for anyway? She had just finished squeezing the lemons and was adding a brimming cupful of sugar when the doorbell rang.

"Pauli, there's somebody at the door," she called, but apparently her brother was too deeply immersed in the wiring of his computer to hear, so she ambled to the entryway herself, swinging the door open wide without so much as a single thought to inquiring who it might be first.

It was with almost a physical blow that she recoiled from the tall man standing before her, dressed stylishly in a smoke gray three-piece suit, his eyes matching the color of the tailored suit precisely. The stranger's dark hair hung long and layered, nearly reaching his shoulders, and he carried a briefcase in one hand and a newspaper in the other. He appeared startled at her appearance and his eyes flicked downward to the newspaper folded in quarters in his hand as if he'd made a serious mistake.

10

Love Never Dies

"Um, is this the Morris residence?" he asked hesitantly in rich tones.

"Yes it is," answered Julia, noting the serious glint to his eyes and striking features of his face. Lean and broad-shouldered, he carried himself well, though his face was a bit too somber and reserved for complete attractiveness. That incredible reserve suggested a man most would find frustratingly difficult to know, and Julia decided then and there she wished to become better acquainted.

"I'm here to answer the ad about the condominium..." he questioned tentatively, and suddenly Julia realized he was one of her twin's prospective roommates.

"Oh, please come in. You're looking to rent one of the rooms. I'll get Paul." She rushed away, suddenly conscious of her worn sweatpants and oversized t-shirt, never realizing his lips twitched appreciatively at the sight of her bare, hurrying feet. Her brother squatted upon the plush carpet as he bent over his uncooperative computer mumbling incoherently to no one in particular.

"There's a man here about the room and I let him in. I don't know what his name is, but he looks really interested." And *interesting* Julia added silently to herself.

Paul jerked up so rapidly that he hit his head on the desk and rubbed it absently. "So someone finally came. If he asks, tell him there's furniture coming," he muttered conspiratorially to his sister as he preceded her out the doorway to survey the tall serious man standing in the foyer.

"Hi," said Paul, wiping his hand on his blue jeans before extending it to the stranger. "My name's Paul Morris and I take it you're here about the ad?"

"Yes I am," returned the businessman. "I'm seeking a place that is quiet and removed from the city center and your ad suggested this place has lots of great amenities."

"This place is peaceful all right, mostly because the condominium next to us isn't even occupied yet and the zoological gardens border our grounds. If it's quiet you want you've come to the right place. You are?" her brother asked politely.

"I'm sorry," said the other man contritely, "my name is Seth Hayes. I'm a junior architect with the firm Bastam, Hughes, and Glickstern. I'm new in town and desperately need a place to live. I've been camping out in a hotel and was hoping to find a place right away."

"You could have immediate occupancy here, though as you recall from the ad, you'll have to supply your own bedroom furniture."

"I can do that," said the man mildly, and flicked his eyes over Julia who smoothed the front of her droopy sweats and wished the floor would swallow her up. Never before had she met a man so attractive or with such a beautiful a voice and of course she looked positively despicable herself. However, he seemed to take no notice of her appearance in the least and returned his silver gaze to her brother.

"So you still have a room available?"

"Two as a matter-of-fact. You can have your pick. Would you care to see them?"

Seth nodded and followed Paul down the wide hall. Paul opened the first door on his right, which revealed a spacious bedroom with immaculate en-suite bathroom facilities. While it didn't have a view of the Zoological gardens, the large balcony overlooked the complex's huge oval pool, tastefully manicured gardens, and an unusual waterfall feature connected to a Koi pond. Seth surveyed the large room with its built in bookcases and wide window seat before opening the mirrored doors of the huge walk-in closet lined with cedar.

"It's truly an exceptional room," he commented. "I believe this would do nicely."

"I think before you make a decision you should check out the other room," said Paul. "It's located at the end of the hall and just down from my office. My room is the last one on the left and there's a guest washroom just there. One of the reasons I bought this place is that three of its rooms have a view of the zoological gardens; the master bedroom, the office next door, and this bedroom on the right."

13

The next chamber, though slightly smaller than the beautiful suite already shown to Seth, had a similarly wide balcony with a lovely view of the vast gardens and its towering trees, brick walkways, and occasional peacock. Sunlight poured into the large room and an open doorway revealed a modern, spacious bathroom with a skylight and sparkling chrome fixtures.

"Very tasteful," said Seth, after emerging from the tiled bathroom complete with clean gray tiles, huge built-in Jacuzzi tub, and double spray shower.

A medium-sized brick fireplace faced the room, which also contained a nice-sized nook leading onto a huge balcony whose wide expanse could easily house a table and four chairs and whose view could not be faulted. Seth stood quietly and observed a stately peacock strut under a gum tree for a moment while a trio of mallard ducks quacked in the distance.

"You're asking two hundred and twenty-five dollars a week, and half the utilities?"

"Yes. The only drawback is the place is pretty much unfurnished."

Seth set down his briefcase and analyzed the room once again, his silver eyes appreciating the vaulted ceiling, numerous plant nooks, and subtle mushroom-colored walls.

"I suspect you use the office yourself. Would there be any way I could get a telephone line in here?"

Love Never Dies

"It's not a problem. I was planning to get a DSL line anyway, though it might be a couple of weeks before it's functional. You know how the phone company is."

"Yes," said Seth quietly to himself. "This will do quite nicely. You indicated I could move in right away?"

Paul's green eyes lit up delightedly, "You can move in today if you want, but unfortunately there's no furniture."

"And when will your furniture be arriving?"

Julia crossed her arms and glanced down at the floor, but not before Seth caught her muffled grin.

"Well," stumbled Paul, "the furniture is coming in stages."

"I see," said Seth, and Julia was certain he did.

"Let me show you the rest of the place," said Paul eagerly, afraid his prospective roommate might vanish because of the so obvious lack of furniture. Seth followed him into the beautifully modern kitchen with its double oven, center island, and walk-in pantry; the lovely empty dining room; and finally, the echoing living area with its massive fireplace and lovely timbered ceiling. Paul even showed him the hall closet and guest bathroom.

"So the furniture is coming in stages," observed Seth. "You know, I have a few additional pieces just sitting in storage. Would you mind if I brought a dining room table, a few chairs, and some miscellaneous pieces until your other furniture arrives?" His handsome face remained serious, never once reflecting the humor of the moment.

Paul cleared his throat, his cheeks slightly pink. "Furniture would be appreciated."

"Then I'll move in this weekend." The two men shook on it and as Seth retrieved his checkbook from his briefcase to write Paul a deposit, Julia decided it was high time to leave.

"I've got to go," said Julia suddenly. "I'll see you tomorrow Paul." She placed an arm around her brother and kissed him soundly on the cheek.

"Give me a call later," said Paul, so obviously relieved by his incredible luck that Julia found it hard not to laugh.

"Of course." Julia nodded a head to the professionally dressed Seth, once again acutely aware of her sloppy but comfortable attire. "It was very nice meeting you Mr. Hayes. I hope you enjoy living here with Paul." Her brother walked her to the door and she whispered under her breath for only him to hear. "You lucked out you this time Pauli! See if you can get him to sign a year lease."

With that she departed as quickly as decently possible. As she hurried out to her aging Taurus she determined that she'd have to visit her brother again very soon with some sort of housewarming gift. Next time, his new roommate Seth Hayes, would catch her in something much more stylish than discarded gym wear and bare feet.

Seth Hayes remained true to his word and moved in within forty-eight hours, bringing with him a lovely dining room table and six chairs in beautiful mahogany with a matching sideboard, as well as a large and ornate mirror, which he and Paul hung in the living room. He also supplied two dark brown recliners, an overstuffed rust-colored leather sofa, and an incredible ornately carved grandfather clock. His generosity also included a unique Indonesian end table, a glass and oak coffee table, a full set of copper cookware, a coat rack, and Paul's favorite items; two large beautiful and worn Persian rugs, one which he spread under the dining room table and the other before the comfortable leather sofa. Its muted red designs complimented the couch and the room, and suddenly the condo had gone from bare and echoing to warm and homey.

Seth furnished his own bedroom with a beautiful mahogany bedroom set whose high four-poster king-sized bed dominated the lovely room. A matching dresser and chest of drawers hugged the left-hand side wall and a huge entertainment center, upon which rested a gigantic TV, DVD player, and stereo system, set near the alcove by the window. Seth used the comfortably sized nook as an office and placed a large ebony desk near the French doors. He set up his own computer and promised to wait patiently for the new telephone line. Best yet, his check for the first and last months rent, as well as a hefty deposit, had already cleared the bank. Paul could now afford to pay the mortgage and eat!

On Monday night Angie and Julia put in an appearance. The dark-haired Angie strolled around the condo in justified amazement at its incredible transformation.

"This place is absolutely stunning," she said after kissing her lover and admiring the Indonesian table with its delicately curved legs and intricate carvings of exotic birds.

"It is indeed," said Julia, gazing first at the beautiful mirror and secondly at the healthy philodendron resting on the end table near the tall coat rack.

"So where's your new roommate?" she asked her brother, who sniffed the air appreciatively before answering. His sister smelled very nice indeed.

"Not home from work yet."

"So what's he like?" asked Julia, as nonchalantly as possible.

"Ah ha, so you *are* interested!"

"I never said I was interested; I just wondered if he's working out that's all."

Love Never Dies

"Oh, he is," said Paul grinning. It wasn't often he'd seen his sister so dolled up or so inquisitive about a member of the opposite sex. "He seems to be the quiet sort. I don't hear much from him because he rises early each morning. Seth takes an early morning jog, eats yogurt and fruit for breakfast, dresses to the nines for work, and takes his very expensive briefcase along with him with little or no fuss. He's not very chatty, but when he asks a question, I get the feeling he actually *listens* to the answer. He's not a very smiley man if I do say so myself, but his money's good and the place looks great. Best yet, do you know what he can do?"

"What?" asked Angie, placing an arm around Paul's slim waist, delighted her boyfriend appeared so thrilled.

"He can cook! He asked me yesterday morning if I'd like him to whip something up for dinner, and lo and behold when I came back, he'd made this incredible lasagna with a tossed green salad and garlic bread. I didn't even know he'd gone to the market. I had leftovers today at work and it was absolutely wonderful. There's still some in the refrigerator; would you like to stay for dinner?"

"Maybe his culinary skills will rub off on you," said Julia, always amused by her brother's hopeless attempts at cooking, as she helped her brother and Angie set the table for dinner. Within minutes Seth arrived, appearing slightly put off at the slight of the two girls. Angie ogled the tall man dressed impeccably in a slim black suit with wide lapels.

Paul growled irritably. "This is my girlfriend Angie Carter and my sister's roommate. You, of course, met Julia the other day. I hope you don't mind, but I'm serving up the rest of the lasagna you baked last night."

Seth, strangely disconcerted, glanced from one young woman to the other. Angie gave him a big smile, the pretty dimple in the middle of her chin reflecting her sunny disposition and open nature. Dark-haired and more endowed than Julia, she possessed an attractive smattering of freckles across her nose. Angie had been Paul's girlfriend for over two years and an acquaintance of Julia for nearly five. A devout Catholic, she had adamantly refused to move in with Paul, much to both sets of parents' relief. Seth's steel gray eyes studied Julia's.

"I didn't realize you were Paul's sister," he stated quietly. "I thought you were his girlfriend."

"Nah," said Paul, sidling up to his sister and giving her an affectionate punch on the arm, "she's my little sister."

"Oh give it a break Paul," scolded Angie. "She's only four minutes younger than you."

"Twins," verified Seth softly, a strange expression flitting over his handsome face as he examined them both closely. "Yes, I do believe I see a family resemblance. Twins are an amazing phenomenon and they run in my family as well." He didn't expound on his quiet comment and later, when it was far too late, Julia was going to wish she'd queried Seth more about the twin situation in his family.

Twenty minutes later they sat at the beautiful mahogany table in the newly furnished dining room devouring Seth's delicious lasagna.

"So he can cook too," chortled Angie, smiling happily at Seth who for one had barely touched his food. He seemed rather distant and didn't contribute to the merriment of the trio at the table.

"You're awfully quiet," stated Paul a few minutes later. "Tough day at the office?"

"You might say that," agreed Seth. A man of few words, there clearly existed an overlying aloofness he appeared determined to maintain. Seth put up with the forced company of Angie and Julia, but when the first opportunity arose, he retreated to his room after taking his plate into the kitchen and placing it inside the dishwasher.

"I'm sorry, but I have some paperwork to do. It was very nice meeting you Angie and you again Julia," he said softly before fading into the dim light of the hall and shutting his bedroom door.

"I'll help you with the dishes Paul," said Angie, following her boyfriend into the kitchen.

Julia picked up her utensils and plate, feeling vaguely disappointed. She had consciously made herself more presentable this evening, donning sea foam green pants and a matching top and brushing her hair until it shone before fastening it back with a pretty pearl-beaded clip. She had even filed her finger and toe nails, painting them a subtle pink, but it hadn't made any sort of impression on the aloof young architect so she tossed her head dismissively. He might possess the most incredible eyes she'd ever seen, but he didn't appear in the least interested so she might as well not waste her time.

It was probably better in the long run since she was subject to popping in on her brother unexpectedly, and if there wasn't any attraction between them her constant visits to her brother would be much less awkward. So Julia tried, and nearly succeeded, to put Seth out of her mind.

The next few times she arrived at her brother's condo Seth was home. A reserved man, he never joined in their conversation, often removing himself to his room within a few minutes to do paperwork, or whatever it was he did there. Twice she heard noise coming from his room; once in the haunting lilt of classical music and the other as canned laughter from a nightly sitcom. Seth never made apologies for his behavior or tried to be more sociable; he simply remained distant. His strange behavior caused Julia to wonder if he'd suffered some sort of personal loss, but she decided not to waste any more time speculating upon his anti-social behavior, which was easier said than done.

For Paul, he was the perfect roommate; quiet, responsible, and neat. If Paul noticed his sister's begrudging attraction to the aloof man, he never commented on it, instead focusing his attention upon upgrading his condominium. Angie often visited the condo and Seth seemed more inclined to talk to her, often querying Angie about her hectic job as a pediatric nurse at the Santa Barbara Community Hospital.

Angie told him all about her little patients and how they dealt with life and disease and Julia could hear the depth of his compassion in his beautiful melodic voice. In contrast, Seth neither asked Julia anything about her work as a teacher, nor ever commented upon the warm relationship she maintained with her brother or parents who often visited the condominium as well. It was as if her lifestyle and career were too dull to warrant even a polite question from him and her unbidden attraction to the tall, dark-haired man almost turned into a form of hostility.

Julia's father, much to Julia's chagrin, became casual friends with Seth. Several times Seth shared with Jim Morris some of his blueprints for a local duplex development he was currently working on for Lenny Glickstern. Her dad mentioned him once again as Julia sat at a late night supper with her parents after a back-to-school night. It was mid-November and the weather had turned chilly, raining dismally over the past three nights and dampening her normally upbeat spirits.

"I believe Paul's roommate Seth is one of the best architects I've ever met," observed Jim Morris.

Julia picked at her broccoli and cheese stuffed baked potato disinterestedly. "Is he now?" she asked exasperatedly.

"Yes. He seems to have a real grasp of how to blend multiple building styles, but never disrupt the Mediterranean and Spanish red-tiled standard that has exemplified our city all these years."

Santa Barbara was indeed a lovely old town, originally built around the mission developed by Father Jun'pero Serra and still hosting one of the most famous missions in California. That, coupled with the fact Santa Barbara was a huge university town boasting an extremely lovely beach, made it an enchanting place to reside. Though a bit pricey, Julia balanced that against her evening jogs on the beach, the vibrant night life available from a city that catered to the university students, and the close proximity to her family. Right now, she couldn't imagine living anywhere else.

"Seth's voice is so unusual, not quite northeastern or Canadian. He told me he hailed from upstate New York, but his accent doesn't quite ring true and I suspect he's traveled a great deal. Have you gotten to know him well?" her father asked, as he cut a slice off his rare steak. Jim had managed to coax his wife Helen into giving him steak even though he was supposed to be watching his cholesterol.

"No, I've only seen him a few times and he seems very quiet and distant. I don't think he likes me much at all."

"Really?" asked her father, cocking his head at Julia's mother. "He's queried me all about what you were teaching, that sort of thing you know."

"That's right," asserted Helen. "The last time I visited Paul, he probably asked at least twenty questions regarding you. What you taught, the age group, where you'd gone to university. He seemed very interested indeed. In fact it sounded like you guys were great friends. You know," said her mother, crinkling her sharp green eyes. "You could do a whole lot worse."

Julia frowned at her mother's red hair. "You can quit your matchmaking, Mom. First of all he's not interested and second, remember what happened when I dated Tim Stevens? I certainly don't want a repeat of that situation, so I'll pick my own boyfriends thank you very much."

Tim Stevens had been one of Paul's best friends since high school and currently served as a manager of one of the Rite-On Drugstores downtown. He was well–to-do, tall, and slightly balding. He came across as one of the sweetest men Julia had ever met; sweetest and most boring, until he'd started groping her in his fancy car and wouldn't take no for an answer. To her, Tim was like some sort of Dr. Jekyll and Mr. Hyde character; sweet to her family and a monster to her.

Julia had gone out with him many times at the encouragement of both her brother and parents, who'd been acquainted with his family for years. After one particularly hideous evening where she'd actually been forced to punch him the mouth to get him to back off, Julia vowed she'd never date anyone her parents or brother set her up with again, no matter how well-meaning they were. She realized how a man appears to his buddies and her parents, isn't always a guarantee he'll treat a woman with respect.

Now, because she was attracted to Seth herself and her father spoke so highly of him, Julia felt doubly on guard. It irked her that the young architect always ignored her, which compelled Julia to say something nasty about him.

"He seems very egotistical and stuck up; not my type at all."

Her father observed her shrewdly and set down his knife and fork while Helen Morris made a show of adding more seasoning salt to her baked potato. "I wasn't asking you to go out with him Julia. I just thought that maybe you were friends or something since he's obviously so interested in your routine. It was my mistake sweetie, thinking there might be something more there. I promise I won't bring him up again," he stated, and moved on to other subjects.

Later, however, when she had time to think about it, her father's words disturbed her. Just why did Seth avoid her every time he saw her, but later pump her parents with questions about her life? Could he be interested in her after all? She made up her mind then and there to figure out what made Seth tick, if it killed her.

The Tuesday before the Thanksgiving holiday Julia knocked on her brother's door and he opened it with a wide grin before appearing sheepish.

"Oh hi Sis," he said awkwardly. "You are, um, coming for a visit?"

"Well yes. I thought I'd pop in for a few minutes if you don't mind. I want to talk to you about Thanksgiving dinner at Mom and Dad's and what you're supposed to bring. Are you busy or something?"

"No, not at all," said her brother and let her in. He seemed tense and out of sorts and as she followed him into the beautiful living room Julia observed Tim Stevens sitting upon the couch. He flashed his wide toothy grin and Julia felt her heart sink.

"Long time no see," chirped Tim. "Just where have you been keeping yourself Julia? I've missed your beautiful face Sweetheart."

Loren Lockner

Paul beamed as Julia winced. She'd never informed her brother about Tim's inappropriate advances so Paul smiled delightedly, still hoping Tim and Julia would make the perfect match.

"Been working," said Julia evasively. "How's everything going at Rite-On Drugstore?"

"Great. We're opening another store real soon in Montecito. I may have to go over there and train the new manager. It's quite a position of responsibility you know," he boasted.

"I can imagine."

Tim's eyes focused upon the front of her peach blouse and Julia squirmed. "Anyway, maybe you'd like to check out the new store sometime? It's near the golf course and because of the large retirement community we cater to retirees. We have a larger than usual pharmacy, as well as lots of additional foodstuffs just to help the seniors in case they don't want to run to the market for the milk or whatnot."

Julia pretended interest and settled across from him in one of the coffee brown recliners Seth had added to the room. The chair was comfortable and warm on this chilly day and her brother had lit a fire in the brick fireplace, infusing the condominium with warmth and hospitality. Paul had added a few paintings of rustic mountain scenes and a beautifully framed photograph of her deceased great-grandmother and grandfather who'd arrived in San Francisco by wagon over 110 years ago.

"Can you stay for dinner Julia?" asked Paul exuberantly, warming to his role as matchmaker.

"Uh, well, I'm not sure Paul. Since it's so dismal and rainy, I'd better hurry home before it gets too dark."

"Ah come on. It's going to be simple, just tacos, and then you won't have to cook and eat a meal all by your lonesome. Say you'll stay?"

"Oh alright," relented Julia. She'd secretly hoped to see Seth, determined to get a handle on the mysterious man she was so reluctantly attracted to. "Is Seth here?"

"Nope, hasn't showed up," answered Paul. "I'll just trot to the kitchen now and start getting the tacos ready. Maybe you and Tim can set the table?"

"We'd be happy to," declared Tim, leaping up and following Paul into the kitchen. It wasn't until Paul was halfway through making the tacos that he discovered he was missing two key ingredients; meat and refried beans. This was typical Paul, always plunging ahead without making sure he was really ready.

"Not to worry," he said. "The market is only five minutes away. I'll run down there and if you'll make the salad I'll be back lickety-split."

"Um, maybe I'll go," said Julia, not wanting to be left alone with the over amorous Tim.

"It's my fault that I don't have the ingredients so I wouldn't dream of making you go out in this weather," said Paul, grabbing his coat and keys and scurrying out the door before she could protest. Tim grinned his too-friendly smile and Julia could do nothing but hope the distraction of making the salad would keep the store manager's mind off of her.

After they finished making the salad, Julia moved to the snapping fireplace and held her hands before it even though she wasn't cold, uncomfortable with Tim's close proximity.

"I've missed you," said Tim quietly behind her, placing his hands upon her shoulders. Julia tried to shrug them off but he only moved closer, his breath nuzzling her ear while the overpowering scent of his too-liberally applied cologne clogged her breath.

"I don't know why you keep running away from me Julia. We've always had an overwhelming attraction to each other."

"Speak for yourself," retorted Julia. "I'm not remotely attracted to you Tim. I could like you as a friend but you've made any sort of relationship intolerable because of your continuous advances. Now please could you move away?"

"I know you could love me if you'd just give me a chance," said Tim, moving even closer. "And our families would be so thrilled." He looped his arms around her torso, locking her in an embrace, as he forced her back again his chest. His hot breath was insistent as he leaned forward, whispering dirty suggestions in her ear. Neither heard the door open nor noticed Seth entering the foyer. He stopped to wipe his wet shoes upon the doormat and hung up his umbrella, suddenly tensing as he heard Julia's adamant voice.

"I've told you before to leave me alone, now get away from me," demanded Julia, slamming an elbow into Tim's stomach. He snarled as she pushed away from him, forcibly turning her and kissing her passionately, grinding his teeth against her protesting mouth. Julia leaned back and slapped him violently across the face, which only enflamed him more. He restrained her one arm and reached for her breast, totally beyond reason. Julia fought violently, realizing she was in real danger of being raped.

"Stop it Tim!" she ground out, trying to move her head away from his questing mouth. "I told you before I'm not interested; why can't you get that through your thick head!"

She was suddenly slammed against the brickwork of the fireplace and Tim ground his hips against her while kissing her bruised mouth as she struggled and tore at him, managing once to scratch his face.

"The lady said let her be. I suggest you do it mister."

If Seth's deliberate tones ever penetrated Tim's lustful preoccupation, the store manager didn't respond. Instead he continued groping Julia who fought furiously. Seth placed a hand upon Tim's left shoulder and pulled him back, his fingers tightening cruelly upon the bony shoulder. Tim retorted and swung, hitting wildly at whoever dared try and thwart his enflamed actions. Julia had never seen a man move so fast. One moment Tim struck out at Seth and the next lay flat on his back, his nose spewing blood over his disbelieving face. Tim groaned and grabbed the protruding member between his hands as blood gushed out, staining the parquet floor.

"I do believe the lady said no more than once," stated Seth nonchalantly, peering down at the man he'd just brutally slammed to the ground, a very self-satisfied expression on his perfect face.

"Who the hell are you?" cried Tim, managing to sit up straight though his freckled nose still streamed blood.

"I'm Paul's roommate and a friend of Julia's, and I suggest that if you don't want Paul to personally toss you out of his condominium after using you as his private punching bag, you'd better leave while you can. It probably goes without saying that I don't want to see your face around here ever again." Seth by this time had returned to the coat rack, and picking up Tim's blue windbreaker, waited for the thin man to rise awkwardly from the slippery floor.

Tim gazed long and hard at Julia before finally shaking his head violently. "You ain't worth it babe," he scoffed scornfully; grabbing his coat from Seth's outstretched hand. The door was already open and Seth slammed it behind him. Reaction to the incident finally hit home and Julia, from where she remained before the crackling fire, shivered as if from cold.

Seth approached her, the smug expression fleeing his face. "Are you alright?"

"If you hadn't come along I think . . . I think..."

"I think you're right," said Seth soothingly. "Here, sit down. I'll get you something that's certain to make those shakes disappear." His hands gently pushed her onto the comfortable recliner positioned before the fire and he hurried into the kitchen. Julia heard the slosh of some liquid being poured into a glass as she stretched her suddenly cold hands toward the revitalizing flames.

Seth knelt before her, handing her a brandy glass whose amber liquid beckoned enticingly. "Drink this up, it'll help."

Julia swallowed a gulp of the strong, warming liquid, gasping as it burned its way down her throat.

"Did he hurt you?" asked Seth tightly.

"I think I'll have a few bruises, but I'm alright. Please, please don't tell Paul."

"On the contrary," countered Seth, leaning back to examine her tear-streaked face. "I believe you should inform your brother. He's probably not aware of his friend's unwanted advances, and unless you enlighten him, you can be certain that Tim will do it again, if not with you, then with someone else. It's important everyone's righteous indignation toward sexual abuse is clearly relayed to animals such as Tim."

Julia recognized the validity of his words and nodded, a single tear trickling down her cheek. Seth leaned forward and wiped off the warm drop. "I guess he felt some of *your* righteous indignation," she managed to quip.

Seth grinned smugly and fumbled in his pocket for his handkerchief, which he handed her gently.

"Thank you," Julia mumbled before glancing down, unable to meet those beautiful gray eyes. She blew her nose and wiped her eyes, grateful he didn't belabor the point.

"No thanks necessary. I'm just glad my timing was right. I'll tell you what... I'll relate what happened to your brother if that will make you feel better. You sit here and finish up the brandy. I noticed a couple of blood droplets on the parquet and I'll wipe them up before your brother arrives."

Seth headed to the kitchen and returning with a wet dish towel wiped up the evidence of Tim's broken nose. Later, he sank upon the love seat across from her and analyzed her with his silvery eyes.

"Feeling any better?" Before she could respond the door opened and her brother's loud voice echoed through the entryway.

"I not only got beef and refried beans; I found a little guacamole and sour cream. These are going to be the best tacos I've made in a long time." He stopped short at the sight of a Seth but no Tim. "Where's Tim? Is everything okay?"

"I'm afraid your friend Tim had to go home. Julia, why don't you take the groceries into the kitchen for your brother? Paul, could I speak to you for a moment in my room?"

Paul glanced from Julia to Seth before handing the plastic bags to his sister.

Ten minutes later he emerged from Seth's bedroom, rage reddening his face while his hands curled into white-knuckled fists.

"If Tim ever tries anything with you again Julia, you let me know. He's not welcome in my house, my parents' house, or anyone else I know for that matter! I'm planning to tell mom and dad what he did and ask them to relay his despicable actions to his parents. If we let him get away with this kind of stuff he's just going to do it again. I wish you'd have told me earlier about the real reasons you didn't like him."

"I tried," answered Julia as she spooned the guacamole out into a small blue ceramic bowl and placed it upon the table. "You just didn't want to listen. Mom and Dad knew how I felt but I couldn't seem to get through to you."

Her brother sidled forward to enfold her in a warm embrace and kissed her on the forehead. "I'm so sorry. Sometimes I'm just not alert to things like that.

Please forgive me. Thanks Seth for explaining it all to me, *and* arriving when you did. I'm just glad it put a stop to his unwanted advances and that he took your advice and left."

Julia eyed Seth as he gave a tiny shake of his head, realizing Seth hadn't revealed how Tim had been requested to leave. She smiled broadly. "Yes, it was very fortuitous Seth showed up when he did and since we've made enough tacos for three, won't you please join us for dinner?"

Seth studied her dark green eyes for a long moment before answering half-reluctantly, "I'd be happy to."

Darkness engulfed Seth's room as he sat alone and contemplative upon his beautiful mosaic bedspread. He gazed moodily through the window at the few stars flickering valiantly as they tried to break through the heavy cloud cover. Seth rubbed the back of his stiff neck and sighed. This was a dangerous game he played. He'd knowingly embarked on something best left dormant, allowing himself the joy of Julia's company this evening. It'd been pleasurable to watch the twins banter, so comfortable in that natural camaraderie they always shared. He'd tried to ignore her, to distance himself from her undeniable beauty and wit, but tonight fate had intervened and forced him near the most attractive woman he'd ever met.

Seth had no doubt Julia could have handled the situation by herself and suspected Tim may have achieved worse than a broken nose after she'd finished with him, but had wanted to step in. He'd wanted Julia to know he wasn't immune to her. So he sat forlornly on his big bed, knowing he shouldn't think about her but was powerless to stop. He tensed, suddenly afraid that after all this time he'd finally run across his soul mate and at a time he could least afford.

Chapter Two

Kerry Matthews was used to unusual things happening at Hyatt Elementary School. That morning she'd already dealt with a child who'd swallowed an eraser, a late bread delivery man, a stray dog she'd personally had to chase out of the front office, and the school nurse going home ill. So when at 11:10 that morning, just before the bell announced lunch for the lower grades, a blue-clad flower deliveryman showed up, she wasn't remotely surprised.

"Yes?" she asked sweetly, approaching the L-shaped desk that fronted the elementary office to greet the slightly perspiring Hispanic man who placed a large vase jammed with roses upon the counter.

"A delivery for Julia Morris," he said politely.

Kerry was just a little put out; having secretly hoped that her husband for once had remembered their anniversary. She and Tyrone had been married for almost two decades, which was nearly a record in divorce-torn California, and particularly among African-Americans, and had hoped that just this once he'd remember. So she smoothed back her perfect ebony hair and let herself succumb to blatant curiosity.

"Julia Morris," she said. "My oh my!" She scrutinized the twelve long-stemmed red roses surrounded by baby's breath resting inside the lovely porcelain vase and signed for the flowers.

She left the beautiful bouquet sitting on the counter for a while, knowing Julia and her counterparts weren't due in the lunchroom for another twenty minutes. The fragrance of the roses filled the front office and when the principal, Connie Fernandez, ventured out of her office to ask Kerry something, her dark eyes lit up.

"Tyrone remembered your anniversary?"

Kerry put on a fake pout. "No. If he did he would ruin his track record. These are for *Julia*."

Connie's grin widened. Julia was one of her favorite teachers and after working at her school for nearly five years, had never once received a flower delivery.

"Well it's about time," she observed. "I think the bell's about to ring," and as if on cue the shrill elementary school bell echoed, announcing to students and teachers alike they were on reprieve for a full forty minutes; the children to eat for twenty minutes and then go to recess, and the teachers to wolf their food down before hurriedly preparing for the upcoming afternoon session.

"I'll think I'll take these into her myself," said Connie, who'd always considered herself a good friend of Julia. "I want to see the expression on her face. Is there a card?' she asked.

"Why Principal Fernandez," said Kerry. "You know I'd never peek at the card."

"What does it say?" demanded Connie.

"Thank you for the lovely dinner and is signed by someone named Seth."

"Ooh, I haven't heard of this Seth before. Well," said the principal, hoisting up the large bouquet of flowers, "let's see what her reaction is."

Julia settled herself down to lunch and gazed forlornly at her bacon, lettuce, and tomato sandwich and wondering how on earth she'd forgotten to spread mayonnaise upon the wheat slices. She glanced up to see her principal approach with the largest bouquet of flowers she'd ever seen.

"Well, well," said Connie, a wry look on her normally serious Latino face. "I didn't know you had a secret admirer," and with that she clunked the roses smack dab in the middle of the faculty lounge table.

Julia's counterparts Leroy, Martha, and Tracy all ooh'd and aah'd, appearing thoroughly impressed.

Love Never Dies

"Well aren't you going to read the card?" asked Tracy, frowning. She sniffed appreciatively and leaned forward to snag the card from its holder until Julia deftly plucked it from her hands. Julia read the note and smiled.

"Well?" said Leroy, munching on a carrot stick. "Aren't you going to spill it girl?"

"It's just from my brother's roommate," Julia replied. "His name is Seth and we had dinner last night at my brother's apartment that's all."

"I was hoping that it was going to be a lot spicier than that, and don't you folks believe that it must have been a mighty nice dinner to warrant *twelve* red roses?" said Connie in mock disgruntlement.

"Don't you have some paperwork to catch up on?" said Julia to her principal, refusing to rise to the bait.

"I know you'll tell me all about it later at the racquetball court," announced Connie knowingly before she departed, humming a nauseating little love song Julia had heard on the radio that very morning. Leroy laughed aloud and Martha gave Julia her best motherly know-it-all glance.

The roses' sweet fragrance filled the air and Julia, not able to stand her colleague's comments any longer, lifted up the heavy bouquet of roses, her sandwich, and some papers she needed to photocopy and hurried to the work room. Seth's dark eyes materialized before her as she Xeroxed the worksheets for her twenty students, wondering what on earth had motivated him to send flowers. Whatever the reason it didn't help her overactive imagination.

It hadn't been enough that she couldn't stop thinking about him after she'd returned last night or that Seth had been her first waking thought this morning. She reread the card and sighed, dreamily lifting the fragrant bouquet to her nostrils before heading back to her classroom, bracing herself for that last energetic burst of energy from her pupils before the four-day weekend.

Her cell phone was ringing as she unlocked her car later that afternoon. She always left her cell phone in its stand because phones were not allowed in the classroom. She braced the lovely bouquet between the door and her tote bag and lifted the receiver to her ear, surprised and pleased to hear Seth's beautiful, even voice.

"Did you get my roses?" he asked softly.

"That I did," said Julia, "and much to the envy of the entire elementary staff. You didn't need to send them but thank you very much."

"I wondered," began Seth tentatively, "if perhaps, even though it's really late notice, you might be free for dinner?" Julia couldn't know that he was mentally kicking himself behind the closed door of his office. He'd been peering sightlessly at some blueprints for the new shopping center near the university and had completed absolutely nothing worthwhile for the past twenty minute in his efforts to predict when she would be finished teaching so he could call her.

"I think an early dinner would be nice."

"Do you like Japanese food?" he asked.

"I love it," she responded simply.

"Then I'll pick you up at 5:30 and don't worry about the directions. I asked your brother how to get to your place just this morning. I'll see you then."

"Until then," she promised, suddenly barely able to wait until 5:30.

The Japanese restaurant was one of those where you sat shoeless on the floor while a Japanese masseuse wandered around the restaurant massaging anyone who decided that their sushi and teriyaki wasn't enough of an oriental experience. Seth, dressed in a dark navy blue suit with a power red tie, appeared the consummate professional and was so stunning that even the Japanese waitress couldn't tear her eyes off him.

Julia had changed into a lovely gray and black sweater dress and wore a simple pearl pendant her grandmother had surprised her with on her sixteenth birthday.

"So how was your day?" he asked casually, after they'd ordered their California rolls and teriyaki chicken stir-fry.

"Busy and hectic as usual," she replied. "Second graders keep a teacher on their toes and I have twenty; eleven boys and nine girls."

"I admire you," he said sincerely. "It must take a great deal of energy and patience to keep up with the likes of... how old are they?"

"Seven," interjected Julia, "and to tell you the truth, this grade is as low as I could go. I truly admire those who can handle kindergartners and pre-schoolers, but I'm afraid I just don't have the stamina. And how was your day?"

"Hectic as well," admitted Seth. "I've been handed a fast-food and mini-market complex near the university and we're running into some problems with the city planning commission. The project should start in about two weeks if we're to have any hopes of finishing on schedule and unfortunately to get permits from the city means a delay. It seems I spent most of that day trying to ward off belligerent contractors as well as city officials, neither of whom have the least compassion or understanding for the other."

"I thought you're just the architect?" asked Julia.

"I am, but I'm what you call a follow-through architect. That is, I follow through the project until the final stone is laid, the electricity, plumbing, and sewers are in, and the final 'i' is dotted. In other words, the building has to be standing upright and functioning properly for me to dust my hands off the project."

Love Never Dies

Julia smiled. It didn't surprise her Seth wouldn't let go of a task until it was completed to his satisfaction.

"Seth, I was wondering," asked Julia hesitantly as she munched on a just-delivered spring roll. "Your voice has a different quality to it, a different accent from what I'd expect from a New Englander. You didn't live your entire life on the east coast did you?"

"No," said Seth vaguely, wanting to drop it there, but realizing she still waited for an answer. "I was actually born and raised in upstate New York, but my father worked in Canada for many years before transferring to the UK for nearly four years. Since all this happened in my formative years, I think my accent got rather internationalized; not quite American, Canadian, or British, just an odd blend of the three. I know I have a tendency to say certain words a little differently, like I say *sch*edule instead of schedule, but I'm trying to reform," he said contritely.

"Please don't," remarked Julia. "It's a refreshing change from the flat tones of California. So what did your father do for a living?"

He allowed the approaching waitress to set down heavy marble platters of sushi before them before continuing. "My dad was actually into bridge construction and generally worked in North America except for the four years he spent in London. My mother, believe it or not, was a civil engineer and fortunate enough to work in the same firm as him."

"And did that create problems?" asked Julia.

"Not in the least. My parents were very compatible and their personal and professional camaraderie was a pleasure to behold." He took a bite of the succulent sushi. "This is delicious. You see my parents were what we call in my family, soul mates."

"Soul mates? I've heard of that phrase before; it's when you believe there is only one person for you in the entire universe and your meeting is predestined."

"Well kinda, but actually it had a very different connotation in my family. Maybe someday I'll tell you about it, but not tonight."

"So you were an only child?" queried Julia as she sampled her teriyaki and rice.

"No," said Seth shortly, but didn't expound upon his brief answer and Julia glanced up to catch a strange expression darken his eyes. Not knowing him well enough to delve deeper into the reason for his stony countenance, she changed the subject.

"So what is your favorite thing to do when you're not designing houses and buildings and all?"

"Well, I do have a hobby. It's just not one I'm certain your brother would appreciate."

"And what could that be, since he is constantly strumming on his guitar and singing off-key at the top of his lungs? What could you do that is possibly worse than that?"

"You brother actually has a decent voice, you troublemaker. It's just that I like to design, build, and stock salt-water aquariums."

"You mean the big ones? Like the aquarium down in San Diego?"

"No, smaller ones for homes and offices."

Julia chewed her California roll carefully. "I would suspect that this would be the place to do it since we are so close to the ocean; it would be awfully easy to get the salt water."

"That's true; the local stores stock jugs of salt water and import all sorts of exotic fish, including my favorite, the yellow tang. If your brother was game I'd design a t-shaped tank of maybe five to six hundred gallons right between the dining room and living room and plunk some coral and fish in it. It would create an exotic accent to an already lovely place. I'm just not so sure he would be willing to allow me to experiment with his beloved condominium."

"It would never hurt to ask."

"That's true, but then again I don't know how long I'll be staying here so I might not want to start something I couldn't finish." A note of melancholy muted the normally rich timbre of his voice, and once again Julia noticed something akin to sadness flit across his handsome face.

Seeking to lighten the mood she declared jauntily, "Well, I have a hobby that's not very expensive and a whole lot of fun. And after this big dinner I wouldn't mind indulging myself. Are you game?"

"Just what am I agreeing to?" asked Seth suspiciously, wiping his mouth with a linen napkin.

"Ice skating! There's a skating rink right at the mall. I don't know about you, but I haven't gotten enough exercise today. Would you like to wander over there and give it a try?"

A peculiar expression passed over his face before he nodded solemnly. "Only if you promise not to laugh at me when I land smack on my bum."

"*Now* you sound British," chortled Julia delightedly as she took his reluctant hand.

Twenty minutes later they laced up their rented ice-skates, Seth appearing quite dubious.

"I'm not exactly sure I'm appropriately dressed for this little adventure," he complained. He had removed his jacket to reveal a snow-white shirt and had un-looped his brilliant red tie, but still looked overdressed in his sharply creased blue dress slacks.

"Don't worry about it," she said dismissively, and grabbing him by the hand dragged him out onto the ice where a couple dozen young people, ranging anywhere from middle school to college age, skated in a counterclockwise loop around the large ring.

"If you feel a little bit shaky, you can either hold onto the railing here or onto me. Have you ever skated before?"

"Once or twice," he commented quietly, watching an energetic young man wink at his laughing brunette counterpart as he zoomed by skating backward. "I suppose you can skate backward as well," he accused and Julia grinned, holding out her hands to him.

He took them gently and allowed her to lead him across the ice. He didn't exactly stagger or fall as he let her slowly maneuver him over the slick ice, thoroughly enjoying the faint breeze lifting her blonde hair, her cheeks taking on a rosy shine. She was absolutely stunning in the clingy sweater dress and he was thankful for the chill air of the ice rink. He allowed her to lead him about like that for three full laps before finally sighing.

"Alright, alright," he said. "That's enough!" and suddenly spun forward to grab her around the waist, and lead her in a smooth swirling circle. Seth had not only skated before but was an excellent skater!

"Why you," she hissed under her breath, but he only chuckled and whirled her around once more.

"If I tossed you would you land on your feet?"

"Why don't you try it?" she challenged, and he gave her a tentative toss of only a foot or so. Julia landed perfectly upon her white skates and zoomed out in front of him. Seth did a nifty spin, and then gliding beside her looped his arm around her waist to skate companionably with her over the next hour.

As Seth later perched on the wooden bench and undid the laces to his hired black skates he admitted, "I haven't skated like that since I was a teenager."

"And how old are you now?"

"Thirty-three. One forgets all those wonderful magical things we did while young and carefree. Thanks for bringing back a very pleasant childhood memory Julia Morris; it's been a lovely evening and one I won't forget for a long while." He remained peacefully quiet on the way home, driving carefully through the drizzle.

"So what are you doing tomorrow?" Julia asked, not caring if she sounded forward.

"I don't know, maybe lounge around," he answered, "and catch up on some reading."

"Why don't you come to my parent's house for Thanksgiving?"

"No, I don't feel that I could do that. It would be an imposition on you and your family."

"Not at all. My dad's already hit it off with you, being a retired architect and all. Besides, no one should have to spend Thanksgiving alone."

"I don't believe you should just invite me at the last minute. It isn't fair to your parents. Why don't we compromise and I'll see you on Friday. You go ahead and enjoy the day with your folks."

"Please, I insist."

Seth shook his head vehemently as he parked his Jeep in front of her complex. "I appreciate your offer Julia, I really do, but I'm not ready to share time with your family. I hesitated even asking you out tonight though I had a truly wonderful time."

"But why?" asked Julia bewildered, hurt distorting her delicate features.

"I hadn't planned on getting involved with anyone right now, but find myself irresistibly attracted to you even though I know I should stay away. So, I sent you those roses and asked you out anyway, knowing I shouldn't. I can't come to your parent's house for Thanksgiving tomorrow; please understand that. I'll give you a call on Friday, if that's okay?"

Seth's defenses remained insurmountable and Julia accepted his compromise. "It is. I'll look forward to hearing from you. Will you at least walk me to my door?"

"Of course." Seth hoisted an umbrella over his head and opened the 4x4's door, the pair hurrying to the front door of her two bedroom apartment as fat raindrops splattered off the black nylon.

"Then I'll wait for your call on Friday," Julia said. "I have to admit you weren't the only one who had a lovely evening. I haven't had better in a long time."

Impulsively she grabbed his lean cheeks between her palms, and lifting herself up on tiptoe kissed him hard upon the mouth, quickly turning the doorknob before he could retort.

Shock mingled with acute desire made him stare stupidly at the closed door. Seth finally folded his umbrella, and oblivious of the rain stepped out into the pounding drizzle, not able to decide if things could get any better or worse.

Thanksgiving was always one of Julia's favorite holidays. With no gift exchange it remained a family time, one she usually spent happily with her parents, brother, and outgoing grandmother. Her Gran talked a mile a minute in the kitchen as her mother, father, and brother helped clear up the dishes. Julia removed the table cloth and prepared it to be washed; it, as always having fallen victim to that one tell-tale stain of gravy.

But instead of feeling content this sunny cool Thursday, she felt oddly sad. What was Seth doing now? Did he sit alone in that beautiful three bedroom condo working on blueprints for somebody else's deadline? Or perhaps he picked at an overheated TV dinner as he watched a football game on the tube. Or maybe he just reread yesterday's newspaper or scanned the Internet in his boredom.

Love Never Dies

Julia moped for over an hour and then couldn't stand it anymore. Her brother, about to leave for Angie's house, said goodbye to Grandma Rose who cautioned him about eating too much during his second feast. This was his yearly ritual now. He'd spend the first part of the day with his own kin before heading over to the Carters to share evening supper with Angie's family. After Paul departed, Julia and her mother sorted out different tubs of Tupperware stuffed to the brim with leftovers. Julia stared at the tasty contents for a moment before finally making up her mind.

"Mom, do you mind if I take a plate of leftovers to a friend? I'm afraid he didn't have anyone to spend Thanksgiving with and I would like him to have a traditional dinner."

Her mom smiled knowingly and winked at her own mother who stood at the sink refilling ice cube trays. "And just who might that be?"

Julia ignored her mother's too-knowledgeable face. "Paul's roommate, Seth. I'm just worried he didn't have a proper Thanksgiving dinner and it seems a shame to freeze all this food when I could take him over a hot meal."

"I think you should," said her father, drying the gravy ladle. "He seems like such a nice young man. Fix him up a big plate and don't forget to give him lots of cranberries." Cranberries were her father's favorite.

Loren Lockner

After the kitchen was tidy her mother and grandmother relaxed in the living room watching *Singing in the Rain*. Her father stretched out upon the couch, his newspaper open, and soon dozed off. The time was ripe to leave so Julia gave her mother a light kiss on the cheek and her grandmother an affectionate hug before loading up the Taurus and heading toward her brother's pricey condo.

Julia hesitated on her brother's landing before the beautiful oak door, balancing the overladen plate to pause before the brass knocker. Before allowing herself to retreat Julia lifted the heavy fixture three times. There was no answer. A wave of acute disappointment washed over her and on impulse she turned the knob. The door opened silently into the still, dark condominium. If Seth had ventured out he hadn't gone far, and Julia quickly decided she would write him a brief note and leave the Thanksgiving dinner. Whether he chose to eat it or not was his own decision.

The house echoed hollowly and unable to stop herself Julia walked down the wide hall toward Seth's door. Underneath the wood paneling a light burned and she pushed open the door. Seth was seated at his desk, his computer screen glowing as he worked on some current architectural program. Black headphones enfolded his dark head and even from where Julia stood the pulsing vibrations reached her. He couldn't have heard a knock upon the door to save his life.

Love Never Dies

Julia cocked her head and listened, smiling as she recognized the rock 'n' roll sounds of John Cougar Mellencamp. Seth seemed lost in a trance as he stared at the lighted screen, his fingers making no effort to change or alter the design before him. Dressed in a warm gray pullover and faded blue jeans; his feet rested upon the desk top. She recognized the song called *Hurt So Good*, and gliding over, placed her slender hands upon his shoulders. He instantly bolted upright, tearing his headphones off before turning startled gray eyes toward her.

"Good God woman, couldn't you knock!"

"I tried," she retorted, "but you had John Cougar so loud your entire house could have been totally emptied by thieves and you would never have known it."

"What are you doing here?" he said quietly, pulling away from her gentle hands, his voice now completely under control. "Shouldn't you be with your family carving up a turkey?"

"Been there, done that," replied Julia. "I brought you a plate of food which is now setting upon the kitchen counter. I wasn't certain what you had for lunch and thought you should at least have a turkey dinner to celebrate since you wouldn't honor us with your presence today."

"That's very kind of you," he said stiffly, and rose awkwardly. Was it her imagination or did he back away from her? He managed to place a full five feet between them before he could retreat no further, his back pressed against the lovely French doors.

"So Paul is here as well?" he asked, glancing toward the bedroom door.

"No, he's at Angie's. That's always the tradition now. He does the early feast with us and then heads to the other side of town for turkey soup and cornbread with her family. He gets along really well with the Carters, who simply adore him."

"Paul's a fortunate man all around. Well, thank you for the plate which I'll sample later. I have some work to do, so if you'll just let yourself out." He gestured vaguely to the glowing screen of his laptop and that was when it happened.

Later, Julia couldn't quite describe what passed between them at precisely that moment. As she witnessed his curt dismissal, the rational part of her mind demanded she leave while the irrational part gazed at this tall quiet man who'd backed as far away from her as possible, and cried out to him with every fiber of her being. As Julia gazed into Seth's lean face, she recognized the strong defensive wall he'd erected, as well as the desperate longing lurking behind those shuttered eyes.

It struck her like a bolt of lightning that Seth was afraid; afraid of her, of commitment, but mostly of himself. Something held him back and if she didn't take the first step he never would. So Julia moved forward until close enough to touch him; his face not more than five inches from hers. She peered upward to connect with those silvery eyes and placed her arms around his taut neck before kissing him long and sweet and hard. Seth resisted at first, as if he, by pure willpower, could push her away both emotionally and physically. But Julia never allowed herself to close her eyes during that first real kiss, instead pleading for him to give himself completely to her.

Seth jerked violently and pulled away, placing another three feet between them as he moved to the back of the bedroom.

"Why do you run away?" she asked, noting his incriminating pulse throbbing strongly.

"I do not run away," he denied.

"I say you that do because you are a coward." She eyed him fiercely, daring to provoke him.

His dark gray eyes smoldered. "I am not a coward," he hissed, "but am aware, unlike you, that what you desire from me has far-reaching consequences."

"Such as...?"

"I do not easily let go of those I care about."

"I never once believed you were of a casual nature. It's one of the things that attracted me to you in the first place."

Seth swallowed roughly and Julia once again scrutinized his handsome features. His ebony hair hung haphazardly about his face and she noticed a discreet hole in his left earlobe, bereft of an adorning earring.

He in turn gazed as if disgusted into her dark green eyes flecked with golden brown. Her streaked blonde hair was tousled and her cheeks flamed pink with undisguised desire. Julia's tense face and rigid body, so luscious under the thick lavender sweater, demanded a response to her declaration of desire.

"I do not do one night stands," Seth whispered, gradually moving closer.

"Neither do I."

His hands suddenly darted forward, drawing her to him in a devastating kiss. Julia pressed her searching lips against his and dared him to deny the sexual surge igniting her whole body. It proved his undoing and suddenly Seth kissed her again, this time opening her full lips with his insistent tongue as he plundered the sweet depths of her mouth.

Seth teased her mouth and then moved his lips onto her ears, her neck, and the recesses of her throat. His hands stroked and searched, finally plucking up the hem of her sweater and rubbing his gentle fingertips over the bare flesh of her back.

Julia in turn ran her hands over his solid chest before sliding them under his pullover, seeking the warm firmness of his toned body. His hairless chest was hot and her fingers delighted in the contours of his muscles as she rubbed her hands down the stiffness of his spine. He gasped and pulled her even closer, enabling Julia to feel the hard length of him crushing into her pelvic bone, and she shivered delightedly.

Her sweater was removed in one deft yank and landed on the floor in a heap of lavender folds. Seth's fingers cupped her breast and stroked the nipple under the lacy beige bra. He suddenly released her and backed away again.

"No," she cried involuntarily, and stretched out a trembling hand to urge him back. For the first time ever, Seth truly smiled, suddenly looking ten years younger and far more approachable.

"Don't fear, love, I would not leave you now," he said, briskly moving to lock his bedroom door before dropping his soft gray pullover onto the floor beside her crumpled sweater as she devoured the sight of his smooth toned chest with her emerald eyes.

Seth hooked a finger in the front clasp of her bra, releasing the tiny catch and allowing the thin garment to fall to the floor. He gazed in open admiration at her lovely full breasts which ached for his touch.

"So beautiful," he whispered, and bent to take a pink nipple between his lips. He suckled and caressed and guided her toward the expanse of his bed, gently lowering her upon the silvery bedspread, his mouth never ceasing its insistent conquest of her breast.

Seth's hands now roved freely, gently massaging her legs under the soft cotton of her tailored pants until his fingers found the snap and zipper and expertly pulled the shielding fabric from her expectant body. Seth's finger looped into her beige bikini, and giving her the gentlest, most reassuring smile, he tugged it downward.

"Ever so beautiful," he repeated, gazing at her trim legs and flat stomach.

"Not as beautiful as you," she whispered, touching the beating pulse at his throat, and tangled her hands in the silk of his hair. "I want you," she whispered, and Seth rose to his knees, slowly peeling off his jeans and blue boxer briefs.

It was amazing how this quiet, often remote man could love so gently. A delightful feeling of completeness washed over her as they became one, his sweet breath fanning her face, his gray eyes smoldering but tender. Later he held her for a long time, his body slack against her. His lips nuzzled her hair and finally he spoke, so quietly she strained to hear.

"I love you," he said. From that moment on her fate was sealed.

"I love you too," she managed, and without meaning to at all, fell into a blissful sleep, never once loosening her grip on the man she'd loved since the moment he'd walked into her brother's door.

The phone's shrill ring caused Julia to gasp and bolt upright, but Seth stayed her, nestling her slim frame once again upon the expanse of his chest as he answered the call in his rich, melodious voice.

"It's not a problem," he said patiently after a while, stroking her silky blonde hair and nesting his nose into the tangled curls. "Of course I'm listening. I'll bring the updated blueprints in on Monday and brief you before the meeting. I've already made the changes, so you're not to worry. I'll see you then."

"Your boss?" murmured Julia drowsily.

"Yes. Lenny is a typical 'type A' personality and frets over every detail. I'll have to go in early Monday and reassure him the designs are up to snuff before the city planners arrive."

"I'm sure they are," she stated, positive anything he produced would be of the highest quality.

"Speaking of designs," he said casually. "One of the drawing points of this condo was the lovely Jacuzzi built for two. May I show it to you?" Seth hitched himself up on one arm and smiled down at her.

"I would love to see your Jacuzzi, kind sir."

Suddenly Julia was lifted into his strong arms and with an excited screech was carried naked into the gray-tiled bathroom. Seth lowered her gently onto the thick bathroom rug and reached over to twist the taps. He nuzzled her ear as the water steamed and filled the lovely tub. They finally lowered themselves into the swirling water of the Jacuzzi; Julia propped against his exhausted body until Seth languidly reached for some herbal shampoo and began to lather up her hair. His fingers massaged, smoothing back the foaming strands, until laughing she suddenly submerged herself to rise a few moments later with water streaming down her face.

"I love your laugh," he said seriously. "It fills me with joy every time I hear it. I wish I could laugh like you."

His melancholy tone bothered her so she bent forward and kissed his too-tight mouth. "Then I shall laugh for the both of us. Now let me wash those dark locks of yours sir."

Twenty minutes later they finally retreated from the pruning warmth of the small pool and dressed languidly after rubbing the moisture off each other's body.

"I promised my mother I'd come over to help make the turkey soup," said Julia reluctantly, straightening her lavender sweater. "Would you care to come along?"

"I have a bit of work to do on those blueprints before Monday."

"We make a mean soup."

"No sweet girl," he said shortly, bracing himself for the hurt look in her sea-green eyes. "I need some time to myself, but perhaps you'd find it in your heart to stop by tomorrow evening or Saturday morning?"

"I'll find it in my heart," she promised.

Love Never Dies

It was barely seven a.m. before she knocked on his door. Seth answered her insistent pounding with a sleepy hello and pulled her back into the warmth of the condo, before discarding her clothes on the smooth parquet. His bed was warm and tousled and she gloried in making him gasp, his dark eyes glowing in contentment. For some, it may have seemed they had moved too quickly, but Julia instinctively realized they had spent way too much time waiting, hesitant to fulfill their needs. She refused to be hesitant any longer, and straddling his lean hips caused him to moan and gasp out her name. It was a Friday to be remembered.

It was late Friday afternoon when Paul finally wandered into the condominium and threw down his overnight bag. Upon observing Seth cleaning up the kitchen he said, "I'm going to have to go on a diet. Two turkey dinners was way more than enough."

Seth gave him a half-smile and waited until his roommate had poured himself a glass of diet soda and eased his long frame onto the comfortable couch before approaching him.

"There's something I need to talk to you about Paul," uttered Seth quietly, sinking down into the coffee-brown recliner positioned directly across from his roommate.

"And what would that be?" asked Paul, only half listening. He was just more than a bit sore his favorite football team had lost by a mere three points. He took a sip of his cola.

"I'm in love with your sister."

Paul didn't plan on spitting out the liquid like some poor B-grade movie, but shot the soda all over the legs of his pants and upon the rich red tones of the borrowed rug from Seth. "You *are* what?"

"I'm in love with Julia and she loves me. I just thought I'd let you know so it wouldn't take you by surprise the next time you saw us together."

Paul watched Seth in stunned silence as his roommate rose and gave him a half-smile.

"Julia and I are having dinner and might catch a movie. We probably won't be back till late. Have a good evening Paul."

Seth once again retreated into the sanctuary of his room, certain that while events moved way too fast, he was helpless to do anything more than enjoy the sensation of being finally and completely loved.

Chapter 3

And so they became a pair. Seth's quiet reserved nature slowly blossomed under Julia's laughter and sweet touch and one week after his declaration to her brother, he visited her parents.

Jim Morris gave him a knowing glance. His daughter's unbridled happiness had not gone unnoticed and Helen Morris could barely restrain herself from giving the handsome architect an impulsive hug. She waited as patiently as possible for the methodical man to finally seat himself upon the couch after accepting the cup of hot cider offered him.

"Julia and I are seeing each other and I just wanted you to know that I would never do anything to hurt her."

"I never thought you would," answered Jim Morris, liking the confident tone of Seth's voice.

"Things are progressing rather rapidly and I just didn't want you to be startled."

"We are not remotely startled, only delighted," chortled Helen. "You'll be joining us for Christmas of course?"

"Of course," answered Seth, and they settled into normal conversation about weather and politics and work. Seth promised Jim to return for a game of chess later that week and the pair watched him walk down the damp walkway to his car after a pleasant thirty minutes.

"I'm so pleased," said Helen, sighing in happiness.

"I am as well. I just hope he doesn't dim her lights; he's so serious."

"June is a nice month for weddings," said his wife, ignoring his cryptic comment.

"Helen!"

"Just enjoying a pleasant daydream Dear, since I've never seen Julia so happy; you'll just have to let me indulge myself."

"I think it's a little early to start picking out china."

"You'll see. There's no one else for either of them," returned Helen, humming happily as she picked up Seth's empty mug and took off for the kitchen.

The next few weeks passed in a dreamy haze for Julia, as gradually some of Seth's clothing and personal belongings ended up in her room, as did hers in his. They often accompanied Angie and Paul on double dates, as Seth loosened up and allowed himself to enjoy the bubbly Angie and her impulsive boyfriend. Seth had managed to convince Paul to let him design an aquarium for the condo and he worked on it each weekend, adding pounds of reef rock and coral until finally, the beautiful tank was complete. They added countless gallons of salt water and eight frisky damselfish in varying shades of blue and black, which now darted about in their new home as they helped mature the saltwater. Within a week the four planned to head to the local pet store and pick out more exotic fish.

There was no hesitancy on Seth's part now. He'd made up his mind and didn't try to hide his affection from Angie, Paul, or Julia's parents. He always walked with his arm draped across her shoulder or held her hand. He sat close to her in booths and theatres alike and each night was glorious in their shared intimacy and warmth. One evening, right before Christmas, the foursome sat down in a Mexican restaurant after some frenzied late afternoon gift shopping. Paul grimaced at the large heap of packages beside him before Angie laid a single piece of paper on the table.

"What's this?" asked Paul, as Julia leaned over to see.

"It's a china pattern Paul." Angie stumbled. "I was thinking that maybe someday, that is if we ever decide to get married, you might like to order it."

"Our wedding," mumbled Paul. If Angie didn't watch it, she was going to take all the fun out of his impending proposal. "Well, maybe someday. Never hurts to dream I guess."

Seth gave him a conspiratorial glance and tapped a finger upon the bronze and black geometric pattern before commenting casually.

"Very elegant and tasteful indeed; it's a fine choice Angie." Angie beamed across from him. She truly liked her roommate's boyfriend and secretly hoped they might have a double wedding.

"I don't know," said Paul, studying the sheet of paper. All this wedding business laid heavily on his mind. It wasn't that he minded getting married; he just didn't appreciate all the malarkey that accompanied it. Las Vegas sounded like a better choice every day.

"Did your father have to succumb to buying china?" he asked Seth, who leaned back in the booth, a casual arm draped across Julia's shoulders.

"I really can't recall," he said, "not having been born yet, but I'm sure he wouldn't have minded since he and my mother were soul mates."

"Soul mates," repeated Angie. "I've heard that term before. Isn't that when someone is destined to be your mate? One true love for each of us?"

Love Never Dies

"That's only half of it," said Seth, gazing intently at Julia's best friend. "Being a soul mate actually entails a lot more than that."

"You really believe that nonsense?" cracked Paul. "I thought you were much too serious to fall for romantic gibberish."

"It's not gibberish," replied Seth quietly. "My father told me himself that my mother was his soul mate and that he'd given her half his soul a year before I was born."

"Gave his soul to her?" repeated Paul, glancing at his sister and shaking his head like Seth had gone daft or something.

"Oh shut up Paul," said Angie, "this sounds interesting. What do you mean he gave his soul to her?"

"Well it's actually a physical thing," stated Seth, suddenly seeming reluctant to expound further.

Julia was suddenly alert, remembering their earlier conversation at the Sushi restaurant.

"My father told me about it several times, but I've never discussed it outside the family; though I'd heard of the phenomena before."

"Now you've really got my interest up so you can't just stop now. Go on Seth," urged Angie, ignoring Paul's snort of disgust.

"What do you mean a physical thing?" asked Julia, watching her lover's face intently. "I thought a soul mate was just someone you wish to remain with for the rest of your life."

"Well, that's a big part of it," responded Seth, "but there's an actual physical act needed to exchange part of your soul with another. My father explained he'd exchanged souls with my mother when only twenty-three."

"What did he do? Take a knife and cut out part of his soul and give it to your mom to eat?" Seth appeared vaguely disgusted at Paul's flippant comment.

"Oh Paul, just be quiet. Tell us about it and just ignore him," said Angie, putting her hand over boyfriend's mouth to silence him. "I really want to know how it's done."

"Here we go," moaned Paul through her hand.

Seth sighed and began quietly, his voice almost melancholy. "When my father met my mother he knew he was doomed to love her from the moment he laid eyes on her. He was twenty-three at the time and she about twenty."

"What were their names?" whispered Julia.

"My father's name was Frank and my mother's was Jenny. He met her during a summer postgraduate course at NYU. Anyway, as soon as dad met her he knew that was it; he would never want to be with another woman. Within weeks there was no question that their involvement was going to be permanent.

Love Never Dies

"This was in 1967, mind you, and a lot of strange ideas had made the circuit. There were mind bending drugs, psychedelic hallucinations, and free, uninhibited sex, but my father, being the more contemplative type, had read a magazine from the far east about exchanging souls and was fascinated, not being the type to go in for the other excesses of the sixties. He was passionately in love with my mother and decided to try it if she was game.

"The process is relatively simple. The first thing is to agree to exchange souls unreservedly with your chosen mate. The second part's even easier yet; while making love you vow eternal devotion to each other and as climax approaches you transfer part of your soul to your mate. My father said that he and my mother were making love passionately in his apartment. He gazed into my mother's eyes and said, 'I love you and I give you the other half of my soul.' An excruciating pain exploded in his chest and as he climaxed he felt as if a twisting knife had been thrust into his heart.

"He glanced down and saw my mother struggled with some intense, overwhelming pain, and he was deathly afraid he'd somehow killed her. Mom's hand flew to her chest and she gasped out his name. A couple of minutes later, when both could finally speak, Dad noticed a warm feeling stealing over his chest, as if a vessel that had been partly emptied was once again being refilled with a liquid that warmed and soothed like a good cognac, for she too had given him her soul. Mom had silently called out his name and had taken his soul back in to herself."

"Wow," said Angie, as Seth paused. Paul leaned back in the booth, his arms crossed defensively before him. He clearly didn't believe a word of it

"And I thought you were a sane, rational man."

"Paul, shut up!" exclaimed Angie. "And...?"

"Later, when they were calmer, they spoke about it. My father, always the skeptic, didn't really believe that it happened and wrote off the pain in his chest as some sort of fluke during lovemaking. But that evening as my mother returned to her dorm room, my father felt a strange pang in his breast as if he couldn't bear for her to be apart from him. Mom whirled about and gave him a halfhearted wave from the downstairs landing, a strange expression flitting over her face. That night a soft despair settled over him and all he could do was think of her, visualizing her stretched out upon her narrow bed, eyes fastened upon the ceiling as she fantasized about him.

"Suddenly Dad realized that part of her was in him, and he was in her. It was almost as if some sort of telepathy had instantly developed between the two. When she entered a room he didn't have to turn around to instinctively know she was there; he could feel it by the warmth in his chest and the glow in his heart."

"You have got to be kidding," said Paul disgustedly.

Love Never Dies

"I wish I were, and it's that unbreakable bond between my mother and father that finally killed him."

"What?" gasped Angie, her dark brown eyes widening.

"It's true. When I was twenty-four my mother was diagnosed with ovarian cancer. From the time of her diagnosis to her death, only a scant five weeks elapsed. My father had no time to prepare himself for her death and upon her passing sank into a deep depression. I myself was too aggrieved to understand that my father needed help. One day, four months later, when I returned home after an evening of drinking and carousing with my buddies in an effort to forget the memory of my mother's frail face and wasted body, I saw my father hunched over in his comfortable old chair where he'd watch TV beside my mother when she was alive. He had aged ten years in those four months, his hair turning prematurely white even though he was only fifty years old.

"He sat in the chair with a picture album spread open upon his knees and scanned photographs of our family. I remember kneeling down to watch his fingers caress a worn and cherished photograph of my mother; one that had been taken in 1967 right after he'd met her. The sadness in his eyes was so pathetic that I wanted to cry at his obvious despair."

"'She's gone now,' he said to me, as if I didn't realize my own mother was dead. 'I know,' I answered, and reached out a hand to pat his thin knee."

"'There's no more warmth,' he moaned. 'When she died she took half my soul with her and I can't exist on this earth without her; without the other half of my soul. What am I to do son? Where am I to go and who am I to talk to? There's no comfort in my life, my bed, or my heart. '"

The air hissed from Angie's lungs but Seth continued, oblivious to her distress.

"I remember I uttered some useless words of hollow comfort, but they did nothing for my father and the next day as I left him to go to work, I never realized it was the last time I'd see him alive. That evening, when I arrived home, I found him sitting in his office with his head drooping; a bullet-hole placed accurately through his skull. His note was brief and to the point. 'When your mother took my soul, I didn't realize it would take my life as well. I cannot live without her, so I must seek her.' He was only fifty years old."

Angie gulped and whispered softly. "So you really believe your father had only half a soul when your mother died?"

"Yes. I believe that when she died the essence of his soul went with her body into her grave or even perhaps to heaven. I'm not sure about the hereafter, that's a whole other realm to contemplate within itself, but I do know my father was an empty shell after she died. Without his soul mate there was no reason for him to linger upon this earth any longer."

"So what you're really saying," said Paul, trying to lighten the somber mood and the expressions of horror mirrored on his sister and girlfriend's faces, "is that having a soul mate has certain drawbacks?"

"And certain benefits," responded Seth. "But it's not for the faint of heart. We all believe that when we love and marry we will love forever, living to ripe old age and dying within a couple of weeks of each other to rest side by side in a cemetery of our choice. That's a wonderful fantasy, one I cherish myself; but you see, they didn't bury my father in a churchyard next to my mother where he belonged. Because he committed suicide and was a Catholic, Dad couldn't be buried inside the church walls."

"That's terrible," exclaimed Julia, watching Seth's face narrow grimly at the remembrance of his father's fate.

"So what did you do? I can't believe you couldn't bury your father next to your mother! That's ludicrous!" exclaimed Angie heatedly.

"I had her disinterred and buried her and my father side by side in non-denominational cemetery. It was the least I could do in honor of their undying love. I would expect my children to do the same for me if that happened."

Paul seemed about to retort but the waitress arrived, laden with heavy plates of steaming Mexican food. The four ate quietly, Julia occasionally stealing furtive glances at Seth's quiet serious face. The sad story of his mother penetrated her heart and she recalled some previously forgotten words he'd stated at the beginning of their love affair.

"You're my soul mate," he had said, and suddenly Julia realized Seth expected her to share her soul with him, just like his mother and father had done so many years before.

"So are you ready for my family's Christmas Eve madness?" asked Paul, collecting the four gifts he'd wrapped just that afternoon and depositing them into a large red paper bag with handles.

"I think so. I've been warned about what to expect," replied Seth, adding another log to the fire he'd built only minutes before. It now burned brightly in the lovely living room, casting dancing shadows over the fragrant Christmas tree they'd erected only three days previously.

"Remember that my Grandma Rose is nice, but nosy. She will be asking everything about you from your deodorant brand to if you ever had braces. I swear she works for the CIA."

Seth laughed. "I'll be on my guard. So you're off to Angie's now?"

"Yeah, I need to deliver the gifts for her folks and then head over later to Mom and Dad's to finish putting together Mom's exercise bike. Dad's about ready to pull out his remaining hair. Julia's coming here right?"

"In about forty minutes."

"Don't tell Angie what I got her. If you do I'll kill you!"

"I would never spoil another's special moment. She's one lucky lady and the diamond pendant is lovely."

"I like it too. Ah, Seth? About that stuff you said the other night. Angie's been going on and on about it and, well, I'm just more than a little distressed about her fascination with your *story*."

"It's not a story, it's the truth."

"Yeah, well. I think she wants me to exchange our souls or something. Look, I love Angie and all, but I'm not sure I want to die if she kicks off."

"No one can force you to do anything you don't feel comfortable with."

"But I'm not like you Seth; so intense and determined about everything." He paused and gazed at his friend who poked the healthy glowing fire. "You're planning to do it with Julia aren't you?"

"It's crossed my mind."

"Does she want to?"

Seth straightened and shrugged. "I haven't asked her, but I get the feeling she would."

"Shouldn't you get married first or something?"

Seth grinned. "You know Paul; marriage is second to exchanging your soul and one doesn't depend on the other. Marriage is for others—the lawyers, the children, the parents. A soul mate, that's just for the couple, no one else. Don't worry about it Paul. You know I would never do anything Julia didn't want."

"It's just that you've become so close so quickly."

"That's true." Seth sighed. "You know Paul that I would never intentionally hurt your sister."

"But if you become soul mates and you die, what's to become of her?"

"It's not going to happen. I take my vitamins every morning," Seth quipped, but Paul didn't laugh.

"Don't joke around. She's my twin sister you know. Sex is one thing, but this soul mate stuff is scary. I love Julia and just want what's best for her. Please Seth; think long and hard before you make an irrevocable decision for her."

"You're afraid I'll leave her?"

"No. I'm confident you wouldn't do that. But everyone dies someday and Julia's already involved beyond any chance of recovery." He snorted and shook is brown head. "Listen to me, preaching to you like I'm some sort of paranoid minister. I'll see you tonight around six then."

"We'll be there."

"I hope you like clam chowder, because if you don't you're in big trouble. It's a Christmas Eve tradition at our house; fresh sourdough bread and New England clam chowder. If you don't like it, I'm warning you as a favor, just force it down. It's only once a year after all—but it's Grandma's recipe and she doesn't take kindly to dissenters."

Seth grinned again. "Warning noted and palate prepared. See you tonight." Paul shrugged into his wool overcoat and disappeared through the door whistling a poor rendition of *Joy to the World.* Seth swung into action. He had only thirty minutes to prepare.

Julia didn't bother to knock, confident Seth would have left the door unlocked for her, and she entered the warm hallway and hung her coat. The condo was peacefully quiet and filled with holiday cheer. She and Angie, under the benevolent gazes of their football-watching boyfriends, had decorated the flat with wreaths, tinsel, and red velvet bows. Yesterday, Julia noted, the men had erected a five-foot tall tree and placed roughly thirty ornaments among its fir branches glistening with tinsel and dozens of multi-colored flashing lights. She'd brought a few old wooden ornaments carved as Santa's, elves, and angels to finish off the tree.

"Seth?" she called. When no reply was forthcoming she ventured further into the cheery condo.

"Seth?"

It was then she noticed the glowing fire and involuntarily moved toward it, passing the stately tree to gaze at the makeshift mattress placed before the hearth, rose petals adorning its snowy white sheets. Seth had spelled out the simple words 'I love you,' in red blossoms and her heart swelled. She noticed an ice decanter near the fire housing the telltale foiled neck of an expensive bottle of champagne. It might be only one p.m. in the afternoon, but Seth had planned his seduction well.

"So you're here," murmured his rich voice behind her and she turned and gaped at him. Seth was dressed only in faded blue jeans, his ebony hair brushed away from his forehead as his slate gray eyes ate her up.

"Yes," she managed. It didn't matter how many times they had lain together, the impact of his physical being always profoundly affected her. After each time, Julia would swear that love-making could never get any better, but that was a lie. Each encounter was awesome in its intensity and passion, and she knew this time would be no different.

Seth didn't hesitate. "I want to give you my soul." The soft words were shocking in their simplicity and directness and she dropped her forgotten carryall bag on the floor.

"Alright."

Julia didn't remember him moving, but suddenly Seth was so close she could smell the vanilla lotion he preferred as she gazed into his gray-flecked eyes. His head bent down, his sweet kiss removing any remaining doubts she might have had.

Seth's hands were slow and deliberate as they gently removed her white blouse and let it float to the floor. He propelled her to the dancing fire and in the flickering light of the hot flames he removed all her clothing and lowered her down among the rose petals.

"I love you so much Julia. Please don't be afraid because I'll help you."

His reassuring words were followed by his lips trailing over her body and visiting those places he'd enjoyed so often before. His mouth lowered and she gasped, arching for him. He was almost lazy in his seduction and she wanted to beg, to cry out for him to hurry, but he was not to be rushed. His fingers and his mouth made sure she was ready and finally, an eon later he poised above her, suddenly taking her with sweet intensity.

"Oh!" she cried out, and then begged him to never stop.

"Never," he whispered hoarsely, driving faster and then slowing, always staving off his climax as he waited for her, patiently anticipating the right moment. Finally she was close and Seth peered intently into her passion filled face.

"Now!" he cried, "take my soul sweet love," and Julia willed her life to him. A stabbing, heart-rending pain tore at her chest and she gasped in agony, vaguely aware that the same excruciating pain was mirrored upon his damp face.

"Julia," he gasped raggedly, as she whimpered. Then, as suddenly as it began, infusing warmth spread over her like an expensive brandy and soothed her torn heart. It flowed and surrounded the stricken muscle before refilling the empty space.

"Ah," she gasped in relief.

"Much better," Seth sighed, his powder gray eyes closing for a moment and savoring the encompassing warmth of her freely given soul. He opened them to find her dark green eyes gazing at him in wonder.

"You've given me half your soul," she whispered.

"It's true my love. Our souls are intertwined now, mingled together for eternity and never to be parted until death. Thank you my sweet, sweet girl. Thank you for your unrestrained gift and because of it, love will never die. We will live inside each other forever." He lowered his suddenly weak body gently upon her and she cradled his fatigued frame, kissing his hair before sinking powerlessly into a numbing, healing sleep.

For two hours they lay thus, the fire ebbing as the room finally chilled. It was the creeping cold that finally awakened him and Seth moved from his soft cushion, pulling her into the confines of his arm. She stirred and murmured his name, nestling against him like a purring cat.

Love Never Dies

"Are you awake, love?" he asked.

"Yes, yes, I think so."

"Any pain?"

"None at all," she answered. "And you?"

"Not now, though for a second I was certain I'd expire inside your arms, my heart torn out by some merciless unseen knife."

"So your father was right?"

"I never once believe he lied, though others in my family often scoffed at his story."

Julia kissed his neck drowsily. "I suppose we should take a shower. I have to drop off those clothes at the homeless shelter. It completely slipped my mind."

"No wonder," joked Seth, sitting up and stretching his long arms. He gazed into the final glowing embers of the dying fire. "Come join me in the shower, love." His eyes were tender as they rose and he draped the king-sized blanket around them before both moved as a unit to the distant bathroom.

It was no different on the surface. They joked in the shower as he asked her how she got the scar on her elbow and they shared childhood bicycle crash stories and tales about family traditions.

"So tonight, you will be subjected to the most ingrained tradition of the Morris household," Julia teased.

"I like traditions," said Seth. "I miss them and would be happy to adopt yours."

"Well then, just a word of warning. I'm sure Paul warned you about Grandma's clam chowder and fresh baked sourdough bread, but we also exchange one Christmas Eve gift tonight and you have to guess what's inside. My father guesses a tie every single time." Seth grinned, truly looking forward to supper at the Morris'.

It was no different as they gathered their clothes and Julia blow-dried her hair. It was no different as he kissed her tenderly goodbye and agreed to meet her at her parents' house in a couple hours. But the moment she stepped out of the condominium door, it became acutely different.

Warmth tugged at her heart, increasing with every step as she moved away from the flat. Julia's heart jolted as she saw Seth wave to her from the white-frosted window she and Angie had sprayed only that week. He was with her and in her, and the love-filled warmth reassured and promised. *I walk with you forever* it pledged and she hugged herself in her Taurus, knowing suddenly that Seth was always going to be there; no matter what.

He watched her from the window as she strolled across the street and lowered herself into the midnight blue Taurus. She raised a hand to him and Seth lifted a hand in reply as she slowly drove off. It was then he noticed the dark gray sedan sitting under a droopy mulberry tree across the street. Someone appeared to be watching the condo and Seth felt his heart quicken. It couldn't be! Seth backed away, fingers discreetly pushing the curtains aside as he observed the sallow face framed in the car window. It was a face he did not recognize, yet instinctively dreaded, and he backed away cautiously from the window. Seth observed the man over the next fifteen minutes, memorizing every feature of the stalker's thin face. He shouldn't have been surprised when the phone rang, abruptly startling him from his focused scrutiny.

"The Morris residence," he answered tersely.

"Seth, are you alright?" Julia's voice held a high note of fear.

"What do you mean?" he asked, already knowing she had tuned in to his nervous anxiety.

"I had this strange feeling or premonition that something's not right; that you're worried or frightened about something." She waited and a long pause ensued as he pondered the significance of her words.

"My father was right then, it is true. We exchanged our souls and now you pick up on my moods. You're not to worry, love; it's nothing. Just anxiety about the day, that's all." Seth wasn't sure she believed him, but managed to pacify her. "I'll be there promptly at five. I love you sweet lady," he said, and rang off.

Loren Lockner

The phone call was desperate and abrupt. "There's a dark silver sedan, California license plate HGJ672 parked in front of my condo. It's a Lexus, recent model, with a sun roof. The man in the driver's seat is sallow-faced and brown haired, wearing a blue sweater. I can't see much more than that. I think my cover may be compromised." He listened a while to the reassuring words, not believing any of them, and interrupted. "I want it checked out and I want it checked out now. There's a lot at stake here."

The monotone words issued reassurance again, and he shook his dark head in frustration. "Now, within twenty-four hours! Call me back on my cell phone," and he dictated the number even though he knew the other party had it.

Chapter 4

Christmas Eve was a wonderful affair at the Morris'.
Jim and Helen Morris made their daughter's boyfriend
feel both comfortable and at ease. Once Angie and
Paul arrived it was merry company and Seth spent
most of the evening sitting back to enjoy the
camaraderie and often tongue-in-cheek exchanges
between Paul and his father, Jim. Julia's grandmother
Rose hovered about, moving between her relatives and
often joining in the banter. She wasn't the typical
grandmother in the least, having lived hard and
traveled widely. She voiced an opinion on everything
from cooking to politics, and even whether Paul's tie
was a tad too wide.

Several times during the evening Seth discreetly
stepped to the oversized living room window and
pulled aside the muted beige curtains. The silver sedan
had parked a hundred feet down the street. He prayed
he was mistaken and wanted to check out the sedan's

license plate number but a heavy drizzle settled over the Santa Barbara coastline and embarking upon a late evening walk was out of the question. So he sauntered back to his comfortable easy chair and watched Julia's slender legs, draped in a festive red sweater dress, help her mother clear up the empty glasses of eggnog.

She was chipper and happy and every once in a while cast a sideways glance to him, bestowing upon him that special sweet smile indicating no secrets remained between them. Of course, she was the only one completely honest and it grieved him that he felt obliged to keep the cause of his anxiety from her. In many ways Seth felt like a traitor, yet in no way wanted to burden his sweet lady's mind by problems that just might amount to nothing. As he pondered his dilemma and practiced shielding his anxiety from the astute Julia, Rose Simpson settled her large frame across from him and began to bombard him with questions.

"So you're an architect?" she asked bluntly, eyeing him with a pair of shrewd blue eyes not remotely dimmed by the round spectacles she wore perched upon her nose.

"That's correct," he answered easily. "I work in eastern Santa Barbara on the other side of the university."

"So how's Lenny?" asked Rose. "He graduated two years before my oldest son. What a prim and proper character he always was. Is he still so politically correct these days?"

"I would say so," laughed Seth, leaning back in the chair to eye the older woman appreciatively. She wore an expensive green cashmere sweater and exhibited a gaudy reindeer pin above her left breast, whose nose flashed every couple seconds or so.

"Is he paying you enough?" asked Rose, examining Seth's subdued gray and black striped sweater and sharply creased wool pants. "He always was a little tight-fisted."

Seth laughed out loud and it took a lot to make him laugh. Julia shifted her French-braided head to watch the lively exchange between her forward grandmother and lover. She listened to his response carefully.

"I've only worked at the firm for a scant four months, but yes, I would say he pays me well." Realizing Rose was not to be so easily put off, Seth quoted his salary and savored the fact her bright blue eyes widened appreciatively.

"That will do," she said stoutly, "and keep my granddaughter very nicely indeed."

"Mother!" burst out Helen Morris who'd just deposited a round rum cake bursting with fruit and nuts upon the embroidered tablecloth; appalled that Rose would even breach the subject of Seth's income. Her daughter's boyfriend only laughed delightedly.

"It's alright," he chuckled, winking at Julia's mother. "She's just taking care of her own. Don't you worry; I have enough money and motivation to look after your granddaughter well, though of course she does just fine as a teacher. I don't think you'll have any worries Grandma Simpson."

"More eggnog boy?" asked Rose deliberately, pleased at the way the quiet young man had held his own, and without waiting for an answer, poured a large dollop of Irish Whisky into Seth's mug. His lips tightened in suppressed humor; if he didn't watch it he'd have to be rolled out in a wheelbarrow.

It was close to eleven before things calmed down and Grandma Rose took herself off to bed. The dishes had been cleared and washed and Seth sat comfortably upon a corner love seat near the lightly smoking fire, his arm draped over Julia's shoulder to enjoy the musical Christmas tree lights. Julia turned toward him and nuzzled his chin, the scent of her clean hair sweet to his nostrils.

"I have to be going," he whispered, as his fingers caressed her hair. She nodded bleakly, not having much choice in the matter since she couldn't discreetly leave for the condo with him. Being at home for Christmas morning was a tradition never to be broken until she'd lawfully married and moved into her husband's house. Seth brushed his lips over her hair; he understood the rules as well as she.

Love Never Dies

"You'll come by early tomorrow?" she asked, savoring his warmth and the faint smell of vanilla lotion that always clung to him.

"I'll arrive around 9:30, and that will give you a chance to giggle and snoop through your stockings, yet enable me to arrive in time for breakfast. I hear your mother makes wonderful Christmas bread."

"It's practically famous," answered Julia, smiling. "She braids the dough into the shape of a Christmas tree and uses cherries and fruit as its Christmas ornaments. She adds cinnamon and honey and the bread actually melts in your mouth. You'll love it."

"Of that I have no doubt so I shan't be late," he said, as she walked him to the door. Julia's arm hugged his waist, her head only topping his shoulder by a mere two inches.

"Till tomorrow then," he said, kissing her tenderly.

Jim Morris, watching the pair from the partially open kitchen door, gave his wife a quick thumbs up accompanied by a broad grin. The relationship between his daughter and Seth Hayes was one he wholeheartedly encouraged.

Seth leaned down and whispered into her ear. "Be surprised at nothing," he said softly, only for her to hear. "It's a whole new world now; everything has changed between us as you will soon see."

Loren Lockner

He opened his umbrella and scurried into the driving rain as Julia watched his lean form head for his Jeep. She missed him already.

As he drove carefully on the rain-slicked roads that twisted from the Morris' house to Paul's condominium, there was no question he was being followed. Seth slammed his fist against the steering wheel of the Jeep Grand Cherokee and cursed aloud. He didn't care that it was the wee hours of Christmas morning on the east coast and that he'd probably be getting someone out of a warm bed to hear his complaint. This had to be taken care of immediately, and if anyone dared suggest he transfer out of the area, he'd tell them right where to stuff it. There was no way he'd relocate when his very soul pulsated with every breath his sweet love inhaled.

Mandy Gaskill was in a bit of a dither. After the demanding call from Seth Hayes at two in the morning she knew something had to be done, and quickly. At the office by five a.m., Mandy pulled out the thick manila file she'd only retrieved a few minutes earlier from the sealed files of the Angus' personal safe and scanned it contents. The incredibly handsome face of a dark-haired man with steel gray eyes glared back at her. His demeanor held the beginnings of a fierce scowl and she could understand his mood completely. Here was a man who'd been forced to do something he hadn't wanted to do in the first place and now was paying the bitter price.

Seth Hayes had asked for answers within twenty-four hours and he was going to get them; no matter if it was Christmas or not. She'd already run the license plate number and discovered the car was registered to one Adam Gable. He lived in a small apartment complex in Stockton, California; employed as an auto mechanic at Speedy Garage in the north of town. The description Seth supplied fit the image she now analyzed of Adam Gable; a man currently on parole for larceny and grand theft auto. He also had prior drug possessions and two DUIs. Adam's sallow, uneven face appeared unhealthy and she wondered if he dabbled in illicit drugs.

While he seemed to hold down a steady job at Speedy Garage, his links with the criminal underworld were well-documented and he had twice been investigated for unsolved assassination-type murders. Apparently a good mechanic, he had a series of regular customers who depended on his expertise with their expensive cars. Speedy Garage held a contract with Emerald Limousine and Adam also worked with the pricey firm, servicing their cars. She noted his salary had been submitted to the IRS as forty-five thousand dollars the previous year, and he'd taken several trips to Mexico and Hawaii.

"Wow," she whistled. That was over sixty thousand Canadian, a heck of a lot more than her pay.

She also noted the brief paragraph regarding Lucas Hayes. As far as she knew he'd been relocated to somewhere in British Columbia as a security measure, though the file didn't indicate where. Seth was justifiably concerned about his cousin's safety if what Mandy had heard about Joe Alletti was even half-true. Mandy hoped some reassurance from Angus O' Leary might help calm Seth down.

Besides, she speculated, maybe this Adam fellow wasn't following Seth for any of the reasons the young architect suspected. Since grand theft auto was the ex-con's forte, perhaps he'd spotted Seth's Jeep Cherokee and designated it for a snatch. Cherokees were at the top of the preferred auto theft list in California, which might explain his surveillance of Seth. The most important thing was to get a tail on Seth as soon as possible and make sure his position hadn't been compromised. It wasn't like they hadn't been keeping tabs on Seth. They knew all about his job, his current housing and roommate Paul Morris, as well as his relationship and subsequent affair with Julia Ann Morris.

As far as Mandy knew, everything seemed legit with Paul, his girlfriend Angie, and his sister Julia, but she'd check again. It never hurt to be too conscientious when dealing with a witness' safety. So, even though it was Christmas, the matronly woman pushed back her mousy brown hair and realized the only way to placate Seth was to work diligently until it was time to leave for her daughter's house for their traditional Christmas dinner. Her face clouded for a moment. Her daughter's divorce had been a nasty blow and a show of family unity at this time in Liz's life was crucial.

The snow blew fiercely across the street from her building, but she set her mind to the task at hand, working uninterrupted for over three hours. At the end, now justifiably concerned and more than a bit apprehensive, she rang up Angus. The muted drone of Christmas music in the background mingled with the laughing frivolity of Angus' many grandchildren.

Angus' voice was steady, as usual, and he didn't seem at all perturbed she'd called him this cold Christmas morning.

"Damn," echoed Angus' succinct comment across the lines. "Are you positive?"

"I've done three hours of cross-checking. Something needs to be done and done today."

"But it's the middle of Christmas," protested Angus, and immediately regretted his words. Without action it very likely could be Seth's last Christmas. "Who's your associate down in the LA area?"

"A man by the name of Stan Garten."

"Put him on it immediately. Arrange a safe house and have Stan transfer Seth tonight."

"Ah, there's a problem Sir; I don't think Seth's going to move."

"What?" came Angus' snort of disbelief. "What do you mean he's not going to move? If I tell him to move he's going to move!"

"He's rather heavily involved with a woman, and from the sounds of it will probably refuse to relocate. I think instead of yanking him from where he is, a more tactful approach might be to check out this Adam Gable more closely and have Stan shadow him. We may also want to check on Lucas. He's stashed somewhere in British Columbia."

"I know," mused Angus, warming to Mandy's idea. He ran a hand through his graying hair as one of his two German Shepherds began barking excitedly at his grandchildren. The place was a madhouse! "Do what you think is right; just make sure you keep that boy alive. Hopefully we won't have to use our backup plan. Get Stan on Gable as soon as possible. Ring Seth and convince him all's under control."

The call came late that Christmas evening, after Seth had returned to the condo, stuffed to the gills with succulent ham and the warmth of a loving, accepting new family. Mandy's monotone voice tried to sound reassuring over the distant phone line. She related everything she knew about Adam Gable, his priors, and suspected affiliations. Seth was not in the least comforted.

"And Lucas, how is he?" he demanded.

"Angus is working on it as we speak. If we have to, we'll move him, Christmas or not. We need to relocate you as well."

"I can't," he ground out between clenched teeth, glaring fiercely at Santa Barbara's holiday drizzle, and fingered the mobile phone. "I have a life here; a chance for a future. You can't uproot me now. I won't let you!"

It was just as Mandy had feared. "If they've found out where you are; even if we get rid of Adam Gable, it's only a matter of time until another one's coming after you."

"I can't abandon the woman I'm involved with now, because if I do I might as well be dead. You've got to find some other way! Keep a tail on this Adam fellow and give me at least until New Year's to decide."

"We'll do the best we can Seth," said Mandy, and hung up.

He wanted, no he needed, the comfort of Julia's arms. He longed to crawl beneath warm covers and seek refuge in her embrace and shut the darkness out. By rights he should tell her everything, but his innate caution, as well as the desire to protect the woman he loved, immediately bullied those immature thoughts aside. Julia wasn't involved in any of this mess, and damned if he'd drag her clean, trusting nature through the muck.

Yet the rational part of him knew it was way too late for any of these futile thoughts. He'd knowingly and arbitrarily dragged her into his world and worse yet, had made her his soul mate. No matter what happened, Julia was trapped and Seth cursed his inability to control his own destiny.

Seth wandered into his bedroom and pulled open the top drawer, where he'd fashioned a secret compartment. He wiggled the thin wooden backing aside and pulled out two items. The first was a deadly blue-black Beretta, loaded and ready. He touched the metal before pushing it aside and lifting the small red velvet box. The lid opened with a creak and he stood for a full minute admiring the exquisite diamond wedding set nestled inside white satin.

He'd picked out a channel setting where a large one carat diamond engagement ring, with two small .25 carat diamonds situated on each side, sat surrounded by beautiful eighteen carat Italian gold. The wedding band boasted seventeen diamonds recessed within its circular channel. It had cost him nearly two month's salary, but was worth every penny. Seth vowed that someday these rings would grace

Love Never Dies

Julia's slim finger. Strangely calm, he replaced the red velvet box next to the Beretta and tapped the gun with his forefinger.

"I will keep what I need to survive upon this earth," he pledged.

It took two full snifters of cognac and three hours of staring sleeplessly at the new aquarium, where a yellow tang, blue angel fish, and Moorish Idol jealously staked out their respective territories, to induce sleep.

Julia arrived bright and early the next morning, a large gaily wrapped parcel peeking underneath her arm. Attired in faded blue jeans, a bright blue UCLA sweatshirt, and comfortable loafers, she looked and felt cozy and warm. Once he released her from a bear hug embrace she grinned impishly.

"I have a little something extra for you Seth; something I couldn't give you in front of my folks." Julia handed him the good-sized present wrapped in bright foil paper and tied with a golden bow.

Seth let her into the inviting living room where he'd already lit a fire. He loved fires. Their encompassing warmth always indicated deep love and acceptance to him. Without fail, his father and mother had built enormous fires in the stone hearth every evening during the fall and winter in Canada. The dancing flames made him recall the memory of exchanging his soul with Julia and he felt his spirits lift.

Loren Lockner

"Another present for me?"

His eyes twinkled and he wondered if Julia felt the same tugging pull at her heart as he did. He'd known when she was about to approach, almost able to visualize her bounding up the steps; and even before her hand lifted the brass knocker Seth could sense her joyful anticipation of being with him.

He sank down upon the couch before the crackling fire, the Christmas tree lights blinking to his right. Julia dropped to the floor in front of him, crossing her legs Indian fashion and cradling her delicate face in her chin. Her dark green eyes sparkled up at him, studying his beloved face.

"Don't even think about it," Julia warned, as he was about to tear off the wrapping. "You know that's not how it's done. In our family the tradition is to always guess what's inside before you open a package, so behave."

"Hmm," said Seth, willing to play along with the game. "Well it's too small to be a convertible," he stated and pretended to pout.

Julia frowned, sniffing scornfully. "You can do better than that Hayes."

"Alright. Let's see... it's way too big for season tickets to the Lakers..." He shook the package, causing her to swat his hand.

"That's not permitted and you know it," she chided, as he grinned.

Love Never Dies

Seth had purposely done it to torment her. He observed all the rules yesterday, noting each step of the contrived game. Starting clockwise, each recipient admired each brightly wrapped package without touching it and then thanked the giver before trying to guess what was inside. It prolonged the enjoyment of gift giving and Seth enjoyed the warm tradition, wishing to embrace it as his own. At her expectant face he decided to give it a genuine guess.

"It's actually a pretty large package and could be just about anything. It's fairly heavy so it can't be an article of clothing. Hmm... I think it's a book," he said, "a skillfully wrapped coffee table book on architecture."

Julia's face lit up in a bright grin. "A good guess Hayes, but no cigar!" Her expression could only be classified as smug.

It was now time to move on to the next stage of the game so he made great fanfare of trying to untie the ribbon. Her fingers twitched in impatience, unable to conceal her acute desire to grab the large package from him and undo it herself because he was so blasted slow! But Julia knew the rules as well as he; one had to be patient. The giver had to suffer while the receiver dawdled and prolonged the gift-giving process, determined to torment the helpless observer.

Seth finally managed to untie the metallic ribbon curled so beautifully around the package before slowly ripping apart the golden red wrapping paper depicting bright Christmas bells. He lifted the lid to the sturdy box apprehensively, staring at the item wrapped securely in bubble wrap. As Seth pulled it out he realized it was a picture frame. Julia had stuffed tissue paper all around the painting to keep it from rattling. As he slowly unwound the bubble wrap his eyes widened in acute appreciation. It was the most beautiful thing he'd ever laid eyes upon and Seth gulped painfully.

The black and white pencil sketch was simplistic in style but precise in detail and he remembered the pose from an almost forgotten photograph. It had been one of those unique results from Paul's countless random snapping of the trio as they worked on his condominium. Seth had taken a breather and Julia had flounced down beside him, wrapping her arms around his waist and leaning back her head while he gazed down at her. Paul had immediately dubbed it 'the moment before a kiss.'

Now a beautiful sketch someone had painstakingly drawn from the original photo and enlarged to a full eighteen inches by eighteen inches emerged from the wrap. The artist had skillfully captured the love and adoration in Seth's eyes as Julia had smiled back, serene and content in her lover's arms.

"This is the nicest present I've ever received," said Seth sincerely. He leaned over the beautifully framed sketch cradled in his arms and kissed her tenderly upon the lips.

"You must help me find a special place to hang this lovely piece of art. How did you manage to find someone so skillful?"

"Down at the beachfront," Julia replied, gazing up at him from her position on the floor. "Lots of artists along the promenade sell their wares and I watched this one man for a long time as he sketched a little boy on a tricycle from a photograph. I realized this would be the perfect present to give you for Christmas. Johan was all booked up, but when I returned with the photo he agreed to try to complete it by Christmas. I only got it back two days ago. You do like it don't you?"

Seth touched her hair gently, tucking a wayward blonde strand behind her ear. "I love it," he said sincerely. "Help me find a place to hang it." They strolled through the condominium hand-in-hand to determine which wall would be the best to display his prize. Seth finally decided upon the spot right above his bed.

"This way I can gaze at it every night before I go to sleep," he stated. Within minutes they'd found a hammer and nail; and the Monet print, previously hanging above his bed, was dispatched to another open section of the room. "Lovely," he said sincerely, giving her a warm hug as they wandered back to the warmth of the fire and sank upon the couch.

Loren Lockner

Seth suddenly snapped his fingers. "Oh no! I forgot to give you your special gift."

Julia's face lit up and she clapped her hands delightedly. "I just knew it! I knew there had to be something else."

"Greedy little thing. Didn't you like the set of cookbooks you requested, or the gift certificate for that trendy bookstore you're always spouting on about? And I thought the jacket was simply stunning."

"Oh it was," she agreed enthusiastically. "The red wool coat feels just like cashmere and is so stylish, but I had an inkling there was something else. So what is it?"

Seth gave a secret smile and disappeared for a few moments, finally returning from the recesses of his bedroom with a long slender package resembling the kind a florist uses when they deliver a dozen long-stemmed roses. The package was feather-light to her touch and Julia caressed the gold foil before venturing a guess.

"Well it's very, very light. Perhaps it's some sort of garment." Seth leaned back upon the beige couch and folded one leg across the other before giving his dark head a resolute shake.

"Wrong. Would you like to venture another guess?"

"What is this, twenty questions?" snorted Julia in mock grumpiness.

Love Never Dies

"I'll give you two more guesses and if you don't figure it out I'll just have to take it back."

"Wise guy huh? Okay, so it's not an article of clothing? Ah ha," said Julia, lifting a red polished fingernail. "You know that I have been dying to see the new production of *Evita* at the Dorothy Chandler Pavilion; is that what it is, a pair of tickets?"

Seth mimicked a fake game show buzzer. "While that's an excellent guess, I'm afraid you're dead wrong. I will, however, keep that in mind as a future excursion for us."

"Alright," said Julia, ticking off what it was not upon her fingers. "It's not an article of clothing, a fancy little negligee or something?"

Seth lifted his eyebrows provocatively. "Now that's an idea," he quipped.

"And it's not tickets to any production at the Dorothy Chandler Pavilion. Hmm, that doesn't leave much."

"Just the whole world," reflected Seth watching her with affection.

It was time Julia got down to some serious guessing so she pushed up the sleeves of her UCLA sweatshirt. "Alright, this guess is going to be it, and if I win and discover the right answer you have to give me a hundred kisses."

"Ooh," said Seth, "am I allowed to give you some hints?"

"Nope, no cheating allowed. I either do this legitimately or not at all. Let me see," she tapped her cheek thinking hard. "It's got to be something I *really* like from that overly smug expression on your self-satisfied face. Let me see, let me see." A strange idea passed over her face and she shook her head as if chiding herself. "No, you couldn't possibly have done that; besides it wouldn't be allowed, not in the least."

"And what is that?" asked Seth, almost afraid she'd somehow guessed his special gift.

"Do you remember when we were in the mall a couple of weeks ago and popped into the pet store and saw the cutest little puppy in the world?"

"Really," said Seth nonchalantly, brushing an imaginary speck of lint off his spotless white shirt. Suddenly Julia knew she'd hit the nail right on the head.

"It's a gift certificate for some sort for a puppy isn't it?"

Seth cleared his throat shakily. It was as if Julia's thoughts had meandered through his mind, and try as he might to disguise the perfect gift, she'd still stumbled upon it.

"I think you'd better open the package," he said softly, and Julia made swift work of it. Inside the florist box nestled another smaller box also beautifully wrapped in gold foil. Julia chortled in delight and unwrapped the next package. Inside lurked another; a small square box so lightweight it clearly contained only paper. She lifted the lid and inside, rolled like a precious piece of parchment bound by gold foil ribbon, was a white piece of paper. Julia slid the ribbon off and unrolled the letter, reading the short note out loud.

"My dearest Julia. You're to be the happy recipient of a new Keeshond puppy, available for immediate adoption upon the sixth of January. The litter contains four females and two males, and you're allowed to pick the puppy of your choice." Julia shrieked and threw herself onto his lap as Seth rolled back his head and laughed, his straight teeth parted in utter contentment.

"It's the perfect gift, the perfect gift! I've always wanted a puppy but..." Her voice trailed off and she froze, still perched upon his knees. "We live in an apartment and I don't think they allow pets."

"Well your landlady, Mrs. Nelson, seems to think otherwise. I told her I wanted to buy my girlfriend a puppy for Christmas and the lovely lady indicated she might make an exception since she herself has two poodles. Then I started telling her all about the Keeshond breed; how they originated in Holland and were used to patrol the barges as they drifted down the canals. To make a long story short, she as a girl raised many Keeshonds of her own. In fact, her father had been a breeder of the furry dogs, and when I mentioned what kind of puppy I'd chosen, she agreed you could have one, declaring the Keeshond is the most noble of dogs since it rarely barks and is always polite to strangers and other dogs. We'll pick up your present on the sixth since the puppy will be eight weeks old. I just hope Angie doesn't mind her roommate receiving a Christmas present that isn't housebroken."

"She better not mind," growled Julia, looping her arms affectionately around his neck and giving him a long sweet kiss. Seth enjoyed the first kiss so much he bent his lips down for another until the distant shrill jar of his cellular phone caused him to flinch.

"Saved by the bell," he chuckled, and gently moved Julia from his lap onto the soft leather cushions of the sofa. "Now just don't forget where we were. I'll be back as soon as I can."

He dashed to his cell phone which rested upon the mahogany dresser next to his bed. It was Mandy Gaskill.

"We've got a tail on Adam Gable," she said without preamble, "and I just wanted you to know that your cousin Lucas is safe and has been moved to another province in Canada, though I have no inkling as to where that might be." Seth gave a sharp sigh of relief.

"If anything I think we've bought you some time. We're going to tail this Gable fellow and find out what his game is. I still wouldn't be surprised if he's after your vehicle."

Love Never Dies

Seth gave what could only be classified as a dismissive grunt. "I have my doubts about that."

"Anyway I want you to watch yourself. You have a weapon?"

"Yes," said Seth slowly.

"Then I suggest you start packing it. One can't take their own security for granted. Like I said, we'll tail him and do the best we can to keep you safe until we find out what is going on. Have you told the woman?"

"You mean Julia," he said softly, her very name a caress upon his lips. "No I haven't. I'll wait until I get your final report. Just keep my cousin safe."

"And regarding the other party? What do you want me to do about him?"

Seth gave a sharp intake of breath. "Don't move on that at the present moment. And whatever you do, don't tell Lucas what's happening. Let him live thinking I'm safe. Promise me that okay?"

"He, as well as *all* your family, has a right to know," said Mandy stiffly.

"Neither he, nor *anyone* else for that matter, has a right or a need to know. You and Angus promised me to keep all this quiet and I'm going to hold you to that. I'll stay in touch."

"I'd like you to fax me tomorrow with all the names of people employed at your firm, even though we may have already checked them out; we're going to double check again. And Seth, the woman you're involved with, do you think you could possibly see a little less of her or maybe...?"

"When hell freezes over! Whatever you're contemplating just put it out of your mind! There's no way I'll stop seeing Julia Morris, now or ever. And about my tail Stan Garten? He needs to reveal himself to me so I know friend from foe. Tomorrow morning, at seven a.m., I'll make a trip to the mini-mart at Cornwall and Fifth to buy a newspaper. Have him relate the code word to me so I have a face to go with the name."

"Got it," said Mandy, deciding she'd gotten off easy, and hung up on the phone.

The next morning Julia barely stirred as Seth kissed her on the forehead. She opened her eyes languidly.

"You sleep, love; I'm just whisking off to get a newspaper. When I return, I'll make you breakfast in bed. Would you like that?"

Julia sighed and reached a finger up to caress his cheek. "I'll be waiting," she answered sleepily before drifting off once again.

The Quick Stop was already busy for a Sunday morning. At 7 a.m. Seth moved to the magazine section and browsed the sports and car magazines, keeping a watchful eye upon the stream of customers who sauntered in on their countless Sunday morning missions. One harassed lady wearing outdated sharp-pointed reading glasses bought a can of cat food and a plastic container of orange juice. Another balding man, who looked like he hadn't gone to bed the previous night, headed toward the antacid section and purchased two packages of the strongest tablets available. Seth watched all in a bemused manner, waiting for the one person who could give him some peace of mind.

Definitely not that one thought Seth, as a harried mother with two toddlers trailing her and crying for breakfast scooped up a loaf of bread and a half-gallon of milk before hurrying to the cash register. An older man waltzed in and slammed down twenty dollars on top of the counter.

"Unleaded," he shouted before running out as the overworked sales clerk wagged her red-tinted hair and punched at the computer keyboard. Seth noticed a skinny man with a huge Adam's apple, dressed in blue overalls, pick out two blue energy drinks. Because of his preoccupation he totally missed the next man who quietly entered the store. Tall and in his mid-to-late thirties, he wore a heavy black motorcycle jacket. A bushy black moustache and thick hair growing slightly silver at the sides afforded him a distinguished appearance; though the dimple in his chin suggested a reckless nature. His eyes surveyed the store's few customers before zeroing in on Seth. He studied the tall architect for a long moment before finally strolling over to the magazine rack to pick up a computer gaming magazine. He cast a sideways glance at Seth and nonchalantly winked one brown eye.

"You wouldn't by any chance know if they have any articles on the computer game *Simon Says*?"

"I wouldn't know," said Seth, eying the muscular man. He noticed the telltale bulge inside the biker's leather jacket and immediately relaxed. "I'll certainly keep an eye out for any articles on that game and let you know." He replaced his roadster magazine, and picking up a Sunday newspaper paid the overweight clerk before waltzing out the store. So that was Stan Garten and suddenly Seth felt immensely relieved.

Chapter 5

The next few days were an immensely pleasant aftermath of the Christmas holiday. There was shopping with Julia and her mother, a couple rounds of golf with Jim Morris, and on the thirtieth of December a visit to Gaviota to look over the six puppies, one of which Julia planned to adopt within a week. Twice Seth spotted Stan Garten in the distance, and while unobtrusive, he was an obvious presence. Seth did not observe the stalker's silver Lexus again and began to relax.

As they walked up to the Mediterranean house with its well-manicured lawn Seth gave Julia a word of advice.

"I've heard that when picking a puppy you should sit down on your haunches, outstretch your hand, and see which puppy comes to you first. That's the one you'll want."

"Like the puppy will pick me? So you *are* an expert," she said, giving him a warm hug, her arm remaining to drape loosely around his waist. She could never get enough of touching him and that warm tug signaling his undying devotion was always present in her heart, whether with him or not. So, as she and her soul mate waited before the elegant oak door after ringing the doorbell, Julia realized she'd never been happier in her entire life.

A petite woman with short gray-brown bobbed hair and standing scarcely five-foot tall beckoned them inside.

"I'm Mrs. Alistair," she said, her chin dimpling, "and you must be the lucky young lady who's waiting for her brand new puppy. Come inside and I'll show you the lot."

They followed her though a well-furnished open plan house with cool wicker furniture and spotless cream tiles leading to wide sliding glass doors opening upon a spacious grass lawn. Six furry little puppies whose tails curled over their furry backs frisked about a makeshift pen under the shade of a large mulberry tree as their proud mother sniffed around the expansive garden.

"Oh, they're adorable!" cried Julia, resisting the urge to claim each and every one.

"I'll tell you what I will do," said Mrs. Alistair. "Just sit over there on that lawn chair while I open the little gate here and let them out. Watch them play and interact with each other until you decide which one you want. There are four females and two males. If you're not planning to breed your dog in the future you might want to pick one of the females. Both the males are show quality."

"Don't get a male," suggested Seth quietly. "Choose a nice sweet female; they'll be smaller and easier to manage in your apartment." He gave no other advice, content to fold his arms and watch Julia delightedly examine the gray puppies. The minute the gate creaked open the six shot into the huge yard as if they had never been free before in their lives. They sniffed about, dashing here and there, their hind legs often functioning separately from their forelegs, which occasionally caused the overeager pups to land in jumbled heaps upon one another.

Four of the rambunctious puppies totally ignored them but two of the smaller females hovered about, examining the quietly observant humans. Finally, one of the awkward females tentatively moved forward. Her short gray puppy fur had not yet given way to the long silver and black fur of her proud mother. She edged closer and peered directly at Julia before giving a high little bark and sitting down upon Julia's foot. Delighted, Julia swooped down and snatched up the puppy that wiggled her short legs wildly. As Julia pulled her closer the dog leaned forward and gave her newly chosen mistress a quick lick of her small pink tongue.

"This one," Julia announced excitedly to Seth. "This is the one I want!"

Seth smiled indulgently. "Compared to the others she seems quite peaceful," observed Seth, watching the other puppies dash about. The little Keeshond seemed content to be held upon Julia's lap. "And just what are you going to name your new found friend?"

"Hmm," mused Julia. "Such a peaceful dog needs a special name. We've been reading Russian fairytales in class and..." Julia snapped her fingers and the little puppy's head shot up. "Mira! Doesn't Mir mean peace in Russian? Since this is a girl, I'll just add an 'a' and call her Mira." She nuzzled the dog's soft fur and received a quick lick as a reward.

"I see you've made a friend," said Mrs. Alistair, who'd arrived with a plate of cocktail sausages cut into bite-sized bits. She whistled to the dogs scurrying around her feet to greedily snatch the tidbits from her fingers.

"Why don't you give your new puppy a piece?" Mrs. Alistair asked Julia, handing her a sausage.

Mira took it delicately from her fingers. Even at seven weeks this Keeshond was a real lady.

It was with great reluctance, over thirty minutes later, that they left the puppies.

"You'll remember which one it is?" asked Mrs. Alistair, "because if you can't, I'll place a little red collar on her."

"I'll remember who she is," answered Julia confidently. "She's the one with the four dainty black feet and silver-tipped ears. There'll be no mistaking my Mira."

Seth once again felt the complete blanket of contentment wash over him. It was the same delicious feeling that had resided within him ever since he and Julia had exchanged souls. There was no way on God's green earth he was going to lose all this now, and as he followed the gaily chattering Julia to his Jeep he realized it was time to call Angus O'Leary.

Angus seemed hesitant to follow through on any of Seth's options until the young architect nearly slammed the phone down in frustration.

"Blast it man," he snarled across the long-distance line at the portly police officer who he knew sat mildly at his desk. One thing Angus had gained from his many years of police work was the ability to stay calm. Seth felt that he was essentially a calm person as well, but not where Julia was concerned. If things weren't resolved over the next couple of weeks, Seth didn't know what he was going to do.

"Be patient man, we're working on it," soothed Angus. "Adam Gable completely dropped out of sight until the Stockton police spotted him at a local bowling alley. I've sent Stan up there so don't you worry, we'll keep a tail on him. We've relocated Lucas to a new province so everything's going to be just fine. Just keep your head low and your eyes open. The Santa Barbara Metro Police have been alerted to a possible stalker staking out your girlfriend and I've placed a female undercover officer in her building to keep an eye on her. Contact me after New Years and we'll revisit your situation."

And so the days swirled by in a happy haze. New Year's Eve was a joyous affair. The Morris' and a few family friends celebrated New Year's Eve with dancing and singing and the blare of horns at midnight. Later, in the dimly lit living room, the old black and white version of *It's a Wonderful life* with Jimmy Stewart caused Julia to fall asleep in the crook of Seth's arm. Seth drifted off, only to awaken at dawn with an old thick comforter placed considerately over them as the rest of the house slept.

Over the next couple of days Seth accompanied Julia to her classroom and helped change the bulletin boards and cut out letters. They sat companionably by one another, cutting out stars and moons for the bulletin board she prepared for her upcoming space unit. As she stapled on the planets Seth examined the large cork bulletin board filled with photographs of the round faces of her pupils. They were of every color; black, white, brown, and many had not yet lost the baby fat some seven-year-olds still carry. One particular little boy resembled Julia, with curly blonde hair and wide blue-gray eyes and Seth felt an overwhelming longing to have a son. As he watched the woman of his dreams putter around her tidy classroom he prayed he'd live to see their child.

It wasn't until January fifth, the day before they were supposed to pick up the Keeshond puppy, that a momentous event happened. They'd all been invited over to the Morris residence, that final Sunday evening before school began, for a wonderful dinner consisting of ham drenched in honey and pineapple, baked potatoes, fresh sourdough bread, and an unusual green bean casserole whose secret ingredient seemed to be onion rings soon loaded their plates. Jim Morris filled their glasses full of a light California White Zinfandel wine and toasted his lovely wife, who still managed to blush after thirty years of marriage.

Both Angie and Paul disappeared into the lounge directly after dinner to peruse some old photo albums while Seth and Julia retreated to the kitchen to relieve Mrs. Morris from dish duty. Halfway through the dishes a shout and roar of laughter issued from the front room, followed by a definite whoop of joy that could only have come from the boisterous Jim Morris.

"What on earth can that be?" asked Julia, drying her hands upon a strawberry-colored hand towel. She scurried out of the kitchen with Seth close behind.

Angie, lovely in a midnight blue silk dress, held her left hand up for all to see.

"He did it," she stammered. "He did it, lookie here!" and there on her slim white finger was the largest emerald-cut diamond Julia had ever seen. Julia's hand flew to her mouth and her eyes widened while Seth grinned knowingly at Paul. So he'd *finally* popped the question.

"Hmm," said Seth quite seriously after everyone had calmed down. "So I guess I'll be looking for new digs pretty soon?"

"Hold your horses Hayes; the wedding won't happen until June or July, but I just couldn't hold off asking her any longer. I had my proposal all planned for Valentines Day, but that ring's been burning a hole in my pocket for weeks, and Angie was making such a fuss over my parents' wedding pictures that I couldn't resist."

"He actually got down on one knee," burst out Angie, who looped her arms around Paul's neck and kissed him tenderly.

"This calls for a celebration," declared Jim Morris, hugging his wife impulsively, and within five minutes the pop of a Brut Champagne cork bouncing off the ceiling echoed through the merry house. The evening was a lovely finale to a beautiful holiday break and as Julia walked Seth to his car she sighed in perfect contentment while he tightened his arm around her shoulder. He kissed her gently on the forehead before unlocking his Jeep.

"I'm delighted to know that Paul is planning for his future. He couldn't find a better girl than Angie." said Seth.

"He appeared so happy, and did you see the look on my parent's faces; they couldn't have been more overjoyed if it was their own engagement."

"So he planned to propose on Valentines Day," commented Seth mischievously. "How very original." He sent her a searing look before turning away and Julia's heart leaped.

"You rarely speak of your family," Julia commented one misty evening in early January, as Seth lounged across from her at his favorite sushi restaurant. Sushi was a passion with him and he popped a crab California roll happily into his mouth after adding a healthy dose of wasabi and ginger to the concoction. He rolled his gray eyes in ecstasy. Julia relished his simple enjoyment of oriental food, thankful a wonderful sushi bar was located only ten minutes from her flat so Seth could get his weekly fix.

"You know about my mother and father."

"Of course, but were you an only child?" Julia suspected he wasn't, but had been afraid to pursue the subject before. She had a premonition his sibling was dead, but Seth was part of her and she had to know.

A shadow darkened his face and he took a swallow of green tea before answering.

"No. I have a brother and a cousin."

"A brother? What's his name?"

"Can't be trusted."

"That's his name?"

"No, but it's what I prefer to call him."

"Ooh. Do I detect a bitter note at the mention of him? Is this subject taboo?"

Seth shrugged and mixed more wasabi into his soy sauce before dipping a portion of a prawn sandwich into it. He let it soak up the hot juice for a moment.

"Let me put it this way. He's not my favorite subject *or* relative. Maybe, in a few months, I'll tell you more about him, but for now I prefer not to ruin my evening, the delicious sushi, or your sweet company by thinking about him."

Julia decided it was best to move on to the other relative. "And your cousin?"

"The salt of the earth. The kindest, most dependable cuss you'd ever have the honor to meet. He is, however, a rover, a wanderer, and just a bit of a cad; at least where women are concerned."

"Where does he live?"

Love Never Dies

"I'm not certain. I believe he's traipsing about Canada somewhere, probably with a couple of redheads keeping him warm at night."

"I take it he's not a one-woman man?"

"Not in the least. Of course, he's a full four years younger than me, a mere twenty-nine, and isn't ready to settle down like your old staid Seth. I'm not sure he ever will be."

"And what's this character's name?"

"A family secret."

"Seth!"

"It's true. I've got to make sure you're the forgiving kind before introducing you to the black sheep in my family. I prefer you judge me on my own merits, not by my two miscreant relatives whose reputations with women leave something to be desired."

"You're afraid I might like them!" she laughed.

"Nope. I'm afraid that they, with all the valiant Hayes blood flowing through their veins, will find you as irresistible as I do. Perhaps someday, after the noose of marriage has tamed your wild, passion-eliciting eyes, I'll introduce you to them. In fact—I promise you'll meet the dynamic duo on your wedding date. I'll make them swear to bring a clingy date and keep at least three meters away from you!"

His tone, though mischievous, reflected a strange deep-seated pain in regards to his brother and cousin, which he couldn't hide. So she reached across the black shiny table and squeezed his tanned fingers in her own. A warm glow tightened her chest cavity, as his soul responded and burned like a high-quality cognac neither had the desire nor power to resist. Love pulsated between them, turning his dark gray eyes silver with desire.

"I've had enough sushi," he said gruffly. "Would you care to join me for a nightcap in my room?"

She nodded warmly as the dark-haired waitress removed their heavy sushi boards and deposited the bill upon the table.

His joy joined hers in the dark less than thirty minutes later as his lips trailed down her neck and hovered over her heart.

"I can feel the beckoning warmth here," Seth whispered, kissing the tender skin where their two souls basked in the entwined fire of her pulsing heart.

"Yes," she panted, and let his body join her in a sweet symphony of motion, her chest burning and glowing as he took her roughly, crying out her name in joy.

Later she held him close and kissed his damp forehead as he sighed deeply, relaxed and content in the confines of her arms. Life could not be more glorious than this, she thought before drifting off, never suspecting a grim-faced man in a big silver car watched and waited for his opportunity to kill that which she held most dear.

Love Never Dies

The next morning, as Julia straightened the lapels of his tailored gray suit jacket, he promised, "I'll be by your house just after five and we'll drive to the beach and pick up the puppy."

"I can hardly wait," she answered, and he knew she wasn't just referring to the arrival of the eight-week-old puppy, but to the promise shining in his eyes.

That evening the gray fur ball curled itself upon Julia's lap as she stroked its soft springy fur. The little puppy immediately dropped off to sleep while Seth drove the twenty miles back to Santa Barbara. As soon as Julia had gotten home from work she'd made sure everything was ready for the new arrival; from the extra newspaper she'd retrieved from school to the softly cushioned basket where the puppy would sleep. Julia had filled the water and food bowls and the puppy sniffed at its new environment and lapped some water before falling asleep on the rug near the kitchen door.

Seth glanced around the immaculate flat Julia shared with her roommate. "Where's Angie?"

"Oh, I forgot to tell you; Angie and Paul drove down to see her grandmother in Ventura to show off her new ring. It wouldn't surprise me if they don't return tonight."

"Oh really," said Seth suggestively. "You know you may need someone here tonight since a puppy can be just like a newborn child, whining and needing to be let out. I should probably stay and help out."

"A newborn child whines and needs to be let out?" An impish grin crossed Julia's pretty oval face. "But I can see your point. I really *might* need some help, kind sir," and pulling at his arm, left the sleeping puppy snoring blissfully in the warm kitchen.

Julia woke peacefully that morning and stretched, Seth's warm slumbering body stretched out beside her. She gave a deep sigh of contentment before bolting upright in bed as the puppy's muffled whining and scratching penetrated her bedroom door.

She shook her lover awake. "Seth, how did the puppy get out of the kitchen?"

Seth quickly donned his briefs and trousers and rushed to the bedroom door. As soon as it opened the little Keeshond bolted across the carpet and leaped onto the bed. Julia, cradling the puppy in her arms, rose and followed Seth into the kitchen where he stood laughing and pointing.

"I think you have adopted a bit of an imp; look there. She's managed to push aside the baby gate you installed. Luckily it appears she hasn't had an accident yet. Quick, take her outside and sit her on the patch of grass near your car and see if she will do her business. I'll clean up the newspaper in here."

Love Never Dies

They bustled around that morning taking care of the puppy, fixing each other toast and three-minute eggs, and dressing for work. Seth donned a navy blue suit he'd left in her closet, and appearing professional and well-groomed, kissed her on the cheek tenderly as she grabbed her lunch off the counter.

"Why don't you come over to my place tonight?" he suggested, "and I'll fix you some dinner. I make a mean beef stroganoff. You can bring your bodyguard of course." The little pup cocked a head and gave a small bark as if in approval.

"I'll be waiting," said Julia, and kissed him full on the mouth, savoring the sweetness of his kiss. Later, she noticed the tug at her heart as he stepped up into his Jeep Grand Cherokee and lifted a hand to her. He adjusted his sunglasses and headed off to his firm as she put Mira outside and locked the apartment.

Her day was busy; Stephen Susiku had a bloody nose within the first hour at school and she got a stain on her pale cream dress that no amount of scrubbing could get it out. Later that day, a classroom bookcase collapsed, nearly striking one of her little girls, who sat crying on her lap for a good fifteen minutes as Julia tried to soothe her. In the afternoon she received a call from an irate parent who demanded that her son, who honestly was one of the most spoiled and overly pampered children Julia had ever had the displeasure to run across, be given special treatment during the upcoming Standard Achievement Test because he was traumatized by the school's rough handling of his delicate nature.

Julia tried to placate the parent and looked forward to seeing Mira and enjoying some of Seth's beef stroganoff. She wondered if it was wise to take her puppy to her brother's condominium and knew she'd have a lot to answer for if her puppy soiled her brother's beautiful beige carpet or parquet floor.

At just a few minutes after five she let herself into her brother's condominium, using the key Seth had given her, having left the whining puppy at home. It wasn't worth Paul's displeasure to risk an accident. Neither Seth nor Paul had arrived yet and the day had turned cloudy and overcast with a slow soaking drizzle. Julia strolled to the fireplace and using what few skills she'd acquired during her Girl Scout days managed to start a fire after fifteen minutes of frustrated stacking. It was at exactly 5:23 p.m. that early January evening that a monstrous pain ripped at her heart.

One trembling hand flew to her chest while the other groped for support. A red haze flashed before her eyes and she was unable to breathe. In that moment of agony Julia visualized a shattered windshield and blood trickling down through splintered eggshell cracks. She screamed, Seth's name reverberating through her brain. Julia dashed to the phone, not sure who or what to dial, and suddenly remembered her lover always carried his cell phone in his briefcase. She punched in his number, striving to regain a normal steadying breath. There was no answering tone or activation of his voicemail; only a lifeless silence that filled her entire being with a horrible chilling numbness.

Julia hysterically called her mother, who answered the phone after two rings and spent the next few panic-filled minutes trying to calm her distraught daughter.

"I'm sure there's nothing wrong dear. Please calm down; he's going to walk through that door any minute. Would you like me to drive over and stay with you? Is Pauli there?"

"He hasn't shown up," gasped Julia, a vice constricting her chest and threatening to suffocate her.

"Why don't you call Angie? I'm sure she's home by now and you can ask her to come over until I get there. When Seth arrives you four can have a nice dinner party. I'll show up later on the pretext of bringing some of my angel food cake. You wouldn't mind that now would you?"

Julia barely heard her mother's soothing words, her heart throbbing as if she bled inwardly. "I'll see you soon," was all she could manage before hanging up the phone. Five minutes later the phone rang ominously and she snatched it up.

"Hello."

"And to whom might I be speaking?" stated an official voice on the other end.

"My name's Julia Morris."

"Are you by any chance acquainted with a man by the name of Seth Hayes?"

A debilitating horror crept across her. "Yes, I'm his girlfriend."

"I'm sorry to inform you Ms. Morris that there's been an accident. I'm Officer Rodriquez from the California Highway Patrol."

"Is he hurt? Where is he? " Her first hysterical reaction was to dash where ever and check upon him.

"I'm afraid," said Officer Rodriquez hesitantly, "that after the collision, his vehicle was hit head on by a semi-truck carrying petroleum and his car burst into flames. I'm afraid Madam that..."

Julia didn't remember the receiver dropping from her fingers as the tinny voice continued in that dreadful monotone. Julia didn't know that she started to scream, the tones reverberating through her brother's condominium and echoing down the hall. She had no idea that people stopped what they were doing in the complex to open their doors, peering out to try and distinguish from where the anguished cry originated. The screaming still hadn't stopped when her mother arrived ten minutes later.

Helen Morris scooped her daughter up from the tight fetal ball she'd adopted upon the floor, her knees

Love Never Dies

clutched tightly within rigid arms as her screams methodically pierced the air with each breath. Helen frantically replaced the now dead receiver and called her husband, pleading for assistance while trying to soothe her hysterical daughter. Julia didn't notice when her brother and father arrived, or recognize they'd called 911 in helpless despair. The screams kept on until a prick in her arm took away that last shrill outburst and she faded mercifully into unconsciousness.

Chapter 6

Over the next couple of days Paul and Angie noted Julia's hands kept straying to her chest, plucking at the loose NYU sweatshirt of Seth's she'd donned after coming to herself and refused to remove. They couldn't know she kept pulling at it as if Seth's blood drenched the front. Her heart throbbed in such acute agony that she believed Seth was trying to reclaim his soul so he could move on to the afterlife, but she couldn't help him; her heart simply refusing to release that precious piece of him.

At night, when she managed to doze with the help of medication, Julia dreamed she saw him floating above her like a cloud, begging her to return his soul, but even in her dreams she staunchly refused. Over that first week the details of the crash were gradually released to Julia's grieving family. The fog-hampered road was treacherous, exhaust rendering the highway dangerously slick. The semi had slid across the center line and plunged headlong into Seth's Jeep Grand Cherokee. His car had spun around twice before crashing into a concrete retaining wall as the truck continued barreling on its relentless path, colliding once more with the 4x4 and causing the Cherokee to burst into flames. It had taken the Highway Patrol and Fire Engines ten minutes to arrive, and by that time the Jeep had been reduced to blackened smoldering metal. Seth had been burned beyond recognition, his dental records required by the coroner to prove his identity.

Jim and Helen Morris arranged everything as they tiptoed around their too-quiet daughter. The somber dignified funeral was a subdued affair as the silver-gilded casket, filled only with Seth's ashes, was lowered into the ground in a cemetery not far from the First Congregational Church. Julia remained deathly silent, watching mutely as Reverend Jacobs gave a brief eulogy for a man who'd died too young. Lenny Glickstern, the owner of Seth's firm, shook her pale hand and promised to take care of Seth's insurance and papers and she remembered stating clearly that Seth had a brother and cousin, but didn't know their names or addresses. Lenny shook his gray head as Julia watched Seth's casket being lowered into the earth. She knew there was no peace for him; not as long as she was alive.

She remembered reading *Wuthering Heights* in high school and recalled how Heathcliff had been doomed to wander the moors without his precious Cathy because she could not go on to her final destination without him, and Julia feared the same fate would be hers. Seth's words regarding his own father's demise replayed itself over and over in her mind and instinctively Julia knew Seth would never want her to do anything as foolhardy as take her own life.

Of course, her family couldn't know that, and no one ever left her alone for more than a couple minutes during those first few weeks after Seth's death. If she lingered in the bathroom for too long, the bottled-up tears finally overwhelming her carefully frozen face, someone was immediately knocking at the door. Julia didn't know her family checked on her each and every night, afraid of her overdosing with the tranquilizers her doctors had prescribed to help enable her to sleep; terrified she'd make a desperate attempt to rejoin her lover.

But as the days gave way to weeks they relaxed somewhat, though she'd lost a full fifteen pounds and appeared pallid and unhealthy. Her principal, Connie Fernandez, had called in a long-term sub and told Julia she didn't have to come back to work until she was ready, so Julia remained in the sheltering warmth of her parents' home, doing little but trying to make it through each day. Her father sat with her in his overstuffed recliner each evening, just like they'd done when she was a little girl, and made a pretext of watching TV. He cuddled his little princess, wishing he could make her pain disappear; not realizing his unconditional love and patience was the best healing salve his daughter could get. And so Julia made no attempt to return to her apartment.

Nearly three weeks after Seth's death Paul asked her to help go through Seth's belongings and Julia reluctantly agreed. She'd not returned to the condo since that fateful night.

"He didn't leave a will as far as I know," said Paul quietly as they entered Seth's room. "At least no one has contacted me, though Lenny Glickstern said he would look into it. He's been wonderful about everything."

The computer sat on the table just as she remembered, and Julia winced at the lovely sketch quietly staring down at her from above Seth's mosaic bedspread.

She took in a deep fortifying breath. "I'm sure he'd want everything to be donated to charity," she suggested bravely.

The next few hours were torture. They quietly went through his clothing before folding it neatly and placing it inside large cardboard boxes. Hanging in Seth's closet was an old denim jacket with wool lining that he'd worn on the weekends during the chilly and foggy Santa Barbara days, so instead of dropping it inside the box along with the other items, Julia placed it on the bedspread, determined to hang it in her closet in remembrance of him. His computer was to be donated to the architectural firm where Seth had worked for only six months since Lenny had expressed a desire to retrieve Seth's ongoing projects. Julia removed a recent photo album, dominated by shots of her family, and placed it atop the jacket.

Seth also had a few books; a worn out copy of *The English Patient*, a tattered and dog-eared edition of *The Lord of the Rings*, a collection of Bradbury's short stories, and two beautiful children's architectural books by David McCauley about *Castles* and *Cities*. They also joined the jacket and photo album. The beautiful sketch she'd given him for Christmas was the last item Julia took.

"You can donate the rest to charity," she said. "I don't want it."

"But what about the stereo and everything else?"

"The Catholic Church near here runs a children's home and since Seth was Catholic, I'm sure they'll especially appreciate the stereo and CD's. As for the furniture, I think you should have it."

"I don't feel right keeping his furniture."

"It was his donation to the house and it makes sense you should keep the lot unless a relative comes forth. I guess your choice is to sell the furniture and pocket the money or give it away. Why give it to somebody who probably wouldn't treat it with the respect it deserves? Seth helped make this condominium a home Paul, so keep those things he shared with you; the pots and pans, the dishes, and the furniture. It seems only right. I've taken the few items I want."

"And his bedroom set?"

Julia blanched. She had lain in that huge four-poster bed with Seth, sharing his body and his love. She'd dreamed about their future under its covers as he lay sleeping, his dark head crowding her pillow. There was no way she could ever use the bed again or enter this room as long as it remained in Paul's condo.

"Sell it and give the proceeds to the Catholic children's home. Don't keep it. Please."

Paul's eyes turned suspiciously shiny. "I'll place an ad in the paper right away. Is there anything else I can do Sis? Would you like to stay here with me for a while? In fact, why don't both you and Angie move in? I have two spare bedrooms and Angie and I aren't getting married until June."

"I couldn't stay here," said Julia truthfully. "Next week I'll move back in with Angie. Hopefully by June I'll feel better equipped to make it on my own, but for now I'm content to remain close to Mom and Dad." She rested a hand on Paul's lean arm. "There's something I need to tell you Paul. You remember Seth's story about soul mates?"

"Yes," said Paul, a frightened look darkening his emerald eyes.

"You recall how his mother's death from ovarian cancer propelled his father to kill himself?"

"Yes," whispered Paul, searching his twin's pale thin face.

"You need to know I'd never do that Paul. Seth wouldn't have wanted me to end my life. He told me once that love never dies and I know that no matter what, through life and after death, Seth will always love me. I have to hold on to that Paul. I'm praying that maybe tomorrow or the next day, or the day after that, I'll feel better. I'm not sure that I'll ever really feel better, but am going to try and maintain hope that I will. I don't want you, Angie, or Mom or Dad to be worried about me. And while each day I wonder how I'm going live without him, I know Seth would have felt that was the coward's way out and I refuse to be a coward!"

Her brother looked so relieved that Julia wanted to cry. She knew she hadn't been totally honest with him, for in her heart Julia understood Seth's father had killed himself because there'd been no other choice for him since half of his heart had been ripped out when his beloved Jenny had died. But as Julia stood in this too quiet room of Seth's, it was as if she could feel his presence everywhere. He hovered above her like some kind of guardian angel and whispered loving words of encouragement into her ear. Julia could not allow herself to perish because she knew she still held a part of his soul deep inside her heart and for now that would have to be enough.

Paul and Angie kept anxious watch over his sister, but outwardly, within a few weeks Julia seemed stable enough. She moved back in with Angie and threw herself back into her work, ignoring the well-meaning gestures of the concerned and forced condolences of the barely concerned. Julia made it through the days by plastering a professional mask upon her face and concentrating all of her attention upon her needy students. However, the nights were an entirely different matter.

As soon as the sun set, gloom spread over her wounded heart. Angie and Paul usually ate dinner with her and helped clean up the dishes, their quiet voices keeping the darkness away. But later, cloaked in the confines of her lonely room, Julia faced a reality without Seth. She learned quickly to muffle her sobs and cry silently so Angie or her brother, or even occasionally her mother, who often dropped by to visit, would not check on her. Her quiet bouts with despair were hidden in the secretive shadows of her own domain. It was during one of these bitter crying jags that her heart burned so desperately Julia could scarcely catch her breath, her shaking hand massaging her chest in a desperate attempt to stave off what she believed was an impending heart attack. The frantic hand soothed and relaxed her heart until finally it eased its desperate constriction.

Julia took to rubbing that spot above her heart each evening until eventually a strange belief regarding the alien piece of soul locked inside her breast overtook her. Seth was not at peace. Julia visualized him locked in some sort of hopeless limbo without a corporeal body and missing a complete soul. He'd lost his body in the dreadful combustion of his Jeep and had given half his soul to her and now was helpless to move on. There was no rest or peace for Seth's wandering spirit as long as she lived.

So, instead of contemplating an end to her life, Julia accepted the fact that some of his living soul remained within her. The soul does not die, as love never dies, and she gradually embraced the belief that Seth waited for her, trapped like some sort of phantom Cathy upon the moors of Yorkshire. She was a female Heathcliff, but unlike that famous character who'd made all around him miserable with his unrelenting cruelty, Julia embraced the thread of pure love Seth had extended toward her in life. He'd given himself unreservedly and completely and there had never been a moment of doubt regarding his devotion or fidelity. Julia was now positive he would patiently wait for her because that was all he could do.

In her dreams his face pale, like some wraith, whispered strengthening endearments to her and

Love Never Dies

begged her to not take the path his father had. Once, in the most precious of dreams, she saw him reclining in the purest of sleeps under the soft spread of a cedar tree, the scent of the bark permeating the air. He breathed softly and deeply, the rich luster of his black hair spread over the emerald grass, and she marveled at his male beauty and serenity. Julia floated down beside him, and nestling spoon style against his relaxed back, draped an arm over his sleeping frame and slept herself within the dream.

Upon waking, Julia determined that every night would begin with that remembered image, of her resting beside her true love in sweet repose, her hand caressing the still-glowing spot of his soul surrounded by her softly beating heart. If she never loved again, the fact that she had loved him so completely was more than she'd ever hoped for or dreamed of. But oh, how her arms ached for his touch and sweet kiss and when, oh when, would her pillow stop becoming soaked with her hot tears? And, in profound moments of helpless weakness, Julia wept for the children they'd never have, the silver hair on his head she'd never caress, and for the life she'd never lead.

It was the students who were her salvation. Their reactions the first day Julia walked back into the classroom to once again take over her duties from the highly efficient substitute was enough to keep her going through the next few months. They threw themselves into her arms, laughing and crying at the same time, and so Julia worked hard with them, listening to their little cares and woes, helping them curve their fingers to hold a pencil often too big for them, and preparing them to move on to the next big step of grade three. And when she returned home each night her little puppy Mira, who grew by leaps and bounds, would jump onto her lap to give her an affectionate lick, her fur turning the silver of Seth's eyes.

Angie and Paul set their wedding date for the following September after Labor Day and Julia, who knew they'd originally planned to marry in June, blessed them quietly for their consideration, ensuring she wouldn't have to survive a summer without work or a roommate. Her parents remained as strong and steadfast as they had always been, never pushing her to recover faster than her heart would bear.

One late afternoon, Paul stopped by the two bedroom apartment on his way home from work.

"I need to talk to you about something," he said quietly, and Julia led him into a bedroom so painfully neat Paul winced. "Um, when I was going through the remainder of Seth's clothing, I found this behind his chest-of-drawers. I think it slipped down the back somehow. Anyway, I think maybe, well... he had planned to give it to you. I've kept it for a while and after speaking to Mom and Dad, determined Seth would want you to have it; so here it is."

He held out a small red velvet case and Julia took it, knowing instantly what it was. Yet, when she opened it, she still gave an uncontrollable gasp; half in appreciation and half in despair.

The wedding set was absolutely splendid. A deep channel-set engagement ring was highlighted by a beautiful one carat diamond glittering in a deep golden groove, surrounded by a circular band of deep-set diamonds. The matching wedding band, whose bright diamonds nestled in a thick channel of 18 carat gold, glimmered in the light.

"Seth always had great taste didn't he?" she said shakily. "Today's Valentine's Day isn't it? You remember the night you proposed to Angie?"

"Yes," answered her brother slowly, straightening his shoulders and peering worriedly down at her from his six-foot height.

"You planned to propose to her on Valentine's Day but were so impatient you couldn't wait until then. Seth mentioned Valentine's was a great time for doing something like that and I knew then this was the day he meant to propose. And here you are handing his engagement ring to me. Somehow, I feel that's what he would have wanted. Thank you Paul for giving them to me."

"Why don't you come out with Angie and me tonight? I don't think it's a good evening for you to be home alone."

"I'll be just fine Paul. I promised Mom and Dad I'd share a glass of wine with them, and then I need to do something I should have done a while ago." She patted his hand. "You're not to worry; remember what I said a few weeks ago. Have a lovely dinner with your sweetheart. She deserves it. It's been a trying time for her as well and she's spent so much time being strong for me that Angie's been rather neglected. I hope you can make up for some of that neglect tonight."

"I'll do just that," promised Paul, giving her a heartfelt hug. "Oh, I almost forgot. There was one other item behind the drawer, along with the box." He handed her a plain white envelope the size of a postcard.

"It's just a little drawing. Maybe because Seth was an architect he sketched a logo or something for someone. See you later Julia." He leaned over and kissed her tenderly on the cheek before enfolding her in another warm embrace.

"You're the best brother Paul and I mean it. Now go show your girl a good time," urged Julia, placing the velvet box and envelope upon the top of her dresser. "I've got to run over to Mom and Dad's; I promised them I'd be there by six. I'll talk to you tomorrow then and it's perfectly alright if I don't see

Love Never Dies

Angie again tonight." Her brother gave her a wicked wink and departed.

Later, when Julia arrived home at 9:30, she moved to the closet where she had stashed the sketch. She resolutely grabbed a hammer, and placing a single nail to the left-hand side of her bed, mounted the special painting of Seth and her. Julia sat gazing at the sketch, remembering how Seth's lips had curved into that loving gentle smile. It was a long time before she rose and removed the single white sheet of paper from its envelope.

The sketch was delicate and lovely, depicting two rose bushes, one pink, one red, whose interlocking branches mingled as if one. Upon the thorny trunk the initials SMH rested above the letters JAM, surrounded by the faintest outline of a heart. Seth Michael Hayes loves Julia Ann Morris; and she clutched the paper to her breast and allowed her tears to flow unabated. Later she carefully refolded the crumpled sheet and replaced it inside the envelope, stuffing it underneath the wedding set she'd hidden behind her socks. It was a long time before she was able to sleep.

That night Julia had the strangest dream. She wandered through a huge white house, opening and shutting hallway doors at random, clearly searching for him. Julia knew she was getting close because the warm glow in her heart ignited and burned ever hotter as she approached a silver door at the end of the vast hall. The metal felt cool as she turned the knob. Seth, dressed in white, stood by a huge window, his ebony hair contrasting greatly with the bleached purity of the cloth.

He turned to gaze at her with silver eyes she'd never forget and Julia noted his face was pallid and drawn. His hair hung long and stringy around his face as if he hadn't washed or trimmed it in ages and a strange bandage covered part of his crown.

"Seth!" she cried out, but he didn't answer. Instead he just moved his too-thin hand over his chest, rubbing the painful spot.

"Seth!" she exclaimed again, demanding he hear her, but no matter how loudly Julia shouted he remained deaf to her cries and she witnessed his head droop in sorrow. Seth leaned against the wall and using it for support inched toward a narrow bed. He limped badly, and finally grasping the cast iron headboard, lowered himself painfully upon the white-clad mattress, his unclosed eyes staring blankly at the ceiling.

His hand began to rub the white shirt over his heart in earnest and Julia willed him to recognize she was there.

146

Love Never Dies

Finally the simple words burst from his lips. "I love you forever my Julia and I will come back for you. Please wait for me my dearest, please wait!"

Julia bolted upright among the damp covers of her bed, her head and heart throbbing. "Take back your soul," she cried to the darkness, begging him to depart the sterile limbo he was trapped within. But no matter how she shouted into the darkness the burning knife in her breast only cut more painfully. "My poor, poor Seth," Julia sobbed, knowing he'd chosen to wait for her; to wait until this life released her.

The days seemed endless as they plodded toward the end of the school year, until finally in May something odd shook her out of her lethargic preoccupation. On that hot spring afternoon she noticed a tan sedan parked outside the school fence. Julia remembered seeing it there before and thought she recognized the muscular dark man slouching behind the steering wheel. He had a wide bushy moustache and reminded her of a photo she'd once glimpsed of an old Greek aristocrat.

Julia had originally surmised he was the father of a student, but he now appeared to just lounge about, lifting a cigarette to his lips as he took a nonchalant draw. The watcher appeared to be in his mid-to-late thirties and as she strolled past, heading toward the copy room, he totally ignored her, instead observing the front office intently. Two days later, as she pulled her blue Taurus out of the teacher's parking lot, she once again noticed the tan sedan with its smoking occupant parked in the shade of a large eucalyptus tree near the east side of the school.

She reversed her sedan and headed back into the office intent upon telling the secretary, Kerry Matthews, there was a man outside who might be stalking some children. Too many horror stories had been broadcast about child molesters and one could not be too careful. Kerry instantly phoned Connie, who was watching the sixth grade boys practice basketball in the gym and the principal immediately instructed Kerry to call their in-house security. Julia and Kerry watched the heavyset Jose Martinez stroll lazily up to the car and speak to the obviously put-out man, who gave a disgusted snort before gunning his engine and roaring down Hyatt Avenue.

"Thanks for alerting me," said Connie, arriving just in time to witness the Chevy's departure. "As you said, one can't be too careful when working with children."

Kerry stepped outside the double glass door and spoke earnestly to Jose, who'd just jotted down the Chevrolet's license plate number and left to phone the police.

"And how are you doing these days?" Connie continued, more softly.

Love Never Dies

"Fine," answered Julia in her most normal tone of voice. She'd discovered most people wanted only a benign answer if and when they asked, but Connie was not so easily thwarted.

"Is it getting any better?"

"I'm able to work and exist on a fairly normal plane if that's what you mean. I suspect that's all I can hope for now. I recognize that there are all these stages of grief; shoot, my mother gave me the book and I've been reading it diligently." Julia sighed and shrugged. "Sometimes I'm not even sure I ever went through denial, though maybe I did. I'm just hoping I can finally achieve the acceptance part and move on with my life."

"Well it's evident to me you've gained back a few pounds and maintain a little more color in your cheeks. Could you accompany me into my office for a moment? I think now might be the opportune time to relay to you something interesting I observed last winter."

Julia sat down heavily across from her principal, a middle-aged Hispanic woman whose full red lips constantly smiled, brightening a luxuriant head of long black hair coiled in an attractive braid at her neck. Connie was well-liked by her staff and students and had apparently been offered an administrative position higher up in the district, but had turned down promotions twice already.

"I don't mind having a long tenure as an elementary principal, so ask me again in five years," she bade the District Office. Teachers and parents alike had breathed a big sigh of relief, Julia being foremost among them.

Connie cleared her throat and fingered her reading glasses among the piles of paperwork littering her desk. "It's about your boyfriend Seth. I saw him do something peculiar and hesitated telling you about it considering the timing. I was wondering; did he go in for tattoos?"

"I beg your pardon?" stuttered Julia stunned, not remotely expecting anything like this.

"Well," said Connie, hurrying on, distressed by the undisguised confusion upon Julia's face. "I was strolling on the promenade by some of those neat crystal and glass shops intermixed with the art galleries and restaurants. A few tattoo parlors are intermingled among the other specialty shops and I had ventured near them to visit one of our students, Carlos Ramirez, who'd broken his leg. I'd arranged a home tutor for him and was dropping off the paperwork at his parent's; they own the taco shop right near the skateboard landing. Anyway, to make a long story short, I glimpsed Seth standing outside Ernie's Tattoo Parlor. He hesitated for a moment and then ventured inside. That was on Tuesday morning, the day he died."

Love Never Dies

"So you think he was going in for a tattoo?"

"He may very well have, but who knows? Perhaps the next time you'd seen him he'd have sported a big old tattoo on his bicep complete with a gaudy anchor and the inscription, 'I love Mama.'"

Julia managed a half-grin. "You're right; that's a very strange and peculiar story, but thank you for telling me. I enjoy other's reminisces about him and add those little tidbits to my memory file. Sometimes people are too careful not to mention Seth so I'm very glad you shared that incident with me."

Connie smiled understandingly and accompanied her to the door, exchanging pleasantries before Julia once again headed for her car. She drove home feeling strangely unsettled and puzzled.

Once inside her room she felt around the back of her sock drawer, her fingers ignoring the soft velvet of the jewelry box and reaching for the worn envelope instead. She pulled out the beautiful sketch of the entwined rosebushes so delicately drawn upon the small white sheet. Julia ran a trembling finger over the drawing and drew in a deep shuddering breath, realizing Seth's commitment had been absolute. She only hoped he'd realized how much he'd meant to her.

In her free time that summer she helped Angie and Paul prepare for their wedding, whose date was set for

September fourteenth. Both her brother and Angie managed to get time off work and her brother secretly told her he'd booked a week in Cancun for their honeymoon.

"Tell Angie I keep talking about Yellowstone or Banff, or something like that." Angie was an outdoor enthusiast and loved to hike and camp. The ploy might very well work, so Julia dropped a few subtle hints to her future sister-in-law about trees and bears and whatnot as her brother grinned conspiratorially.

She also taught summer school and took a writing course in August to help pass the long summer days. During her free time she spent endless hours walking on the beach and collecting shells, helping her mother prepare for the wedding, and performing the simple maintenance needed for the oversized aquarium in her brother's condo. The fish were doing nicely and her brother had added a silver eel and several anemones with their resident tomato clowns to liven up the beautiful tank where red and green algae covered the natural reef rock as the yellow tangs darted about. It was peaceful working on the huge tank, and she recalled the enthusiasm gripping Seth as he designed the perfect saltwater aquarium for the spacious living room.

So the summer speeded toward Labor Day weekend and after school started once again, with a whole new class of small second graders gazing up at her with hope and trepidation, her brother's wedding

Love Never Dies

date arrived. The First Lutheran Church was filled to capacity as the sun streamed through stained glass windows depicting the Madonna and Child gazing lovingly at one another. The rosy rays fell upon the beautiful arrangements of gladiolas, baby's breath, and roses decorating the wide steps of the front altar. Her brother looked splendid in a black-tailed tuxedo, and he, in his typical mischievous manner, had placed a glossy top hat upon his head. On another man it might have looked silly, but on Paul it looked jaunty and appropriate, making him resemble a modern-day version of Fred Astaire ascending the matrimonial stair.

Angie's niece Cindy took her job seriously as the flower girl and dropped fragrant rose petals freely upon the aisle as everybody chuckled at the dainty little girl in her bright violet dress. The music swelled as the pale bride, stunning in an exquisite full-skirted white gown with pearl beading covering the delicate front, approached. Beautiful gathered tucks ran the length of the material in the back and she wore a full see-through veil hinting at the lovely French braid dangling halfway down her back. Angie had never looked more beautiful or more nervous and Julia flashed a reassuring smile at her as Paul straightened his shoulders and received the hand of the bride from her suspiciously shiny-eyed father.

The wedding proceeded without a hitch and Julia noted her mother shed more than one tear as Jim

Morris beamed proudly at his only son. She steeled herself for the reception, recognizing too much genuine merriment and laughter would abound in the church's flower-clad banquet hall. As Julia joined the reception line, she once again felt that strange pang above her heart where Seth's soul lived. He should have been standing here next to her brother, watching the scene with his bemused gray eyes and tossing off cryptic comments as he was inclined to do.

Instead he lay in a grave she secretly visited every Sunday morning to lay two beautiful roses, one pink and one red, upon his mowed plot. Julia would sit and converse with him, even though she knew only his ashes were interred under the earth, and found it comforting to relay her week's business to his ever attentive ears. Sometimes, though not as often as in months previous, Julia cried, but more and more she was able to speak in resigned tones about her life without him. Oh, how she wished he were here!

The bride and groom headed onto the dance floor and did their single waltz together as the festive crowd watched in delighted appreciation before moving onto the parquet floor themselves. Julia found a lonely chair near the buffet and watched her brother laughingly twirl his new wife around the floor.

Julia couldn't know that in a shadowed corner of the reception hall, a sad dark-haired man watched the transparent emotions flit across her face. He shook his head grimly, wishing he could somehow ease her pain. If only he knew a way to make her life easier. Julia was too thin, he could tell, having apparently lost a great deal of weight after Seth's death; and her delicate face gleamed palely against the lovely violet dress Angie had chosen for all her bridesmaids. How he wished he could enter the noisy banquet hall and greet her, but knew that would probably be too much of a shock for her frail system. Instead he'd have to devise a more subtle way to meet her, so she'd know Seth hadn't died completely friendless and without family. Thus determined and fortified, the tall stranger left the joyful reception hall with its one somber inmate, resigned to wait a few more days before he made his move.

Chapter 7

The letter arrived in a nondescript white envelope with only a return address in the upper left-hand corner. Julia opened it with all the rest of mail, which included the electric bill, a short note from her grandmother, and an invitation to attend the upcoming P.T.A dinner to be held at the school within two weeks. Her heart recoiled in shock at the contents and she reread the single sheet three times before picking up the phone and dialing her brother and his new wife. It was October first, and Paul had only just returned from his honeymoon ten days ago, restarting work at Tri-Tek amidst a great deal of grumbling. When he heard his sister's voice Paul instantly knew something was terribly wrong.

"Could you and Angie come over here right now? I received something in the mail I have to show you. Something that is well... almost frightening. Please Pauli?"

Love Never Dies

Paul had not heard that kind of distress in her voice for months and immediately agreed. Angie was in the kitchen chopping vegetables for their late evening stir-fry.

"We've got to go over to Julia's now; something's happened." Angie's brown eyes locked with his and without a word she grabbed her coat.

Within fifteen minutes he and Angie were seated at the small breakfast counter in the two bedroom flat Julia and Angie had shared as roommates only a couple of months earlier but now Julia had taken as her own. Mira lay at his feet as Paul reread the letter twice and shook his head grimly.

"Did you know Seth had a brother?"

"Well yes. Seth indicated he and his brother had had a severe falling out and when I tried to pursue it further, said he'd talk to me about it later. Seth also mentioned having a cousin but never went into much detail about him either."

"But this is not from the cousin, but the brother Simon. He says he would like to meet you but is afraid to do so because you'll be shocked because they were twins."

"A twin!" snorted Angie. "You would have thought that was something worthwhile mentioning to you Julia."

"You're right. It all seems so confusing now," said Julia, pacing the kitchen again for the hundredth time.

Angie scanned the letter again. "I don't know what to say Julia. If it's going to upset you, maybe you should just let us handle it."

Julia wagged her head vehemently. She'd never played the coward before and wasn't about to start now. "It says he has something for me. Do you have any idea what that could be Paul?"

"Maybe some of Seth's personal effects; who knows. So you're going to agree to see him?"

"I don't know," said Julia, wringing her hands. Paul let her pace about, knowing the decision had to be hers. Finally she settled down and inspected the letter again. "I guess I could meet him, but only if the two of you agree to be here as well. I don't want to see him alone. You know if they're twins, they probably look similar."

"What if they're identical twins?" said Angie, the thought just hitting her. "Maybe that's why he's so afraid of distressing you."

"I still can't believe Seth wouldn't have mentioned the fact he had a twin brother to me, though he did mention twins ran in his family. It seems so unlike him."

"Was it?" asked Paul, rising and straying to the window overlooking the sparkling blue compound pool. "Was it really? One of my profoundest memories of Seth was how very private he was. I recall him mentioning once how he'd had a falling out with some people he'd known on the east coast and that's why he transferred here. To make a new start he said. His deciding not to talk about a brother who'd pissed him off doesn't seem unlike him in the least somehow."

"But no one came forward after the funeral. There were no phone numbers or any sort of records indicating relatives at all and suddenly this brother shows up," grumbled Angie.

"Yes, but we also left the search for a will and family members to Lenny Glickstern, remember? Maybe he was successful in his search but never mentioned anything to us because he knew how distraught Julia was."

But Angie's mind had already taken a different track. "Paul, you remember my great-aunt Beatrice and her sister Sharon?"

"Yeah, what of it?" said Paul, drumming his fingers on the window sill.

"They didn't speak for forty years even though only fourteen months separated them. Then one day Aunt Beatrice calls her sister Sharon up just like nothing had happened and asks her to come over for tea. Though they only lived an hour away, they'd managed to avoid each other for nearly forty years. When they finally got together they couldn't even remember the reason they hadn't spoken for all that time. Maybe that's what happened to Seth and his brother. Now it's too late for Simon to make amends to his brother, but he *can* to his brother's girlfriend. I think you're right to meet him Julia, but I also believe Paul and I should be there as a backup."

Paul smiled at his bride. She was always clear-headed and rational, and had that uncanny ability of getting right to the root of a matter. "I believe you've hit the nail right on the head Carter! This Simon has a Santa Barbara phone number so I think you should give him a call Julia."

Julia shifted nervously upon the mauve couch. "No, why don't you call him Paul. I'd feel so much better if you did since I'm just not sure that I could talk to this Simon in any sort of normal manner. Could you do it for me?"

"Alright," said Paul, returning to the couch and smiling down at her. His sister had substantially more guts than he. "When would be a good time to meet him?"

"Tomorrow night, if you guys are free."

"Absolutely," said Paul reassuringly. "Let's make it for 6:30." Paul moved confidently to the phone, his broad forefinger punching in the numbers Angie dictated to him. A voice similar to Seth's answered the phone.

"Simon Hayes," came tersely across the line.

"Hello, my name is Paul Morris and you sent my twin sister a letter indicating you were Seth Hayes' brother and would like to meet her?"

Love Never Dies

"That's correct," uttered the quiet voice across the line.

"My sister's had a rough time, and while she's willing to meet with you she'd like to do so only in the presence of her family. I hope that's alright with you."

"Of course," returned the pleasant voice. "What time is good for you?"

"How about tomorrow night; six-thirtyish? May I give you directions to her flat?" Simon answered in the affirmative and Paul recited the directions to Julia's two-bedroom apartment, gave a brief goodbye, and hung up the phone.

Julia's arms were crossed defensively across her chest but she managed a brave smile. "So it's done."

"He'll be here at 6:30. Don't you worry about anything Sis since Angie and I will be present to back you up. Everything's going to be just fine."

6:30 came way too early for Julia. She straightened the apartment, rearranged the dining room table, adding fresh cut gladiolas as a centerpiece, and even made some cream cheese appetizers for Seth's brother. Around five p.m. she felt that familiar burning pull within her heart; the one that occurred when she knew Seth was near or agitated. Considering his feelings regarding his only brother, she was certain his soul somehow protested his brother's intrusion into her life and was letting her know about it in no uncertain terms. The burning sensation, as well as the clock's persistent march toward 6:30 made her a nervous wreck.

"I have to see your brother Seth," she whispered to the ceiling. "It's the right thing to do and you know that as well as I. I'd appreciate it if you'd try to prop me up for this encounter and be a little supportive okay?"

Amazingly, her chest soothed and she rubbed her yellow shirt front in gratitude before placing four wine glasses upon a white wicker tray.

"Try to calm down," urged Paul nearly ninety minutes later as he approached the wine cabinet and pulled out her one bottle of good brandy, pouring himself and Julia each a stiff dollop.

"You need to drink this down. I'm sure his brother is a nice enough guy and after he's been here for a few minutes and you've exchanged pleasantries we'll send him on his merry way. He just wants to touch base with someone he knew was his brother's girlfriend. It's the proper thing to do so you've got to relax." Paul fiddled with his wedding band, a sure sign he was agitated, while Angie cast her sister-in-law a knowing glance as she placed silver napkin holders upon the glass coffee table.

At 6:30 on the nose the doorbell chimed, and since Julia was too nervous to open the door herself,

Love Never Dies

Paul did the honors. He gasped at the sight of Seth's identical twin, for Simon Hayes was the splitting image of his brother except for three minor details. The first existed in the form of a swatch of silvery hair discoloring his long dark hair near the crown of his head. The second was a thin white scar running from under his nose down to his lip; and the last was the extreme paleness of his skin; a pallor so unhealthy it appeared as if he'd been frightfully ill for the last few months. He immediately stuck out a lean hand to Paul, who shook it warmly.

"I'm Simon Hayes, Seth's twin brother." His voice was slightly deeper and huskier than his twin's but still possessed the unusual rich tones of the international traveler Julia had noticed the first time she'd met Seth. Julia forced herself to meet his face. Thinner than Seth by perhaps ten or fifteen pounds, the strange white swatch of hair sprouting from the crown of his forehead seemed odd and out of place and reminded Julia of a widow's peak she'd witnessed once on a friend of her mother's. Simon's hair fell shoulder length and he wore a single gold hoop in his left ear.

"I've been hoping to meet you for some time," he admitted. Julia noticed a brown leather briefcase hanging like a satchel over his shoulder as Paul moved aside to allow Simon Hayes' entry.

"You must be Julia," he said quietly, and extended a lean hand toward her which she grasped almost reluctantly. When he squeezed the slender appendage, she felt her heart burn painfully. There was no doubt about it, Seth wasn't only a witness to his brother's arrival but seemed highly agitated by his presence.

"I'm so sorry about your loss. I would have come sooner but certain circumstances prevented my traveling down here." He seemed to flounder so Angie piped in.

"We understand since it was such a tough time for us all. Please sit down. Can we get you something to drink?"

"Just water would be fine." He waited as Angie poured his drink, letting his eyes wander around the tasteful apartment.

"Did you hear about his death immediately?" asked Paul, seating himself beside Simon and pouring himself a glass of white wine. He lifted his eyebrows to Julia, but she gave her head a nervous shake. She was in no state to drink.

"No, not until late February. I'd been down in Detroit working on a project before zooming off to Manitoba for six weeks to finish up another. When I got home to Toronto, there was a message on my answering machine from my brother's lawyer informing me my brother had died in early January. I guess his employer had contacted Martin somehow, and now that I was home, there was going to be a reading of his will. By this time my brother had been dead for nearly seven weeks. Less than three days later

Love Never Dies

I was involved in a fluke car accident and was incapacitated for several months. You probably consider me some sort of heartless jerk to have missed his funeral but it was history by the time I heard about it. Once I felt better and could get additional time off work I flew to LA, rented a car, and drove up here. It had been almost ten months, and the more time that passed, the more difficult it was to call. I finally realized a call just wouldn't hack it after all this time and had to meet you in person."

"I take it you and your brother weren't close?" observed Paul, who disliked his sister's tight face and clenched hands as she perched on the edge of her easy chair across from the jean-clad Canadian.

Simon took a deep drink before answering. "Over the past year we weren't, but before that we were inseparable. We had similar tastes and after our parent's deaths we remained physically and emotionally close. We attended the same college and both received degrees in architectural design.

But, about a year ago we went our own ways after having a terrible spat. Seth didn't write me for a full six months and when he finally did, it was just a brief note to inform me he worked for a firm called Bastam, Hughes, and Glickstern in southern California. He said he wasn't going return to the east coast for awhile and suggested we keep up a mild correspondence until we worked out the problems we'd had."

"And what problems were those?" asked Angie, never hesitant to ask a direct question. She sampled the olive and cream cheese appetizers, never once removing her searching brown eyes from Simon's gray ones.

Simon's breath released in a sharp hiss and the trio swore a flush of embarrassment stole over his pallid cheeks. "We had a fall out over a woman," he said reluctantly. "I mentioned we had similar tastes and well, my brother was seeing someone and then..."

"Don't tell me anymore," said Julia abruptly. "I get the picture!"

Simon turned toward her, obviously relieved. "Anyway, I just wanted you to know that in the last few months of his life, from about October to January, Seth wrote me more often, sending me an occasional e-mail from work and indicating he'd met someone and was very serious about her. He told me he was living with her brother and was extremely happy with the arrangement. Seth even suggested I fly down for Easter to meet all of you. I could tell he'd gotten over much of his animosity toward me and was content to let bygones be bygones since he and I were all that we had left."

"I thought you have a cousin?"

"That's true, but Lucas... well, he's a wild one and God knows where he is now. He's a photojournalist and one week he could be in Kenya and the next,

Love Never Dies

somewhere in the Northwest Territories taking pictures of stinky musk oxen. I'm lucky if I get an e-mail from Lucas every six months. Since our family was spread out I wanted to reestablish my relationship with Seth. Lucas' parents died when he was just a teen, and then, well, my mom..."

"We know the story," said Paul breaking in. "Seth told us about your mom dying of ovarian cancer and what happened with your father."

Julia could have sworn that Simon let out an extended sigh of relief. "So he told you that? Well good for him. For years he wouldn't even talk about it. Anyway, when they read Seth's will, we discovered he'd divided up his holdings in Toronto."

"Toronto? Why would he have holdings in Toronto?" asked Julia bewildered, speaking for the first time.

"That's where we lived before coming here."

"I thought he was from New England?"

"Well we did live in New England; several places as a matter of fact. But we have dual citizenship. We stayed in Connecticut for a while and New York later on, before our parents moved to Toronto when we were teenagers. My brother liked it so much he bought a condominium on Lake Ontario. After his death I sold the condo as per the will's instructions, and... um... have the proceeds. I thought that maybe...," he floundered, clearly embarrassed by the whole situation.

"Simon, it's time for a glass of white wine. California makes some pretty nice ones. Why don't you relax for a few minutes and we'll talk about the will later."

Mira whined from Julia's bedroom, desperate to be let out. "I'm sorry," apologized Julia. "But I need to attend to my dog. Please try some of the appetizers. I made them this afternoon."

Simon sampled one of the delicious snacks and sipped a glass of chardonnay as Julia checked on her overeager dog. Angie and Paul engaged Simon in a conversation about the weather and he chattered on about how lovely the weather was in Santa Barbara compared to the east coast and Canada. By the time Julia returned he'd launched into a clever story about how his and Seth's preference for old time rock 'n' roll had nearly driven his jazz-loving dad to gray-haired distraction. Finally, after a few minutes, he sighed heavily and reached for his satchel.

He handed a piece of paper to Julia. "Unbeknownst to me, Seth rewrote his will to include you, sending a certified and witnessed copy to our family lawyer in Toronto. You can see he left half of what he owned to me and the other half to you."

"I don't really... Julia sputtered. "I don't want it!" she cried, suddenly panicked.

"I knew you wouldn't want the condo and since I couldn't bear to keep it I sold it to a friend in the real estate business. It netted me about three hundred thousand Canadian dollars, which is roughly two hundred and twenty thousand U.S. dollars. Half of that is one hundred and ten thousand dollars and I had the bank draw a check in U.S. funds payable to you. It's yours Julia. It's what he would have wanted."

Julia stiffened in her chair, knuckles turning white on the fine wood armrests. "I don't want the money,"she cried, suddenly rising and batting away Simon's hand and the embossed cashiers check. "I just wanted your brother, not his money or anything else. You take it. Give it to someone else, anyone! Please! I don't want it at all!" She bolted from the suddenly quiet room and a few seconds later they heard the slam of her bedroom door.

Simon placed a hand on his forehead, turning even whiter than his previous unhealthy pallor. "I thought perhaps if I waited... if I gave her a little more time she'd be better about this. I was wrong I guess."

"You have to understand Simon that your brother and my sister were inseparable. I have never seen two people more compatible or more in love. They spent every minute they could together and sometimes I swear they could read each other's minds. Neither one cared a whit about money."

Simon's head jerked up and he appeared almost fierce, the pale scar pulling at his lip as he scowled. "Good God, they became soul mates didn't they?"

"We believe so," said Angie sadly. "He told us the story about your parents' belief in soul mates late last October. That's when he related how your dad killed himself."

"I prayed that after what happened to my dad, Seth would be smart enough never to pull that stunt. It's amazing Julia survived. She... ah... never contemplated...?"

"No," shot back Paul. "She believed Seth wouldn't have wanted her to do that. Rest assured she'll never kill herself, no matter how lonely she becomes."

Simon studied his Rockports. "She must be one tough lady and that is admirable in itself. Look," he said rising. "I don't want to take up anymore of your time and I've certainly upset Julia enough. I'm planning to remain in town for a while since Seth's firm wants me to look at some of the projects he started and hadn't been able to complete. I've taken three months off for my health and thought I might be able to help them out. About the money; I don't want it or need it, and hell... it's really hers after all. Please Paul, could you make sure she takes it. I don't really care what she does with it."

"I'll tell you what," said Paul, walking the taller man to the door. "Would you mind if I handed this check over to my mom and dad and explained the situation to them? They have a trust account for Julia that my grandfather started, which totals about fifteen or sixteen thousand dollars which she'll inherit when my grandma dies. My Grandmother Rose has been adding to it for years and is such a steadfast old bird I'm certain she's not going to meet her maker for a long time. What if I take this money and place it into that account? It'll earn interest and a few years down the road, when things are more tolerable, it'll be waiting for her."

"You'd do that for me?" asked Simon, so clearly relieved his cheeks flushed with gratitude.

"I'll take care of it tomorrow. You can give me a call later to guarantee the money is invested. Hell, I'll even send you a statement and you can check on it now and again to see how it grows."

"I trust you implicitly. If you were a friend of my brother's then I know you're a man of honor and integrity because my brother was. I, on the other hand, well that's another story. Do you think Julia will mind if I call upon her in a couple of days to see how she's doing?"

"Don't just stop in to see her," blurted out Angie defensively. "Phone her first. You're a bit of a shock since you look so much like your brother."

Simon stuck out a hand to Angie and Paul. "I'm very glad to have met you after all this time. My brother only had wonderful things to say about you in his e-mails. I'll be giving Julia a call in a couple of days and see if she needs anything. If you want to contact me, this is the number of Seth's firm." He fished a pen out of his briefcase and wrote down a number and address. "This is where I'm staying; it's one of those suite hotels equipped with a little kitchen. If you'd like me to speak to your parents I would be happy to do so."

"I'll keep in touch," responded Paul, who held true to his word.

A few days later Simon called Julia at seven in the evening during a short October squall.

"How are you doing Julia?" he asked tentatively.

"I'm much better now. I'm sorry if I was rude the other night but I was so overwhelmed at the moment I didn't know how to deal with you. While it's been over nine months since he died, in many ways it feels just like yesterday."

"I understand completely. Would you mind if I drop by and give you something? I didn't feel comfortable handing it to you with your brother and sister-in-law present. Seth sent me something and I made a few modifications and would like to present it to you as kind of a memory of him. I also want to talk to you about something that's been bothering me."

"Alright," said Julia evenly, sounding calm, although she actually trembled at the idea of meeting

him again. Her chest burned in warning. "You can stop
by now if you like."

Within thirty minutes Simon stood upon her
doorstep. He'd dressed casually in blue jeans; his dark
hair parted in the middle to allow the dark strands to
hang freely down instead of combing it back as he had
before. He resembled a rock 'n' roll star, not a staid
architect, and Julia smiled. The resemblance between
him and his brother had diminished greatly and she
was certain Simon had planned it exactly that way.
Simon entered her apartment and lowered his satchel
onto the floor beside him before sinking down onto the
soft cushions of the cream couch.

"Would you like something to drink?" she asked
politely.

"Yes, that would be nice. Do you have an iced tea
or something?"

"Yes, but I also have a very nice cognac. In fact,
it's one your brother gave me."

"An iced tea will do."

Simon reached inside his satchel and handed her a
folder after she returned with the glass of icy peach tea. He
sipped at it politely as she gasped at the pictures inside.

"He sent these photographs to you?"

"Yeah, I thought they were lovely. That's the dog
I heard the other night?"

"Yes, she's out on the balcony. Would you like to
meet her? I'm afraid she's not an adorable puppy

anymore and now weighs almost forty pounds. I suggest you brace yourself since she's quite friendly."

Julia moved to the screened patio door and Mira dashed into the room, circling the couch twice before taking two strong sniffs of Simon. She leaped upon the cushions beside him and placed her silver head into his lap.

"Wow," he laughed. "She's friendly alright, and has certainly grown since that photo. Are you able to keep up with the food bills?" he joked.

"Luckily she's nearly full grown. I'm awfully glad she didn't get bigger since this place is fairly small for a dog. I have to be certain I walk her every morning and night." She fingered one of the prints. "These photographs are truly lovely. I remember when Seth snapped this one at the ice rink, but I have never seen the other. Who took that?"

"I think it was your brother Paul. He probably gave it to Seth. I had all of them blown up as a gift from me to you. It's all I really have of him after he moved down here. I hope you don't mind, but I made some doubles. I was supposed to give him the negatives back." Simon reached into his bag and handed her the photo envelope.

"Thank you very much," said Julia, Seth's soul expanding in her heart. She watched Simon sip his iced tea.

"This is quite good. You've done a very nice job with your place and I just love the southwestern photos and all the houseplants. I wanted to compliment you the other night but everything seemed too awkward at the time."

"I understand perfectly. So how's it working out with you at Bastam, Hughes, and Glickstern?"

"I'm only going to be there a couple more days. Lenny Glickstern wanted me to help out with some sort of quick market project Seth was working on. I know my brother always enjoyed Mediterranean architecture so I was able to give them a few pointers though it's extremely uncomfortable working there. Everyone stares at me and whispers behind their hands so I told Lenny I would help out until the end of next week and then take off."

"And where are you planning to go?"

"I'm not sure. There's actually a firm in Sacramento I'm looking into. Like my brother, I'm getting a little weary of the weather on the east coast and my girlfriend... let's just say I'm a bit of a free bird so to speak." The wrinkles at the sides of his eyes crinkled in laughter as he mildly mocked himself.

"I didn't really allow you to explain why you and your brother were not on good terms. Would you care to tell me now?"

"Alright," said Simon evenly. "My brother was dating a girl named Marcie and they were actually quite serious about one another. A graphic artist, she worked near the architectural firm where Seth was employed. I came over to see him for lunch one day and she was there, sharing a sandwich with him. I don't remember exactly what happened really."

Julia understood he was uncomfortable, but wasn't about to let him off the hook. "And...?"

"I guess I've always been kind of a flirt and my brother was always so much more serious than I. Anyway, I begin telling jokes and being my usual devil-may-care self and Marcie gave me a call that evening. Looking back, I should never have responded to that call or met her for lunch the next day. One thing led to another and she ended up dumping him in a kind of brutal way, explaining I was much more carefree and light-hearted than he and she preferred me over him.

Seth was enraged. He accused me of pulling this trick one time to many, and equated it to how I had stolen his toys during our childhood. He said he didn't want anything to do with me from that moment onward."

"It must have been a horrible scene."

"It was. I remember coming to my senses and protesting we were the only family left except for Lucas. How could he just throw in the towel on me? That's when Seth said he needed six months before he'd even think of contacting me again. If I kept the same hotmail account he'd e-mail me if and when he damn well pleased. I didn't hear from him for a full eight months and was nearly out of my mind with worry. I knew he'd relocated to the west coast and was making a good living, but nothing else. Finally, he started writing me again. I take it he'd gotten over Marcie since he'd met you. Seth seemed so happy and everything he said about you was complimentary. He spoke of your sense of humor, your generosity, and how beautiful you were."

Julia blushed and Simon grinned. "I mentioned I wanted to come out and meet you and received a staunch no as an answer. 'You stay where you are' he said, 'and I'll stay where I am. After everything is settled you can come out and visit us but not before.' I guess he still didn't trust me."

"It seems to me you had to work long and hard to earn Seth's trust and devotion. He was a bit wary of me in the beginning as well and after hearing your story regarding Marcie, I can understand why. I'm just glad he finally wrote and you both were on better terms before he died."

"I just wish I'd had an opportunity to say goodbye," said Simon sadly.

Julia tried to stop a defiant tear from sliding down her cheek. "I never got the chance either."

Simon leaned forward, and taking both her hands let her cry unrestrainedly as he cursed life and the uncanny way it dealt out a sour hand to those who didn't deserve it.

Simon made it his ritual to call Julia often over the next few days. He'd ask about her day and casually let her know things were going well at the architectural firm who'd managed to coerce him into working for another week. Julia didn't rebuff him but certainly didn't encourage a meeting either and Simon had to remain satisfied with that for the present.

On October tenth around lunchtime, he wandered into Paul Morris' office at Tri-Tek. Paul was surprised to see him but rose cordially and extended a hand to the brother of the man his sister had loved.

"Please take a seat," he gestured, as Simon sank into the black leather chair across from the broad desk where Paul's computer terminal hummed. "I was actually just about to call you," said Paul, "and planned to stop by your hotel to drop this by." He reached into his desk drawer and pulled out a thin manila envelope. "I had the money deposited."

Simon perused the statement before smiling across the desk at Julia's twin. "I can't tell you how much I appreciate this, and hopefully someday when Julia's married and has children, this money will make a nice college fund or become a down payment on a dream house. I don't care how she uses it; just that she eventually *does* use it."

Paul sank back down upon his own leather chair and steepled his hands before him.

Love Never Dies

"So how much longer are you planning to remain here?"

"My last day at the firm is tomorrow. They offered a short term contract to me, but I refused."

"Too uncomfortable," surmised Paul.

"That would be an understatement," sighed Simon, and Paul noticed his hand absently rubbing his left hip vigorously. He'd observed the mild limp when Simon had first entered Julia's flat over a week ago, but this time the limp was much more pronounced.

"You have an injury?" he asked compassionately.

Simon's head jerked up. "It's just an old ski injury aggravated by a later accident. It makes me realize I'm not getting any younger." His fingers stopped massaging the sore spot near his hip. "Look Paul, one of the reasons I stopped by was to let you know I plan to linger in the neighborhood for awhile. It's always been a dream of mine to explore southern California and now, since I have over two months remaining on my sabbatical, I thought this would be a good time to do it. I'm also just a bit concerned about Julia."

"You're not the only one," said Paul, shrugging. "She's a key topic of conversation every time I visit my parents or run into one of her colleagues. I need to inform you that Julia has more tenacity and courage than I've ever seen in a woman, and I don't say that just because she's my twin sister. I would be lying, however, if I didn't mention how concerned I am about your presence here."

"So you think my staying will upset her unduly?"

"I don't know. In many ways she seems to have gotten over the worse, but there are days when her eyes drift far away and I know she hasn't forgotten him."

"I don't want her to forget him," said Simon angrily. "From everything I've heard and witnessed, he was the best thing that ever happened to her, and vice versa. You must understand I feel some sense of family obligation and believe I owe it to my brother, especially since we parted on such harsh terms, to look after the woman he loved; it's the least I can do."

Paul scrutinized the darkly clad form of Simon, who sat uncomfortably across from him. Simon seemed a man much more at ease in a pair of blue jeans and black leather jacket, but still looked striking in the dark gray suit, the white swatch of hair combed away from his pale forehead. A faint sheen of moisture glistened upon his face and Paul understood his anxiety.

"I realize you may feel some sort of obligation to my sister and that's all fine and good, but if you harbor any other thoughts about her romantically I think it would be best if you put them aside. She isn't interested."

Simon straightened uncomfortably. "You believe I'm going to pursue my brother's girlfriend?"

Love Never Dies

"I really don't know what all your motivations are Simon, and while I appreciate your money and time I'd like you to go easy with my sister. Even though you're very different from your brother, you're still a constant reminder of all she's lost. Yet I'm the first to admit that on the other hand, your presence might actually prove a comfort to her. Sometimes I think my sister is walking through a huge fog she can't seem to find her way out of. Maybe by sharing anecdotes of your childhood, showing pictures of your parents, and proving by your very presence that life does goes on, it will help bring her back to herself. Maybe she will finally be able to face the truth that Seth is never coming back and she has to move on with her life. You knew your brother well; you knew how intense he was. If you can find a way to help ease my sister's day to day path through what she views as a God-awful life, then who am I to question your motives?"

"I would never hurt her intentionally," Simon protested, moved by Paul's pained face.

"All I can ask is tread softly sir, and understand that I believe in many ways Julia will *never* get over Seth. I have forewarned my wife and parents that I truly believe my sister is going to end up a lovelorn spinster, drowning herself inside the memories of a man who's never coming back. And, as pathetic as I believe that is, I'm not sure there's any way around it." Paul was startled to see moisture well up in Simon's eyes.

"She loved him that much," he stated softly. "You needn't worry my friend, I have only her best interests at heart and will tread softly as you say."

Paul gazed for a long moment at the pained man sitting across from him and finally smiled.

"So you finish work tomorrow, do you? Saturday, the girls and I plan to view a small exhibition on the promenade. Would you care to join us?"

"I would be happy too," said Simon, surprised at the invitation. "Paul... please don't worry about my intentions. I only want to do what is right and if I can't make Julia happier with my presence I promise to leave."

"Then how about 9:30? There's an art gallery called *Little Peter's* near the Fish Grill; I'll see you there." As Simon rose, Paul offered a hand. "Thanks for everything Simon. I just had to be frank with you."

"I appreciate that," replied Simon, and took his leave.

Just after five p.m. the next afternoon Simon Hayes met a man whose reputation was well-known to him at a bar called *Miguel's*. The place was crowded and noisy, as all good bars are, and Stan Garten sat at a rear table puffing a slim cigar and adding his smoke to the countless fumes of others.

"Well, well, well," said Stan, as Simon dropped into the rickety wooden chair across the scarred table from where Stan lounged, squinting at him though the smoke of his putrid Cuban cigar. "It's the wayward brother who's the mirror image of his twin. Of course you look a little worse for wear; a great deal rougher I'd say than your suave and sophisticated brother. What's with the leg, an old war wound?"

"Nope," said Simon, "just a ski injury." The two didn't bother to introduce themselves or exchange pleasantries. They knew who each other was.

"So you went against the strict commands of Angus and contacted the Morris twins?"

"I had to," said Simon simply. "I needed to know she was okay."

"Well, I'm sure your dead brother appreciates it, but the concerns and cares of Julia Ann Morris are my responsibility, not yours, as I'm certain Angus has already told you. So why don't you just trot back up to Toronto and let me do my job."

Simon raised a finger to a thin balding waiter who immediately scurried over. "Whatever you have on tap," he ordered, and turned his attention back to the hostile brown eyes scrutinizing his person. "I'm not about to stop you. Go ahead and do your job, but note that I don't feel comfortable with Julia Morris' safety. Seth apparently didn't receive the appropriate 'care' he needed."

"Are you accusing me of something Simon?"

"No, but I'd feel a whole lot better if I could be absolutely certain nothing will happen to Paul, his new wife Angie, their parents, or the woman Seth loved. So I'm making it my personal responsibility to guarantee the entire Morris clan stays healthy."

Stan's straight white teeth clenched as he took a sudden aversion to Simon Hayes. He would have loved to splash his light beer all over that too shiny motorcycle jacket and pinched pale face.

"As I said before, it's my job to look after the girl," he ground out, the threat evident in his rough voice.

"Just as you looked after her lover?"

"That was an accident," said Stan, refusing to be goaded.

"Was it?" countered Simon.

"You need to mind your own business and leave this to professionals." He cupped a hand to his ear. "I do believe I hear Toronto calling."

"Nah, Toronto is getting way too cold this time of year and since I have a couple months free and some physical therapy to attend to, I thought this might just be a dandy time to hang around and soak up the sun, as the song says."

The sweaty waiter placed a pint of golden liquid in front of Simon who dug into his pocket and laid a couple of bills on the waiting waiter's tray. He took three deep swallows of the amber beer and then wiped his mouth with the back of his hand as Stan glowered under thick dark brows.

Love Never Dies

"I'll tell you what. I'm a reasonable man and believe it would be best if we work together. Our goals are the same Officer Garten, so I agree to tread softly and stay out of your way. If anything comes up and you believe I should be alerted, give me a call." He retrieved a thin business card out of his jacket pocket and pushed it across the table to the denim-clad policeman. Stan's black moustache twitched and his only response was to take another deep drag on his foul cigar.

"Keep in touch," said Simon, rising from the wobbly, uncomfortable chair. He left his half-empty pint of beer on the table as he wove through the crowded mass of partying people and disappeared out the smoky entrance of the bar.

Stan cursed loudly under his breath, finally reaching across the stained table to retrieve the neglected glass and lift it to his own lips. He downed it in one gulp. He had to admit the Canadian had guts, and resigned himself to the fact he and Simon were partners. Stan slammed down his beer and pocketed the business card, noting the hotel's nearby address. A shapely blonde eyed him from under lowered lids from the bar, her cosmetically enhanced figure poured into a skintight black dress. Stan smiled across at her, inviting her to join him with the simple lifting of his black eyebrows. There were so many more interesting things to do than worry about Simon Hayes' self-

185

prescribed mission and he raised a finger to the waiter to deliver two more beers as the blonde glided toward his table.

Simon showed up promptly at 9:30 in front of Little Peter's. The art gallery was hosting an impressionistic display of several local artists and Simon stuck his hands into the pockets of his blue jeans and shivered in the October morning. The days were definitely getting cooler and foggier, and while much warmer than Toronto's icy gloom he recognized this beach city also had its share of winter. He watched the trio approach. Angie and Paul strolled hand-in-hand, both dressed casually in blue denims and colorful tee tops under matching denim jackets. Julia was clad in a pair of black pants and a purple sweater, the narrow trousers emphasizing her thinness, and Simon sighed. She had lost too much weight in her ordeal.

The three pulled up in front of Simon, who smiled across at them, recognizing Julia's tentative response. He'd taken care with his appearance that morning, pulling his hair back into a tight ponytail and wearing a black leather jacket over a snowy white t-shirt tucked into faded blue jeans that had a rip in the left knee. While he resembled his more serious brother, his attire, as well as his demeanor, indicated a totally separate individual and Julia visibly relaxed at his appearance.

Love Never Dies

Simon extended his hand to the trio, making sure he didn't grip Julia's hand any longer than the newlyweds.

"Planning on buying some paintings?" asked Paul, his green eyes scanning the easels lining the promenade.

"Some of them are not half-bad," admitted Simon, "but since I'm only renting my suite for the next couple of months, I'm not sure I can load myself down with any artwork right now."

"Let's go in," said Angie eagerly. She had a huge desire to place her own personal mark on the condo she now shared with her new husband, and a fresh new painting was just what she had in mind.

"There's a woman exhibiting here named Gloria Montabelli, who's supposed to have done an exciting series of paintings of ocean birds," stated Julia, smiling gently at Simon, her blonde hair fluttering in the constant wind that battered Santa Barbara's shoreline in fall.

"I'll hold on to my wallet," Simon responded easily, and followed the Morris' into the trendy art gallery.

The exhibition was far more extensive than Simon had anticipated and the four wandered through the crowded promenade, enjoying the paintings and often gasping at the outrageous price tags. Julia remained withdrawn and Simon never tried to force her into conversation, instead chatting quietly to Angie and

Paul who exhibited all the symptoms of newlyweds. They were never able to stop touching, their heads bowed closely together as they spoke in soft caressing whispers. The couple finally settled on a small painting of a Black Oystercatcher, a Santa Barbara native, pecking at a sand crab as the foamy white salt water dashed over its webbed feet.

"That will look lovely in our bathroom," said Angie excitedly, and Simon grinned as they haggled over the price with the eager artist who was only too willing to negotiate.

"So how's school been?" asked Simon quietly as Julia studied an ocean scene depicting a surfer taking his life into his own hands as he topped the crest of a particularly fearsome looking wave.

"Things have been just great," returned Julia mildly. This was her stock answer and Simon cocked an eyebrow at her and though he didn't believe her, gave an equally benign response.

"I'm glad to hear it."

"So you finished your stint at the firm?"

"Yep. Old Lenny didn't want to let me go, but I just couldn't stand working there another day. I did manage to go on site and see the wrap up of the little mini-market complex Seth had designed last year. It was a comforting feeling seeing the beautiful lines of those red-tiled buildings. He did a fine job."

"Where is it?" asked Julia, suddenly interested.

Love Never Dies

"You know where Goleta is? The center is two blocks north of Turnpike Road, right on the corner. Maybe you'd like to drive up there sometime and see how his last job turned out?"

Julia stiffened visibly before letting out a shaky breath. "I think I'd enjoy that."

"Would you like me to drive you up there? I know the way and when you view the center, it's like a piece of him survived somehow. That is if you wouldn't mind putting up with the likes of me?"

Julia peered across at him, studying his handsome face. "I don't think I'd mind at all. Are you busy tomorrow Simon?"

"Nope," he said. "I've currently joined the ranks of the unemployed. I'll bring my camera and take a couple shots. Hey, it finally appears Paul and Angie have stopped haggling over the price and obtained their painting."

Her sister-in-law hugged the small paper-wrapped painting with an air of triumph.

"They got their price," laughed Julia.

Thirty minutes later they sat at a sidewalk café admiring the lifelike painting while Paul boasted about his negotiating abilities. California gulls screeched overhead, while brown house sparrows waited on the white railing of the café, hoping to snag some crumbs. Simon lifted the top slice of his club sandwich and added a lethal dose of hot sauce as Angie shivered.

"Well, that's one way you resemble your brother. He always liked to add spicy sauce to his food. I remember once he whipped up this Thai stir-fry for all of us one Sunday afternoon. I thought I was going to die and must have consumed a gallon of water to wash it down."

"Seth did love to cook, and enjoyed his chilies and peppers. I think we both got that from our mother's side. Her grandfather had been Portuguese and used to do a seafood mix on the grill, adding so much peri peri I swore we'd all expire in one big puff of smoke." He grinned and took another hearty bite of his sandwich.

"I've noticed Simon," said Angie, spreading brown mustard over her tuna melt, "that you walk with a definite limp. What happened?"

"I can see at finishing school they certainly didn't teach tact," said Paul gruffly, frowning at Angie who shrugged innocently.

Julia laughed. Angie's overt questioning skills had always been a sense of amusement to both her and their parents and she sincerely hoped that someday Paul would get used to it. Simon didn't seem to take offense.

"Well that's quite a story," he said, "and one my brother Seth used to tell with relish. I have always considered myself a pretty good skier and on this particular occasion my brother and I had visited a ski resort just north of Ottawa. We both arrived stag and there was this cutest little ski bunny on the slopes. I remember she was dressed in a hot pink jumpsuit with this delectable zipper up the front. She had the mandatory white ski boots, long blonde hair, and the clearest china blue eyes you'd ever seen. I fell instantly in love. I remember Seth warning me about how treacherous the slope was and reminding me to be extremely careful on one particularly sharp turn. But there she was, that pink angel in the snow, and I decided to prove what an expert skier I am."

Angie took a bit of her sandwich and munched happily. This was the kind of story she loved.

"Anyway, I swore I had everything under control, but while heading downhill this tree reached out and tripped me."

"The tree reached out and tripped you?" repeated Julia. "I don't believe I've ever heard of that happening before."

"I swear to God that's what happened," said Simon, crossing his heart. "I'm positive I was at least three feet away from that blasted tree before it just jumped into my path and stuck out a root. My skis got all tangled up and I flew head over heels to find myself embracing the tree trunk. After my brother finally stopped laughing the medical team from the resort rushed me to the emergency ward and I've unfortunately paid for my infatuation with the pink snow bunny by sporting a very unsexy limp ever since.

The leg was coming along just fine until I re-injured it a couple of months ago and now must seek further physical therapy."

"That just goes to show you need to watch out for blondes," said Paul, winking at his sister and taking hearty bite of his reuben sandwich. He followed it up with a large gulp of bottled beer while Angie punched his arm.

"That was a nice story," stated Julia, wiping her mouth and pushing her plate away. Half of her turkey sandwich remained untouched and Paul frowned.

"Ah, that reminds me," said Simon, reaching into his back pocket and pulling out his billfold. Flipping it open he retrieved a glossy photograph. Julia wiped her hands before taking the extended photograph.

"That was snapped just before the ski bunny incident. Would you like to have it?" Both Angie and Paul leaned over to gaze at the glossy photo which showed Seth and Simon, arms about each other's shoulders and dressed in identical white and navy blue ski suits, balancing their poles upon their shoulders. They appeared happy and carefree; Simon laughing while Seth, always the more serious, gazed somberly at the camera.

"I wouldn't mind a copy," said Julia. "But I suspect it's one of the last taken of you two together. I think you should keep the original, Simon. But a copy would be great."

Love Never Dies

"I'll see if I can find the negative for you," said Simon lightly, not enjoying the dark expression hovering over her face. "It's very evident from this photograph that I'm the much better skier."

Angie snorted with laughter and even Julia managed to grin. "Oh really? Is that before or after your leg was placed in a cast?" They all laughed heartily as Simon tucked the photo back into his wallet.

If Julia had been more observant she might have noticed Simon often casting a glance over his shoulder as he scanned the busy promenade of Santa Barbara or even spotted a dark-haired denim-clad man lounging near where they wandered unhurriedly down the long boardwalk. Once, a nonchalant Simon nodded to the mustached man who casually strolled in the opposite direction. Julia never noticed the slight bulge under the left armhole of Simon's jacket for she kept herself respectively distant from him. Perhaps it was best she didn't know that in Seth's brother she had inherited a bodyguard.

Chapter Eight

So began the slow deliberate development of a casual relationship between Simon and Julia. He didn't press any sort of romantic suit, but instead disarmed her into friendship by giving her a casual call, or suggesting he bring over some Chinese food. He called her one night asking for advice about finding a decent physical therapist who could work on his leg.

"I know there's one in a medical park near Pacific Oaks Road on Elwood Beach, just north of the university in Goleta Valley." Julia rummaged around her desk searching for the card given her by a student's mother a couple of years ago. "Here it is," she said, and dictated the phone number. "I hear Sharon Thompson is really good. I taught her daughter two years ago and she's apparently built up quite a clientele."

"Thanks, I'll give her a ring," he stated casually, and didn't prolong the call.

Love Never Dies

The next time she saw him he visibly limped.

"Have you seen the physical therapist?" she asked, alarmed.

"You mean the killer therapist?" stated Simon grimly between clenched teeth. "Yeah, I had my first appointment on the fifteenth and she's arranged to see me three times a week for the next month. She said her torture will help rebuild my strength around the injured area."

Julia had to laugh. He'd met her that evening to enjoy a quick burger and a chat.

"How many treatments have you had so far?"

"Only two thank God, but she's fitting me in on Monday, Wednesday, and Friday next week. I was hoping she wouldn't have a slot open."

Julia laughed because talking with Simon was always entertaining. She sipped her diet soda and watched as he added horseradish to his burger. Julia grimaced; this one trait of both twins she could never actively embrace herself.

"So, have you been keeping yourself busy?"

"I've actually been attending some lectures at the Santa Barbara campus since it's not far from my physical therapy. I've also been doing research on the Los Angeles county area and want to travel south sometime to visit *Disneyland* and *Universal Studios*."

"I remember doing all that," said Julia. "My brother and I used to make it our summer ritual to visit either *Knott's* or *Disneyland*. My parents refused to go to both every summer so we had to alternate. When they finally opened *Magic Mountain* they were relieved because it was so much closer."

"So you grew up in this area?"

"Actually I spent my formative years in LA before moving to Goleta when my dad got a job connected to an architectural firm catering to the engineering research center attached to the university. I think I was probably about ten at the time and from the beginning knew Santa Barbara was where I wanted to live my life. So here I am nearly twenty years later."

"And what a lovely spot it is," stated Simon, gazing out onto the softly rolling hills giving way to the majestic Pacific Ocean.

He had to agree Santa Barbara was one of the loveliest secrets of southern California, located just north of Los Angeles and Ventura. The city, with its old trees and quiet neighborhoods, belied the bustling university and civic center. One could visit the stately mission, attend an amazing variety of activities at the university, or simply drive along the beautiful highway fronting the beach. True, Santa Barbara was pricey and overdeveloped but Julia couldn't imagine living anywhere else.

"So you received your degree from UCSB?"

"Yes I did, though I actually attended UCLA for two years as a freshman and sophomore while entertaining the notion of becoming a screenwriter or cinematographer. However, I gradually changed my mind and decided to be a teacher after working with handicapped children during a special university sponsored program at the UCLA Medical Center. I still love LA and Hollywood. In fact, I'm heading down to UCLA at the end of the month because my principal, Connie Fernandez, is a Flamenco Dancer and she's part of the entertainment during the annual Hispanic festival."

"That sounds like a lot of fun," said Simon. "Just when are you leaving?"

"The day after Halloween. Connie designs the most beautiful flamenco dresses of flaming yellow, red, and white and is quite an accomplished dancer. A few of the staff are planning to head down to watch her on November first and she wants me to film her in action."

Julia continued chatting about her principal, relating how they'd become good friends over the past three years and played racquetball occasionally at the local gym. Simon desperately wanted to ask her more about her jaunt down to Los Angeles, but decided to hold off. It was too soon to tag along, so after dinner he casually walked her to the blue Taurus. Julia raised a hand to him before driving off into the fading light. A movement touched his periphery vision and he observed a man pull away in a silver sedan. Simon's heart lurched since Adam Gable was known to prefer silver vehicles. Unfortunately, the car disappeared before he could take down the license plate number, propelling him to give Stan Garten a call.

Over the next two weeks Simon kept a low profile, continuing his physical therapy doggedly and occasionally visiting Angie and Paul for lunch on the weekends. He was always friendly and disarming, never once indicating any interest in Julia other than casual friendship and saw her only occasionally, always in the presence of Paul and Angie.

On Wednesday, October twenty-seventh, Paul gave Simon a call. Simon had just gotten back from physical therapy and was in a thoroughly rotten mood. There wasn't any part of his body that didn't ache, and while he was certain the treatment would be beneficial in the long run he still cursed his body's inability to heal itself without help. He growled a terse hello into the phone.

"Is this a bad time?" returned Paul's pleasant voice.

"Hey Paul. I'm really sorry, but I just got back from physical therapy and I'm not feeling too chipper. What can I do for you?"

"I actually have a big favor to ask and please feel free to say no if any part of it makes you uncomfortable."

"Go ahead, shoot," said Simon, putting on the kettle.

Love Never Dies

"My sister is heading down to UCLA this weekend to take some footage of her boss' flamenco dancing session during the Hispanic Celebration."

"Yes, I've heard about it," said Simon as mildly as possible, trying to disguise his intense interest.

"You know Julia hasn't ventured out much alone, and well I was kinda hoping..."

"That I'd make some excuse and tag along?"

"Yes, that's it. She staunchly refused having either Angie or I come down, saying she didn't need chaperones, and I know you've been wanting to visit LA and check out Hollywood Boulevard and *Universal Studios*. I thought... well... that maybe you could somehow convince her to let you come along?"

"And how am I going to do that Paul? She's been fine with having lunch occasionally and talking about Seth for old time's sake, but if I tried to join her in Los Angeles, she'd suspect I had ulterior motives."

"But you do have an ulterior motive," said Paul. "To help her recover."

"Okay," sighed Simon, pouring hot water over the tea bag to brew. "And just how do I go about hitching a ride with her?"

"Can't you just show up? She's staying at the Getaway Suites near Westwood and maybe you can kinda check into the same hotel?"

"So the Los Angeles county area has about ten million people right?"

"Yeah," replied Paul.

"And you want me to just *happen* to bump into her? I don't think so."

"You have a better idea?"

"Sure, I'll tell her you're incredibly worried about her and if she doesn't allow me to tag along you'll be in her suitcase."

"I'm sure *that* would work," Paul scoffed.

"Well it better than just *bumping* into her at the Hispanic Festival. If I do that, she'll probably think I'm some sort of stalker and call the cops. You leave it to me; I'll work it out. And Paul, you should look on the bright side. At least she *wants* to venture down to LA; certainly that's got to be considered a breakthrough."

"Yeah, but she seems so melancholy all the time."

"Well, what can you expect? What's it been now, ten months?"

Paul sighed morosely on the other end of the line. "So you'll do it?"

"I'll try but you owe me BIG time. You keep promising to take me to a Lakers game, and this time I'm going to hold you to it. I'll give you a call and let you know what comes of my finagling. Just keep your fingers crossed."

Simon didn't waste any time and rang Julia up that very evening.

200

Love Never Dies

"Do you mind if I stop by?" he asked. "Something's come up and I have to speak with you."

"Alright," said Julia, surprised at the urgency in his voice. "Come right over."

Simon liked the airiness of her modern apartment; its cool cream walls complimented by the bright green drooping stems of healthy house plants. Mira immediately ran up to him and sniffed his leg, giving her curled tail a wiggle before leaping onto the couch.

"Off the couch Mira," reprimanded Julia. "You know you're not supposed to sit there!" The dog sadly but obediently jumped down onto the rag rug designated as her special spot. She circled twice and sank down, resting her beautiful pointed muzzle upon dainty paws before following Simon with her dark brown eyes.

"Something to drink Simon?"

"No, I'm fine," he answered, sinking down onto the comfortable couch after giving the furry dog an affectionate pat. The heavy breathing designating the Keeshond breed proved comforting, enabling one to always know the whereabouts of their faithful dog.

"So what is it?" asked Julia, adjusting the embroidered pillow Grandma Rose had made for her before leaning back in her mauve recliner.

"It's about your brother."

"Paul?" cried Julia alarmed. "Is something the matter?"

"Well not per se. Listen Julia, Paul rang me up this morning, requesting I accompany you to LA."

"What?"

"He's worried about you Julia. He's afraid you'll get all melancholy without some sort of support around and since he knows I want to explore the region, asked if I could somehow hitch a ride with you."

"I see," said Julia carefully. "And were you against this *plan*?"

Simon shrugged vaguely. He wore his normal uniform of a white t-shirt, blue jeans, and a worn pair of trainers. "I wouldn't say I'm exactly against it, but I'm smart enough to know you don't need a chaperone *or* a babysitter."

"Well you can just tell him that I am *a-okay*," said Julia huffily, and rose to snap off a brown leaf from one of her philodendrons. She was clearly seething.

"Maybe we can come to some sort of a compromise. I know you're totally capable of going down and enjoying yourself this weekend. You're spending much of your time with your boss, right?"

Actually Julia wasn't. A fellow flamenco dancer named Alvaro Lopez had attracted Connie's eye and she'd already told Julia she planned on getting to know the middle-aged man better this weekend.

"I'm spending *some* time with her, but believe she has other arrangements as well."

"You love your brother right?"

Love Never Dies

"Why of course." She turned toward him, the dead leaf dangling from her fingers. "Why do you ask?"

"Think about why your brother doesn't want you to be alone and try to understand how much it would mean to him to know you're there with someone you know. It's an easy solution; allow me to visit an area I've wanted to explore anyway and make your brother feel a whole lot better in the bargain. Besides, it's better than his other suggestion."

"Which was?" asked Julia, placing her hands on her hips and shooting him a hostile glare.

"That I was supposed to discreetly bump into you either at the Getaway Suites or at UCLA."

"Of all the nerve!"

Simon chuckled and raised his hands in mock surrender. "The fact you can get so indignant about your meddling brother is probably a good sign. What do you say Julia; do we go down to UCLA and have a good time, making your brother feel good about himself in the bargain, or do you tell him off?"

Julia pursed her lips, not realizing how appealing she appeared in her oversized pink sweater, scruffy sweats, and sheepskin slippers. "You're right. He's only concerned about me." She waved a warning finger at him. "But we're not going together. If you want to follow me down to LA, that's one thing, but I'm taking my own wheels and only spending time with you *if* and *when* I choose. Do you understand that mister?"

"Of course," agreed Simon innocently, "but I was just wondering if you could make one exception to this total independence plan."

"And what is that?" hissed Julia, instantly suspicious.

"Do you think you could spare one hour to escort me to the Avenue of the Stars?"

"I can't believe it. Simon Hayes a pure unadulterated tourist?"

He raised both hands above his head. "Guilty as charged. It's been a lifelong fantasy of mine to stroll down Hollywood Boulevard, visit Grauman's Chinese Theatre, and check out all the famous movie stars' handprints in their forecourt."

"You have got to be kidding!"

"Look, if I'm struggling to pacify your brother could you at least indulge me a bit?"

Julia laughed out loud. "So who's your favorite movie star?"

Simon looked a little embarrassed. "I've always had a thing for Olivia de Havilland. Ever since I saw her in *Gone with the Wind* I was a goner."

"And anybody else?"

"If I could find Bogie's or Cagney's handprints, or actually any of those great forties movie stars, I'd die a happy man."

Julia chuckled. Simon was just full of surprises. "Alright, I'm leaving from school on Friday afternoon. Do you know where Hyatt Elementary is?"

"Nope, but I believe you're going to tell me," he said.

She retrieved a piece of blank paper and gave him brief instructions on how to reach the elementary school. "School is out at 2:15 and I'm hitting the road at 2:30. If you're late Hayes, you're on your own 'cuz I'll be gone. Then you can have the honor of explaining *that* to my overprotective brother."

"I'll be there," he promised, heading for the apartment's front door.

"I suppose you're going to give Paul a call as soon as you get home?"

"I *did* promise him an update."

"Well, you've got to hand it to him; he does have my best interests at heart. But one hour Simon Hayes, that's all I'm spending on the Walk of Fame! Good grief!"

The next day at Hyatt Elementary, Julia loaded her vocabulary tests and weekly journals into the car to grade that night. The weather had turned crisp and cool and she preferred scoring the children's papers in front of a crackling fireplace instead of sitting uncomfortably at her gray metal school desk and wishing she was home. Julia slammed down the trunk lid of her Ford and noticed that a tall, thin man had removed himself from a silver BMW.

"I'm sorry," he said, waving at her tentatively. "Are you a teacher here?" Julia nodded as the man approached and introduced himself.

"My name's Mike Cooper and my nephew Jeffrey Cooper is in Mr. Smith's class. I just got a call from my sister-in-law who's hysterically indicated my nephew didn't make it onto the bus, so I drove down here to check it out. Do you have any idea who I should speak to?"

Julia knew little Jeffrey Cooper well. He was a bit of an overactive boy, but very sweet. The fact he'd missed the bus somehow didn't surprise her.

"Of course Mr. Cooper. If you'll wait right here I'll check in the office and see if he made it on the bus. Do you know what its number was?"

"I think bus three, but I could be wrong. It's the Vera Cruz route."

"I'll be back in just a moment," said Julia, and hurried toward the office. The sallow-faced man immediately moved to her car and just above her back rear bumper attached a small dime-sized metal disk before returning to lounge against the metallic paint of his sedan. Within three minutes Julia rejoined him.

"He did get on the bus Mr. Cooper, so at least we know he's not lurking around the school grounds. Why don't you call your sister-in-law and see if there's been any sort of update."

Love Never Dies

"That's a great idea," said Mike Cooper, flipping open his cell phone. "Hey this is Mike, have you heard anything from Jeffrey? You have... what? Jeez, you're not going to let this go are you?" There was a long pause as Mr. Cooper frowned apologetically to her. "I don't know about you, but I believe this deserves a spanking, not just a talking to." He was silent for a long while and she could hear a female voice on the other end. "I don't care what you say Cynthia, but he's caused a lot of people undue worry. I don't mind if he goes to a friend's house, but shouldn't he clear it with you first? All right, I'll stop by later and we'll talk about it. Yes, yes of course I'll give myself some time to cool down. Talk to you later." He disconnected, flipping the lid of the cell phone closed before tucking it into his pocket.

"I'm really sorry; apparently Jeffrey wanted to stop at his friend Leon's house and didn't bother to tell us until *after* he was already there and gorging down some milk and cookies. I'm sorry to have put you to any sort of trouble."

"Not at all Mr. Cooper," said Julia pleasantly. "I'm just glad to find family members who still keep track of their children. You can never be too careful in a world like this. We hear way too many horror stories about what happens to children because people don't pay attention."

"Well, thank you once again for being so accommodating. Have a good day." The obviously frustrated uncle eased himself into the BMW and pulled away from the curb, raising a friendly hand as a thank you. Julia put the incident out of her mind, not realizing Adam Gable had placed a very sophisticated tracking device on her car and that she was in more danger than she ever could know.

Simon Hayes was not only punctual, he was early. He'd apparently taken her at word that she really might leave him if he didn't show up on time, so his bronze Pajero idled patiently as he watched her swing her school bag into the trunk and place a cool thermos of water onto the passenger seat beside her.

"Alright Simon, this is how it is. The traffic can get really heavy into LA on Friday afternoon so let me explain the route I'm going to take. First, we'll head down the 101 to the city and then take the 405 south. UCLA is located right next to Bel Air, but the Getaway Suites are off Santa Monica Boulevard, so if you lose me just get off at Santa Monica and go northwest toward West Hollywood. The Getaway Suites are on the right."

"Aye, aye Captain," he saluted.

"And I just want you to know, Simon Hayes, that I called my brother last night and he didn't give any indication at all that he knew you were coming down to LA with me this weekend."

Love Never Dies

"He's a sly one isn't he?" said Simon, tongue-in-cheek. "I suppose Paul wants you to call him every evening?"

"But of course. Aargh," growled Julia between clenched teeth. "Sometimes being a twin is so... so infuriating!"

"Tell me about it," said Simon, their eyes meeting over the hood of her blue Taurus. A strange flicker of some strong emotion glinted from his steel gray eyes for a fleeting moment, but whether from sadness or regret she couldn't ascertain. Julia shook off the odd sensation, not realizing her hand automatically touched her chest and the warm glow there.

"See you later Simon," she murmured, and swinging into her sedan, started the engine.

Within seconds, Simon recognized the drifting lyrics of Enya and grinned. He'd been thoroughly and completely dismissed.

Julia hadn't been kidding about the traffic and as he headed down Highway 101, skirting the Santa Monica Mountains, he was thankful he didn't have to drive this highway everyday. As soon as he hit the San Fernando Valley, traffic became incredibly heavy. Contrary to Julia's belief he might lose her, Simon kept close behind as she pulled onto the 405 freeway and headed past Beverly Hills, the traffic becoming increasingly more congested. His cautious nature forced him to continually check the rearview mirror for any car following too closely and he noticed a silver BMW on his right-hand side that had been hanging in that lane for over fifteen minutes. The late model Beamer had dark tinted windows, making it impossible to discern the driver's features.

"You're just being paranoid," he told himself, as the silver BMW also pulled off onto Santa Monica Boulevard as Julia made for the hotel. He breathed a sigh of relief when the silver BMW zoomed past the hotel and continued toward Hollywood. It was probably just another tourist. He met Julia in the reception area as she finished signing for her room.

She grinned at him. "I'm impressed Simon, you didn't lose me; maybe you should consider a career in police work or something."

"It's crossed my mind," he said softly, leaning toward the redheaded desk clerk. "The name is Hayes and I have a reservation for a non-smoking room."

"I'm going to find my room and unpack, Simon. Shall I meet you in the lobby about 5:30? We could have a drink or something."

"That sounds great," he answered enthusiastically, watching her yellow and black clad form disappear through the entryway.

"That will be room 219," said the copper-haired clerk, giving him a pert smile.

"Ah, just how close is that to my friend's room?"

"She's actually around the other side of the building."

"Could I be a bit closer to her if possible?"

"Why certainly, her room is 132, how about 141?"

"That would be great," said Simon, pulling out his credit card.

The room was spacious and comfortable and Simon stretched out on the king-sized bed, rubbing his aching thigh energetically. His wireless phone gave a cell-phonic rendition of the Hallelujah Chorus and he placed the Nokia against his ear.

The first word out of Angus O'Leary's mouth was a foul curse and Simon winced.

"And just what the hell do you think you're doing?" roared Angus. The man may have been located in Toronto, but from his volume it sounded like he was in the same room.

"Thought I'd do a little sightseeing," said Simon, knowing full well Angus knew exactly where he was.

"I warned you before to let the girl alone. There's no telling how you could compromise the situation."

"I see that you've had a friendly conversation with one of LA's finest. Could it have been an undercover detective by the name of Stan Garten by any chance?"

"Stan is a good man and I'd appreciate it if you'd allow him to do his job!"

"I'm not jeopardizing his position in any way," denied Simon. "I just believe that two sets of eyes are better than one."

"Oh really, and what happens if it *is* Adam Gable following her and he spots you?"

"Then he'll realize I'm not in Toronto or wherever anymore."

"Alletti's been looking for you for a long time and if Gable is following the girl you'll have walked right into a trap."

"Strange, I thought it was the girl we're concerned about."

"I can't protect the two of you blast it!"

"You don't need to protect me," said Simon. "I've been taking care of myself for a long, long time," and his fingers reached up and touched the butt of the Beretta underneath his leather jacket. "Besides, Julia's brother asked me to look after her."

"What a bunch of nonsense," hissed Angus across the line. "Anyone can see you have the hots for her."

Simon's voice turned deadly. "That's quite enough, so back off Angus! What I feel or don't feel is my own business, but I have a responsibility to that woman and I'm going to meet it."

"Sometimes I get the distinct impression you don't trust me," said Angus wearily.

"Boy you've got that one right; remember what happened to Seth?"

Love Never Dies

"Okay, okay. So what's your itinerary?"

"I meet Julia for a drink in the lounge at 5:30. I'll try to coerce her into having dinner with me and tomorrow we'll head down to UCLA to watch some flamenco dancing. Her principal Connie Fernandez is going to be there, but of course, if Stan has been doing his job you already know all that."

"Wise guy," snorted Angus.

"Do you have any idea what sort of car Adam Gable prefers these days?"

"He used to drive a Lexus but apparently no longer. The only thing about Adam we know for certain is that he prefers silver cars and changes them like girlfriends."

The image of the silver BMW flashed into Simon's mind. "Could he be currently driving a BMW?"

"Why?" asked Angus, suddenly interested.

"I just thought a Beamer was trailing us a little too closely this afternoon. Maybe you can check on it. Any chance I'll run into Stan tomorrow?"

"Tomorrow? If you're a really lucky boy you'll glimpse him tonight." Angus couldn't see Simon's broad smile, but sensing it, sighed bitterly. Why did his family have to be so damn difficult?

"Well, it's comforting you're doing something right for a change. I'll stay in touch," said Simon, and hung up before Angus could retort.

Loren Lockner

At 5:30 sharp Simon waited in the lobby, eager to have a glass of white wine with the lovely Julia who had changed into a lovely black and white pants outfit with a matching striped jacket and a small little spaghetti tie looped around her neck and clasped together with an onyx pin.

They seated themselves in the busy bar. "What would you like to drink?" Simon asked.

"I think just tonic water," she said to the hovering waiter.

"Bring me a glass of white wine, something dry if you have it. So where would you like to go for dinner?" he asked.

Julia's cheeks flamed and she broke eye contact and concentrated on playing with her coaster. "I'm sorry Simon but I can't have dinner with you tonight. Connie called about twenty minutes ago and indicated she and Alvaro, along with a bunch of teachers from my school, are going to meet at a steakhouse called Jimmy's around 6:30. I, um... well..."

"Don't feel comfortable having me accompany you?"

"I hope you understand," she said contritely. "You see, while I've mentioned to Connie you're in town and resemble your brother a great deal, I've never told my other colleagues about Seth's brother. I think they'd be quite shocked to see you."

Simon felt a tremendous wave of disappointment wash over him, but plastered an accepting smile upon his face. "That's fine by me; you're not to worry about it a single bit, but since your nosy brother is going to ask me to relate a detailed nightly account of your actions could you at least tell me where Jimmy's Steakhouse is so I can let him know you haven't been eaten by a giant ogre or something?"

Julia flashed him a thankful smile. "It's in West Hollywood on the corner of La Cienega. I do hope you understand. I truly meant to have dinner with you. Honest." Her dark green eyes plead for his understanding and Simon reached over and patted her hand.

"Don't worry about it. It'll give me a chance to do some of my touristy-type exploring. Who knows, maybe I'll find a jumping nightclub. I wonder if they have one specializing in eighties and nineties rock 'n' roll. Anyway, let's enjoy our drink and you can tell me all about your week."

They passed the next fifteen minutes comfortably, Julia immensely relieved Simon didn't seem upset. At six o'clock, she swung her handbag over her shoulder, lifted a hand, and disappeared through the slowly filling bar. Simon gave her a full two minutes before sliding into the seat of his Pajero, waiting until she directed her sedan toward West Hollywood to follow her discreetly at a safe distance.

Julia never knew Simon kept to the shadows that entire evening, lingering in the lounge of Jimmy's

Steakhouse, safety tucked out of sight while he devoured a rare porterhouse steak and watched her socialize with her gregarious principal whom he instinctively trusted on sight.

Connie and Julia were joined by her rather portly boyfriend, Alvaro Lopez, as well as three other teachers, all whom Simon recognized from Angus' records. Angus had downloaded the previous year's yearbook and thoroughly checked out all of Julia's school associates once it became apparent she might be in danger. The gay company lingered over their meal and while Julia didn't eat much, only picking at her baked potato and sirloin steak, she seemed to enjoy the noisy crowd about her.

Another watched Julia that night. Adam Gable's watery eyes, hidden behind disguising sunglasses, observed her socializing from a solitary booth, kitty-corner from her. He shook his head in disbelief; not only was the girl here with her friends, but barely discernable in the shadowy bar sat the wayward brother of Seth Hayes, a man who'd been missing for more than a year. This was certainly going to earn him a raise from Joe Alletti, yes indeed. He could have kicked himself for not recognizing the Canadian before.

He sipped at his glass of sweet red wine and savored its fullness. This California lifestyle was one he could certainly get used to. Adam noted that Julia

Love Never Dies

Morris had a very nice figure underneath her less than revealing black and white pants' outfit. She was one mighty fine looking woman and maybe after all this was over and he'd found out what he needed to know from the pretty blonde, maybe he and Julia could have a private session together. The very thought caused him to grin lecherously. Unfortunately, she hung around with too many people tonight and that blasted Hayes followed her, probably keeping an eye on her, which made perfect sense after his brother's abrupt demise.

"You're a cautious one Mr. Hayes," he smirked. "Well, you know what they say; one is more vulnerable in a crowd and she's heading to UCLA tomorrow. Now that's a perfect place for a little lady to get separated from her companions," and he raised a finger to the waitress, deciding a plate of hot, spicy nachos would just hit the spot.

Chapter Nine

The next morning Simon met Julia bright and early for breakfast. They hadn't made any prearranged plans to meet, so he made sure he was present in the hotel's buffet restaurant around 7:30. Julia was already seated, munching on a warm chocolate croissant and stirring her tea. Her eyes lifted in pleasure at seeing him.

"So how was your evening Simon?" she asked, as he sank down across from her. Today Julia was a peach dream, her pretty pearl buttoned t-top open slightly at the neck and tucked into pale orange jeans. Her blonde hair was plaited in a loose French braid and comfortable walking shoes enclosed her small feet. Fresh and pretty, this morning no dark smudges ruined the beautiful symmetry of her delicate face. Julia focused her wonderful emerald eyes upon him.

Simon tore his silver ones away and thought rapidly. "Just wonderful. I drove around and stopped at a few dance clubs, not returning until after one. This town is certainly hopping on a Friday night. What about you?" His blatant lie made him want to cringe, but Julia seemed relieved to hear he'd enjoyed such a pleasant evening.

"I just had dinner with my friends and then stopped off for some dessert. I was back by 9:30. I find I'm not very energetic on Friday nights, but did enjoy seeing Connie moon over her new beau."

"He's a flamenco dancer as well?"

"That's right, his name's Alvaro and he's quite a character. He has a story for every occasion and kept us *very* entertained. I'm just not sure he's such a good choice for Connie. He's been married twice and lost both of his wives."

"To illness?" asked Simon.

"To philandering, though I can't mention that uncomfortable fact to Connie. Anyway, I guess he's one heck of a dancer and they're really going to cut a rug this morning."

"So where exactly are we going?"

"Most of the activities take place at Dickson Plaza in the center of the campus. It's been a while since I've visited UCLA, and even though Connie gave me a map, I need to figure out exactly where she's going to be performing. Once we get to the campus, let's park near the Bruin Plaza in case we become separated. It has a large replica of a grizzly bear that's affectionately referred to as Joe Bruin and everybody uses him as their rendezvous point. If you get lost just look for the Bruin Bear and I'll be waiting."

"Okay," agreed Simon solemnly. "I'll try not to get lost."

Julia grinned. "I was just thinking this is going to be a great architectural treat for you. There are some really unusual buildings on campus like The Viewpoint Lounge, The James West Alumni Center, and Kerckhoff Hall. The latter used to be the original student union and is still headquarters for the Associated Student Body."

"That's right; you'd be really familiar with the campus because you were an undergrad at UCLA for two years weren't you?"

"Yes, it's an amazing place. We've got tons of neat buildings like the Wooden Center and the Ashe Center, which was named after Arthur Ashe, the Wimbledon Tennis Champion. Did you know he was a student at UCLA?"

"He was an amazing man," stated Simon. "I remember when he won Wimbledon; it was a great victory for all African-Americans. It's such a shame he died of AIDS, contracted from receiving a blood transfusion during heart surgery."

"It was sad. Anyway, I thought if you wanted me to, I could take some pictures. You'll get an incredible view of the lower campus at the top of Janss Steps. Much of the campus served as part of the

Love Never Dies

Olympic village in 1984 when the Games were held in LA."

"I think this is going to be a real treat," asserted Simon, "so I'd better fortify myself."

He excused himself, and after obtaining a healthy serving of hash browns and bacon from steaming stainless steel serving dishes, waited while the chef, complete with tall white hat, whipped up a ham, mushroom, and cheese omelet. It was strange, Simon thought as he watched the chef beat the egg batter into a frothy mixture before pouring it into a hot oily pan, that after all that had happened to Julia, she was still able to think of others. She'd gracefully included him in her trip to LA, had seemed genuinely contrite when he couldn't have dinner with her, and now was eager to snap photos of some of UCLA's architectural wonders. It was no wonder Seth had loved her so much.

Simon didn't get lost, in fact, with a bit of luck, he found a parking space before Julia did and leaned nonchalantly against the bronze bear statue at the foot of Bruin Walk. Already the strum of Spanish guitars floated from the Plaza while many gaily-bedecked dancers passed by them on their way toward the festivities. Julia and Simon followed a glossy-haired dancer to the commons above Janss Steps. As soon as they turned the corner, countless booths featuring items from lacy Spanish blouses and hand-dipped candles, to a booth serving genuine fajitas appeared. Mexican music surrounded and penetrated the busy plaza and their attention focused upon a makeshift stage erected directly in the center of the square. Two yellow-skirted women, hair pulled back into sleek buns, clapped their hands and stomped to the wonderfully energetic Spanish music.

"When's your boss scheduled to go on?" called Simon over the loud music, as he watched a teenaged dancer tap her feet to the rapid rhythm. He wondered how the dancer managed to keep a perpetual smile upon her face when Simon personally knew he would have been exhausted beyond belief.

"She and Alvaro's troupe start at 9:45, but I thought it might be fun to explore the campus and observe some of the sights before they begin."

Simon agreed and for an hour they strolled through the lushly landscaped campus. Julia had been correct about the architecture, which was indeed lovely. They passed by Moore Hall and spent thirty minutes in the Powell Library as Simon examined the building's famous ornamental tile work. The architects, George W. Kelham and David Allison, had proposed using the Romanesque style they'd observed in the Lombardy region of northern Italy, and finally managed, after a great deal of effort, to convince the university's founders, Edward Dickson and Earnest Moore, to embrace it as the new university's style.

Love Never Dies

"It's so lovely," said Julia, gazing up at the rounded ceiling.

"It's true Romanesque," stated Simon, "and I can see many of the older buildings have adopted this style as well. Do you know when the campus was originally built?"

"I think in the 1920's. If you like this then I'm sure you'll enjoy the painted ceilings of Royce Hall. The Loggia is supposed to depict the twelve medieval professions. I used to stand under it as an undergrad between classes and marvel at the amazing architecture."

"In many ways you sound like a frustrated architect yourself?"

"No, not really. I truly enjoy teaching, although I admit Seth inspired me to have a greater appreciation of architecture. Every building here compliments the basic theme of the campus, though very different from UCSB which was developed along the Spanish Mediterranean style using the original mission to set the tone for subsequent buildings. Seth was adamant about following regional themes and he'd probably be delighted that UCLA was so carefully designed to follow the classic ideal."

"Wow! You *are* an amateur architect!"

She laughed at Simon's amazed glance. "Okay, okay. I admit I remember that from my high school tour of the campus when I was considering UCLA."

"So what made you leave UCLA?" Simon asked, examining the octagonal dome of the Powell Library.

"After deciding I didn't want to go into film after all, my mother became ill at the end of my sophomore year and I wanted to be close to her. It's not like UCLA's that far from Santa Barbara, but it seemed reasonable at the time to transfer to UCSB. I've never regretted the choice though I still harbor warm feelings for UCLA. Would you like me to take some pictures?"

He nodded and over the next twenty minutes Julia snapped several shots of the Janss Steps, the lovely domed interior of the Powell Library, and was just heading toward the Alumni Center when she glanced at her watch.

"Oh no! We've got to hurry back to the plaza since it's almost 9:45. Connie will be starting her routine any minute!"

Simon had difficulty keeping up with Julia as she sprinted toward the commons, his injured leg hindering his progress.

Julia positioned herself near the stage and sure enough, exactly at 9:45, Alvaro and Connie stepped onto the wide platform accompanied by two other couples. Connie leaned her head back to gaze lovingly at Alvaro, who stretched out a hand to the comely principal who wore high-heeled tap shoes; a yellow and scarlet flounced skirt topped by a beautiful low-cut Mexican blouse, and a beckoning smile. Connie had tied her shiny black hair back with lovely tortoiseshell combs and grinned down at Julia as the music cued. Her warm brown eyes suddenly widened at the sight of Simon. He nodded pleasantly to her and discreetly backed off, not wishing to distract her.

It was an amazing performance as the energized pair flawlessly executed a synchronized rendition of the famous hat dance and three other pieces Julia didn't recognize. Simon observed the entire proceedings bemusedly, remembering his own college days while casting appreciative glances at Julia. The faint breeze tugged at her long blonde hair, loosening it about her face and tingeing her cheeks pink. Her peach outfit skillfully disguised her too-thin figure and Simon sighed as Julia snapped several pictures in rapid succession. He scanned the boisterous crowd, suddenly noting a dark sun-glassed man leaning against a pillar across the plaza.

Stan's thick moustache twitched in recognition as Simon sauntered over to the leaning man, who slowly and deliberately lit an unfiltered cigarette.

"Having a good day Detective?"

"Ah, this is the life. A sunny clear morning on the beautiful grounds of UCLA; it reminds me of my own college days. The tantalizing odors of fajitas and tacos, the sight of beautiful dark-haired women strolling by, and the rhythm of ethnic music... ah, it makes me long to be an upperclassman again. It also almost makes one forget how a certain rash young Canadian is compromising an innocent woman's position."

"You're wrong on both accounts," said Simon. "I'm not Canadian, at least I'm only half one since I carry a dual passport, and I'm not compromising anybody's position."

"Hum, tell that to Angus. I hope you're aware, Simon, that Adam Gable would love to see you just as dead as your brother. Seth wasn't the only 'black-listed' man in your family from what I've heard."

"Hopefully Adam will never get his wish. So you're keeping a good eye out?"

"But of course," said Stan, "that's what I'm paid the big bucks for." He took a deep drag on his cigarette and grinned, blowing smoke into Simon's unflinching face as the two examined each other.

Not so very far away, under the shadow of an enormous Eucalyptus tree, Adam Gable lifted his cell phone to his ear and called in a debt owed.

"Roy, this is Adam."

"Nice to hear from you bud, I've been waiting for your call," returned a heavy Alabama drawl.

"I'm currently at UCLA at the Hispanic Arts Festival and need that favor. Where are you hanging right now?"

"Westwood; there's a nice little joint here that serves up real biscuits and gravy."

Love Never Dies

"How convenient. I need you to take care of an annoying problem that's popped up for me. It has something to do with the police."

"I get to whack a police officer? Today *is* my lucky day."

"Hold your horses. All I want is for this guy to be incapacitated for a few hours while I take care of some unfinished business. Hey," he protested, to the nasal whine that hummed across the line, "it's good money for doing almost nothing." Adam listened for a while, his mouth twitching in distaste. He never really cared much for Roy, but beggars can't be choosers and Roy *was* very efficient.

"I'll meet you in front of the Bruin Statue in fifteen minutes. Of *course* I've got a photo of the guy. I just took a Polaroid and you can't miss the jerk with his big ugly mustache. All I'm looking for is a diversion. Roy, I told you, you don't have to kill anybody. Jeez, aren't you aware if you kill a policeman it's the gas chamber. I've got a much better idea. Yeah, see you soon."

Adam flipped his phone off, tucking it into his black jeans' pocket before leering again at the oblivious Julia, who kept snapping pictures of her energetically dancing boss. If only Seth had been forthcoming about the true nature of the game, the little lady might have been forewarned about her current danger. So much for true love.

Loren Lockner

It was purely a fluke that Simon spotted Adam Gable at all. He'd left Julia to Stan's diligent watch and headed toward the Franklin D. Murphy Sculpture Garden, which is renowned as an open-air museum, and even though the jacarandas were not in bloom he ambled about, examining the works of many notable twentieth-century sculptors such as Henry Matisse, Jean Arp, and Henry Moore. He needed to place some distance between him and the young elementary teacher he so desperately wanted to protect, so he wandered through the heavily vegetated path, enjoying some of the often odd-shaped sculptures.

Simon suddenly noticed a tall pallid man hovering near the scaly trunk of a sleepy jacaranda tree. This time his eyes didn't deceive him; it *was* the same man from the silver BMW and matched to a 't' the snapshot Stan had flashed him several minutes earlier. The gaunt man watched him intently and Simon pretended not to notice, his heart thudding painfully as he headed back toward the Dickson Plaza, pretending to search for the men's toilets. He quickly scurried into Royce Hall and hid inside the first archway. Sure enough, the hurried steady tread of the quickly moving man passed by the entry he'd just ducked into.

"Damn," he cursed. They'd been followed, and what better place for Adam Gable to strike than in the middle of the UCLA campus amongst thousands of people. Simon hurried back toward the stage where Connie and her troupe had just finished their performance. He searched vainly for Julia, finally discovering her near a jewelry stand fingering a heavy amber necklace.

"Julia," he tried to say nonchalantly. "I think I've had just about as much culture as I can stand and I'm dying to see Tinsel Town. Are you ready to take me to Hollywood so that I can get my fix of celebrities on the Walk of Fame?"

Julia glanced up and smiled. "There's still a lot to do here. Are you sure you want to take off now?"

"Positive," stated Simon firmly. "It's just that my hip is really bothering me and I need sit down for a while. I thought maybe we could have some lunch somewhere. I'd stay here, but this loud music is really getting to me."

Julia grinned. "So mariachi bands are not to your taste, kind sir?"

"I like them in small doses; *very* small doses. I know that you might want to come back here later so why don't we take my car and leave yours here?"

"Whew," said Julia after a particularly loud trumpet blast. "I can see your point. I'm ready to go as well. However, I'd rather take my car back to the hotel since I wouldn't mind retrieving a sweater. It can get quite chilly here in the evenings, being so close to the ocean, and I'm sure we'll be out for a while."

"Alright," said Simon hesitantly, casting a glance over his shoulder. Neither Stan nor Adam Gable was anywhere to be seen. "We'll meet back at the hotel then."

While it went against his better judgment, Simon followed her as she headed toward the Getaway Suites. Julia took her own sweet time too, and for the first time he felt some impatience with the seemingly content woman. Simon watched as she parked her car and disappeared inside her room lugging some of the heavy photographic equipment. He made a quick dash to his own room, picking up his spare cash and an extra box of cartridges. Five minutes later, jacket in hand, he met Julia at his 4x4.

"If your leg's hurting I can drive if you want?" Her handbag and a brown wool coat hung over her arm.

"No, I think I'd like to drive."

"But if you're in pain it would only make sense for me to drive. C'mon?"

"Then why don't you take a spin in my Pajero?" he asked. He'd feel more secure in the bronze off-road vehicle.

"That sounds like fun," said Julia, smiling at the truck. Within moments, she'd hoisted herself up into the driver's seat and adjusted the rearview mirror. "This is a very nice truck. I can see why both you and Seth enjoy 4x4s."

Love Never Dies

"Yeah," croaked Simon, peering about the nearly empty parking lot. Luckily for them the silver Beamer hadn't shown up yet. "Do you want me to navigate?" he asked.

"C'mon now, you're talking about a southern California resident here. I can get you to the Strip with my eyes closed."

Julia was an excellent driver. It took only a matter of moments before she acclimated herself to the heavier steering mechanism of the truck and Simon breathed a sigh of relief as she pulled out of the parking lot and turned onto Santa Monica Boulevard. Within fifteen minutes, he was convinced they hadn't been followed as she parallel parked on Hollywood Boulevard, only two blocks from Grauman's Chinese Theatre. They strolled down the star-studded lane, pausing every few steps to read the famous and sometimes nearly forgotten names from Hollywood's golden age.

"Wow," said Simon, quite impressed by the splattering of stars extending down the sidewalk. As they approached the famous theatre Julia recited the names.

"Look Simon, here's Kevin Spacey. Oh, and one of my favorites, Spencer Tracy. Remember Groucho Marx and his crazy brothers?"

They passed Julie Andrews and Greta Garbo, William Shatner and Tom Cruise. Even singers such as

Loren Lockner

Elton John and Michael Jackson had added their stars to the famous Walk of Fame. Julia paused before the Chinese Theatre's gaudy facade and pointed to the forecourt housing 173 star's footprints and handprints.

"This is the priciest real estate here Simon. If you make it to Grauman's forecourt, you're truly a superstar." Julia swung the camera off her shoulder as Simon knelt by Clark Gable's square as she snapped a photo for memory's sake.

Simon shook his head in amazement. "I'd read about this place, but had no idea it was so extensive. Look, here's Judy Garland who wrote, '*For Mr. Grauman... All Happiness,*' and it's dated 1939. There's George Lucas and Tom Hanks, and near him, Arnold Schwarzenegger. Thanks so much Julia, you don't know how much this means to me."

After finishing their often-amazed scrutiny of the forecourt, they continued their quest for quite a while, still enthusiastically reading the stars until Simon, his leg truly aching, asked if they could rest and have something to eat. They sat upon canvas director's style seats in a sidewalk cafe and sipped diet sodas while sharing a plate of nachos as they watched tourists from all over the world stroll by. A particularly excited group of Japanese tourists halted at every star and snapped a picture.

"You'd think it would be cheaper to buy the book," murmured Simon, as he placed a crunchy tortilla chip smothered in olives, guacamole, and sour cream inside his mouth. "This is definitely something Toronto is missing; good authentic Mexican food."

"Maybe you should change your career line and open up a Mexican restaurant. I'm sure you would make a fortune."

"Oh, I don't know. French cuisine as well as seafood from the Maritimes dominates most restaurant fare." He scanned the busy sidewalk for the skeletal Adam Gable and relaxed when the gaunt man was nowhere to be seen. For the time being they seemed safe, but his fingers itched to call Angus.

After their delicious snack, Simon excused himself and headed for the men's room. Once inside, he flipped open his cell phone and gave Toronto a call. Angus' answering machine locked in after only four rings and Simon left a terse message. Simon then dialed Stan Garten's cell. The phone rang endlessly but never logged onto any message system. A wave of trepidation passed over him. It was not like Stan to disregard calls and as Simon hurried out of the men's room his eyes immediately sought Julia. She was window-shopping, her camera looped over the shoulder of the pale peach top.

"Is your leg well enough to continue?" she asked sympathetically.

"I think the rest did help, but I feel like strolling back to the car."

"Will you look at that," stated Julia's amused voice ten minutes later as they paused in front of a trendy clothing store. "Isn't it amazing?"

If Simon's attention hadn't been directed to the huge glass store front, he'd never have glimpsed the reflection of the silver BMW gliding slowly down the street. The blue-haired mannequin sat perched on a red chair in a shimmering lime-green dress and glass hat while blowing huge pink bubbles out of a toy pipe. The Beamer slowed down to get a better view as it headed in the opposite direction. The narrow face of Adam Gable peered out of the open car window and once he'd spotted Julia and Simon he speeded up, searching for a place to make a u-turn. Simon immediately jerked Julia around and hurried down the sidewalk, avoiding tourists who'd paused to study the imprints upon the sidewalk.

"We need to go," he hissed under his breath, and Julia jerked her arm away from him, surprised at his bullying manner.

"What on earth?"

Simon realized that in less than two hundred yards the BMW would be able to make a u-turn and dragged Julia to the Pajero, pressing the security system and thrusting her toward the car after the telltale beep.

"Get in," he demanded.

"What do you mean? You were all fired up about visiting here an hour ago and now you want to leave?"

Love Never Dies

"I said get in the car," he ground between his teeth, and practically threw her onto the passenger seat. Her face paled as he jumped up as quickly as his hurt leg would allow into the driver's seat and ground the gears in his haste. Simon waited until the BMW headed toward him and then suddenly pulled out, gunning the engine before engineering a severe u-turn in front of a city transit bus. Julia shrieked as he streaked in the opposite direction from the BMW, the impatient bus driver blasting his horn at the 4x4. Simon immediately hung a sharp right.

"Where's the nearest on-ramp?" he demanded, realizing they had only a minute or so to lose the silver BMW.

Julia frantically buckled herself in before backing against the car door as if he were a madman.

"If you make a right over there it'll put you on the Hollywood freeway. Simon, what are you doing?" The last came as a frightened shriek as Simon pulled onto the ramp, his foot ramming the accelerator and they hurled full throttle onto the freeway, barely missing a red Subaru as he merged into the traffic. "Now you're starting to frighten me Simon, what's going on?"

"We're being followed," he shot out, casting a quick glance at her shocked face.

"What do you mean we're being followed? Followed by whom?"

"By a man named Adam Gable who works for another man called Joe Alletti."

"Adam Gable and Joe Alletti? I've never heard of them, so why would they be following us? Are they the police?"

Simon snorted depreciatively. "Not in the least. And they're following you because of Seth." The confused expression passing over Julia's face was enough to plunge Simon into despair. So much for her emotional recovery.

"But Seth... Seth's been dead these past ten months. I don't understand!"

Simon changed lanes and studied the rearview mirror. "I can't talk to you about it right now and while I know it's a hard thing to ask you, I'm begging you to trust me Julia. Trust me because you loved Seth." Julia didn't appear trusting in the least; in fact she looked about to leap from the vehicle. "Please Julia, you've got to help me since I'm not familiar with this area. If we continue heading south on the 101, where's the best place to get off if I need to exit quickly?"

Julia shivered and grabbed the dash as Simon swerved around a Ford Bronco. "If you keep on this highway you're going to run into the Burbank Freeway or 134 toward Pasadena, but our hotel is that way. You're going the wrong way Simon!" she cried.

"I'm fully aware our hotel's in the opposite direction, but I can't worry about that right now.

236

Love Never Dies

Toward Pasadena; that sounds as good a choice as any. Isn't that where the Rose Parade is held?"

"Yes," whispered Julia, scrunching back as far away from him as the confines of the 4x4 would allow. Simon immediately veered north and within a few miles looped onto the 134. His eyes continually returned to the rearview mirror and Julia became so paranoid she began peering out the rear window of the Pajero, clueless as to just what she should be looking for. One thing was for certain, the man beside her had changed from a casual carefree tourist into a man she didn't remotely know. Her chest burned in fright and Julia kept whispering Seth's name, hoping he could somehow protect her against his maniac brother.

"I have an important question to ask you Julia. Has anyone unfamiliar approached you within the last few days for any reason; perhaps to strike up a conversation with you, or ask for your help or something?"

"I'm... ah... not sure. I talk to a lot of people; I'm a teacher for God's sake!"

"This man would have been a tall, dark-haired fellow with a sallow face, way too thin for his height."

A sudden image of Mike Cooper flashed into her brain. "Well on Thursday after school a man by the name of Mike Cooper approached me regarding his nephew who apparently hadn't gotten on the bus."

"And just where was this?"

"In the parking lot at school when I was getting ready to go home. That's when he approached me."

"And did you stay with him the whole time?"

"Uh no... I went back into the office to check if his little boy got onto the bus."

"So you left him alone near your car?"

"Well I guess so. Yes, yes I did."

"Thank God we're in my Pajero."

"What's this all about?" Her words no longer sounded frightened, only angry, her fingers locked around her handbag. Simon was certain she would use it on him if he didn't manage to placate her soon.

"Please allow me to explain it all to you later," he asked gently. "I need to concentrate on my driving, but believe me when I say I only have your best interests at heart. You've got to help me though. If you see anything resembling a silver BMW let me know. The man inside... he wants to kill me for sure and very likely you as well."

Julia began to hyperventilate; her hand vainly searching for the warmth of Seth's soul, but no comfort was to be had, only a severe tightness indicating intense anxiety.

"Okay," she croaked, struggling to breathe. "I guess I'll just have to trust you for now." Julia swiveled in her seat and searched the busy freeway with anxious green eyes. Thus occupied, she managed to calm herself enough to ward off her previous lightheadedness. A full twenty minutes later, Simon pulled off onto Lake Street in Pasadena to search for a secluded hotel.

"Ah, this will do," Simon said thankfully, after driving for several minutes along the beautifully treed streets of Pasadena. A low-roofed motor lodge stood on the right-hand side near Altadena Drive. He pulled up promptly before the reception area, removed the keys from the ignition, and ordered Julia to stay put. She closed her eyes and leaned back against the headrest, unwilling to meet his concerned stare. Within five minutes, Simon returned with a hotel key dangling from his fingers.

"I managed to get us a room around the back. There's parking right by the room so no one can spot us from the road." He maneuvered the truck around the back and parked under the shade of a mulberry tree just beginning to lose its broad leaves. Simon stiffly removed himself from the Pajero as Julia's voice floated over the top of the bronze vehicle before she slammed the door angrily.

"I need some answers now Simon."

"And you're going to get them, but inside the hotel room. C'mon." He unlocked the door, throwing his key atop the TV set before moving to the drapes. They slid shut with a hiss. Julia watched his movements, staring at him as if trapped in some sort of surreal dream. This was the kind of scene from some sort of grade-B movie, not her well-structured life, and suddenly a hot spurt of anger threatened her and she barely maintained control.

"I think you have a lot of explaining to do mister," she snarled, ignoring the burning sensation in her chest that suggested caution, and Simon turned bleakly toward her and nodded grimly.

Chapter 10

Simon sat across from her, his chair facing backward while his arms leaned across the pine top. He gazed intently at her pinched face that somehow managed to be frightened and angry at the same time. Julia perched upon the edge of the bed, her hands twisted in her lap as her confused face demanded credible answers.

"About sixteen months ago," Simon began, "my brother Seth worked for a firm called Girard and Tierney. They are a large architectural company in Toronto and serve some of the main business interests in the city. Seth worked for the firm for over two years and had bought, as I mentioned before, a condominium on the shores of Lake Ontario. He enjoyed working for Lou Tierney and the two men became personal friends.

Lou had been son of a well-known businessman and seemingly entered the field of architecture through love, not obligation, having decided to reject ownership of his father's successful textile business.

While Lou Tierney played at architecture, his firm was actually a front for other lucrative business holdings he held, unfortunately not all of them legal. Unbeknownst to Seth, Lou was a chronic gambler and to pay off his debts his well-established business was used by the mob."

"Good God, the mob's involved in this?" asked Julia, turning white.

"Unfortunately yes, and that's where Seth comes in. His computer, having unfortunately crashed, severely set him behind on some plans he was designing. To catch up, he decided to work late and use his secretary's machine. While using her computer, he noticed some files that, well, didn't fit and realized he'd stumbled upon some very incriminating information. That night, by chance Mandy Gascone, whose real name was Mandy Gaskill and an undercover cop, came back to retrieve some papers and caught him at her machine."

"I bet that didn't look good."

"You've got that right. She instantly thought he was involved with Lou Tierney and it took all of his sweet-talking skills to convince the middle-aged woman he wasn't. Anyway, to make a long story short, Mandy enlisted his aid, asking him to keep an ear out for any additional information. Seth was simply going to be a source, nothing more, until a fluke accident occurred. As you probably have guessed, Toronto winters can get pretty chilly and icy. It was during a brief thaw that Mandy slipped upon the steps leading to the building and broke her leg in two places. Realizing that the carefully constructed sting intended to trap Lou Tierney in his money laundering business was about to go awry, she enlisted Seth's aid again, placing him in contact with a man by the name of Angus O'Leary."

"O'Leary? I never heard Seth mention either him or this Mandy."

"I'm sure it's because Seth didn't want you to know Julia. All I can say is that things went terribly wrong. Seth's cover was blown and even though Joe Alletti was arrested, a leak in the Toronto Police Department indicated that Seth and I, as well as our cousin Lucas, had been involved in the entire undercover operation. Our cousin Lucas had been down visiting us and some of Tierney's associates took a snapshot of Seth and him. Of course, at the time, Joe Alletti couldn't be sure if it was Seth or me who was involved because we were identical twins. As the trial approached and one government witness "mysteriously' disappeared, the Toronto Police Department realized Seth's life was in danger and because of our close relationship packed all three of us off. Lucas, I later found out, was stashed somewhere in British Columbia and I was sent down to Detroit.

Seth of course wasn't speaking to me at the time because the incident regarding the girl, Marcie, so I didn't know he'd been stashed in Santa Barbara. Seth began a new life down here and in mid-October, flew up to Toronto to testify against Joe Alletti. No one knows how he was pegged, since his testimony had been sequestered, but when Seth returned to Santa Barbara he was tailed by the man following us now; Adam Gable. I'm not sure Seth became aware of his presence until December and by that time was hopelessly in love with you. He was instructed both by Angus O'Leary and Mandy Gaskill to relocate, but refused." His voice tailed off and suddenly Julia realized what Simon hadn't said.

"Oh no! He refused to find a safe place because of me?"

Simon glanced down sadly, his fists clenching the chair top. "It was a stupid mistake, one that cost him dearly."

"So what you're saying is that the collision between the semi-truck and his Jeep was no accident?"

Simon swallowed deeply. "I'm so sorry Julia."

"So the man I loved was murdered?" Julia suddenly rose, staggering blindly about the small room before backing into a corner of the room. She sank to the floor and leaning her head against the wall, cried silently.

"Oh Julia, please..." Simon rose awkwardly and knelt beside her, placing gentle hands upon her

244

shoulders. At first she resisted but finally, turning stiffly, sought the comfort of his arms.

"They killed my Seth," she gasped. "They killed him, those bastards."

Simon held her for a long time, soothing her hair and allowing the hot tears to rain down upon his chest. When Julia became calmer he lifted her from the floor, steering her toward the bed. Simon looped an arm over her limp shoulders.

"Julia, I hate to say it, but there's more. Joe Alletti was to stand trial on further allegations. Seth found out that Taylor Reynolds, an accountant with the firm, had access to a disk detailing Lou Tierney's monetary connections with Alletti. Taylor didn't trust the Toronto police, certain there was a leak somewhere in the department and unbeknownst to the police, mailed a copy of the disk to Seth, instructing him to hand it over to Angus personally if anything happened to him. Taylor was killed in January, just before he was about to testify, and because of his death part of the charges against Alletti were dropped. Within a day of Taylor's 'accidental fall' from the balcony of his high-rise apartment, Seth's Jeep burned to a crisp on a damp California highway.

Alletti received information that Seth had secreted the disk of Lou Tierney's workings somewhere in Santa Barbara. You probably didn't know that Bastam, Hughes, and Glickstern suffered a burglary less than three days after Seth's death. Seth's desk was rummaged; his computer files pillaged, and his hard drive stolen."

"I never knew that," gasped Julia, peering up at him with red swollen eyes.

"I'm sure no one wanted you to know; particularly as the police began to put two and two together. Unfortunately, Alletti's convinced that Seth made you privy to his secrets, which you and I know isn't the case."

Julia wiped her blurry eyes. "He never told me anything about it. I wish he had."

"I wish he had as well. While I'm proud he wanted to protect you, his mistake has unfortunately come back to haunt you. And the reason it has is partly because of me."

"Why?" she asked simply.

"When we heard through the grapevine that you might be in danger, Angus O'Leary suggested you go under police protection. Both Lucas and I protested, realizing what you had just gone through. Were we now going to tear you away from all those people who served as your support system? It was hoped that when no disk surfaced, Alletti would assume the truth; that you knew nothing. Therefore, it was instead agreed by the powers that be that you'd be watched."

"Watched?" she repeated numbly.

"Yes, by an undercover detective named Stan Garten who'd been in contact with Seth. He drives a brown Chevy sedan and is a tall man with a bushy moustache."

Suddenly Julia gasped. "He's the man I had removed from the school grounds because I thought he was stalking children."

"Yeah, and actually was your own personal bodyguard. That tale certainly made its way around the circuit. Anyway, Stan was at UCLA today watching over the two of us. It's likely Adam Gable placed some sort of tracking device onto your car the afternoon he pretended to be the uncle of the missing student. Gable clearly wanted you out of Santa Barbara and away from your family and friends so he could ransack your flat after you left and then approach you."

"Approach?"

"Maybe that's too mild a term," said Simon.

"So you just didn't come down here to tie up Seth's loose ends at the architectural firm?"

"I came to watch over you Julia."

"Because they failed to protect Seth?"

Simon's gray eyes were bleak. "That was only part of it Julia. I felt a responsibility for you. You were like some sort of lifeboat set adrift, alone and needing my help. Shoot Julia, you were practically family! How could I sleep at night knowing you might be in danger? It was bad enough you were so despondent over Seth. For months we worried that maybe you would..."

"Do what your dad did?"

"Yes," he voiced sadly. "That's before it became clear to everyone you had the strength and courage to go on. You can't imagine how much I admire you for that."

Julia's hand rose to her breast and rubbed. Seth's soul had calmed, reassuring her that what Simon had just related was the complete truth. Simon noted the action and turned his head away, swallowing down the horrible lump in his throat.

Julia noted the muscles in his jaw tensing. "All this must have been horrible for you as well; to lose your brother, knowing he'd been murdered and that this Alletti would stop at nothing to silence your entire family, including me. So what do we do now?"

Simon reached under his black leather jacket and pulled out the Beretta hidden in his shoulder holster. "The first thing we're going to do, Julia, is give you a quick lesson on how to use this." Her dark green eyes widened, but if she felt fear or panic she kept it to herself.

"I'm ready," was all she said, and Simon understood Julia would valiantly face whatever happened next. That was the kind of woman she was.

Two hours later Julia lay sound asleep upon the queen-sized bed dominating the small motel room. Simon rested uncomfortably in a low chair by the window, occasionally flicking the curtains aside to check the parking lot while he observed her sleeping form. Her blonde hair spread over the pillow in glorious disarray, her hand twitching occasionally as she slept soundlessly. She'd cried before falling asleep and Simon wished he could have comforted her, but such a move was highly inappropriate. This was simply a hands-off operation, but that couldn't stop him from fantasizing about her.

His stomach gave a telltale growl and Simon rubbed the hungry spot in disgust. This motel wasn't equipped with any of the modern conveniences like room service, but did have a telephone, and within a couple of minutes he was flipping through the yellow pages searching for a nearby pizza delivery service. Julia awakened as he dialed the number.

"Pizza?" he mouthed and she nodded. Julia was also strangely hungry and quietly observed Seth's brother order two large pizzas; one pepperoni and one vegetarian, and a couple of soft drinks along with a Greek salad. Simon recited the address and room number and hung up the phone before flicking on the TV. Watching him now, Julia had a better understanding of Seth's hesitancy about getting involved with her initially.

"Simon," she asked, willing him to talk to her. "You never told me how you got that white streak in

your hair. Was it from the same snow bunny incident?"
Her reference to the pink-clad skier caused him to
smile.

"No, I was in a minor automobile accident several
months later. Well maybe not so minor. I re-injured my
leg and fool that I was, wasn't wearing my seat belt
and flew right through the windshield. I received a
nasty gash on top of my crown and low and behold
when the hair finally grew out again after the stitches
came out the strands were as white as snow. I feel like
Leticia from the Adams' family."

"I'm sure it is quite appealing to the ladies."

"Oh yeah," said Simon, "they've been flocking
around me in hoards. Haven't you noticed how I've
had to beat them off with a stick?" His tone was light
as he gently mocked himself.

Julia sat up on the bedspread and tucked a couple
of pillows behind her. "I think Seth would be very
proud of you Simon."

His eyes, so like Seth's, peered back at her. "You
think so, eh?"

"Now you sound Canadian with your 'eh's. I have
the sense Seth always felt you were a little immature or
self-serving. That's just my impression, since he didn't
speak about you much. But here you are, risking your
own life to watch over someone you don't even know."

"I know you," he said quietly.

"What do you mean?"

Love Never Dies

"Seth wrote me all about you. It wasn't always what he said; it was what lay between the lines. He used to go on and on about your natural easy style with children, about how quick you were to laugh, and how beautiful your hair was. I'm not surprised he made you his soul mate. Do you still feel it Julia? Do you still feel him inside of you?"

"What do you mean?" she asked, turning her face away as she plucked at the rust bedspread, suddenly embarrassed.

"My father used to talk about a burning glow in his chest and said how he always knew when my mother was near. Do you still feel it there?" His silver gaze eyed her chest.

Julia touched her breast with two fingers and caressed the spot lightly. "Yes," she admitted. "I do still feel his presence. You know Simon, I used to believe Seth was trapped in some sort of self-imposed limbo as he waited for me to pass on to the hereafter, yet always felt he didn't want me to die before my time. But, while I lay here thinking about what you told me, I've formulated another concept to explain why his presence remains so strong inside of me."

"And what is that?" asked Simon hoarsely.

"He knows I'm in danger and that's why you felt you were needed here, because Seth sent you. The first time I met you I felt a tremendous jolt in my heart and thought he was warning me about you, but I don't believe that now." She paused and gazed at Seth's twin intently. "I've read there's an intense connection between twins and admit I've often felt Paul and I are nearly one even though we are not identical twins or the same sex. During Paul's wedding, I *felt* his intense joy. I've separated from him somewhat as I've gotten older, but know Seth's death hit him harder than the rest of the family because he could literally feel the pain I was going through. If that's true for Paul and me, then what about you and Seth, who were identical? You originally came from a single egg that split in your mother's womb. Could Seth be dictating what you do, or perhaps urging you to look after me?"

An odd expression passed over Simon's face as his silver eyes shimmered in the artificial light of the cheap motel lamp. "I'm positive you're right; I have been propelled and motivated by what Seth wanted. I admit everything I'm doing now is because I know that's what he would want and I owe it to him. I owe him Julia because he loved you more than life itself."

A sharp rap came upon the door, saving her from responding to his intense statement. Simon rose, and peering through the eyehole, opened the door to a red-shirted pizza delivery man with a jaunty striped hat. A minute later two huge cardboard boxes full of savory smelling pizzas, a large salad, and two ice cold drinks were spread upon the round table near the air-conditioning unit.

Love Never Dies

"Your gourmet meal awaits, my lady," Simon bowed, as Julia rose to join him at the small table to devour their feast.

"I have to go out," Simon said a full twenty minutes later after wiping his mouth on a paper napkin. Julia felt a cold wave wash over her as icy prickles of fear stiffened her back.

"Why?" she asked simply.

"I have to find out what happened to Stan Garten and since I can't seem to get hold of Mandy or Angus, I need to use an alternate method of contacting them. I don't want to use the hotel phone or my cell in case we're being traced. I'm also almost out of money after paying for the motel room with cash and buying your expensive and sophisticated dinner."

"I might be able to remedy that," stated Julia, glad to be able to help with something. She rose from the uncomfortable chair provided by the motel and rummaged through her handbag before finally pulling out her kidskin wallet. She peered inside the bill compartment.

"I went to the ATM yesterday and have about a hundred and eighty dollars remaining. Will that help?"

Simon watched her warmly, his too-long hair sexy and inviting, and she suddenly felt uncomfortable under his silver gaze.

"You keep that for an emergency. I'll come back and get it if I need it."

"But can't they trace ATMs?"

Simon leaned forward and tapped her lips gently with his finger. "Don't you worry about that," he said. He reached inside his jacket and pulled out the Beretta. "I'm leaving this here with you just in case."

"No!" Julia denied, suddenly worried about what might happen if he ran into Adam Gable and didn't have a weapon. "You keep it."

"No, you're defenseless here without the gun."

"That's just what you think!" Julia bent over the tan handbag again. "Ah ha! My mother gave me it a couple of years ago and I'm certain it still works." Julia pulled out a small gray can of mace and squinted as she read the directions. "Hmm, just point and shoot the spray into the assailant's face. I can do that!"

Simon's lip twitched under the thin disfiguring scar as he battled a smile at her valiant declaration. "Alright, but I must admit I'd feel more comfortable if I left the gun with you."

Julia eyed the blue-black gleam of the revolver upon his outstretched palm and shook her head. "I'll take my chances with screaming and mace," she answered, and Simon knew her mind was made up.

"I should return within thirty minutes. If not, I'll phone you on my cell. You're not to leave this hotel or call anyone. Is that clear?"

Love Never Dies

"You sound just like a second grade teacher," retorted Julia mildly. "Don't worry Mr. Hayes, I'll behave myself."

"Good girl." Simon suddenly felt an uncontrollable impulse to kiss her gently on the forehead so he backed away.

"Take care of yourself," she whispered.

"You're not to worry Julia, I'll be back before you know it my...," his voiced trailed off as he thrust the Beretta violently back into the shoulder holster hidden underneath his leather jacket and marched out the door. Within moments, the roar of the Pajero's engine throbbed, only to diminish rapidly as the 4x4 drove away.

Julia perched on the edge of the bed for a long time, staring sightlessly at the pizza boxes and remains of their dinner strewn over the low table where they'd shared their last meal. Her heart tugged and glowed, forcing her to reach up and rub the agitated spot. An inspired thought suddenly struck her. What if Simon also shared a portion of Seth's soul? She'd been so involved in her own personal grief that Julia had never really delved into the true relationship between Simon and Seth. They'd been identical twins and must have been close. Hadn't Simon mentioned how their similar tastes had gotten him into trouble and hadn't both studied to be architects? They'd grown up in the same house, witnessing their parents' true and undying affection, and it must have shattered Simon as much as Seth to have his father kill himself.

True, they'd had their problems, as Simon was quick to point out, but certainly there must have been a deep emotional bond between the two. Simon seemed so different from Seth, more carefree and quick with the jokes and one-liners, while Seth had been so serious and almost remote. Nevertheless, they were identical twins, as their shared love of hot sauce and women clearly indicated. A strange fluttering fear hovered at the outer edge of her mind and Julia suddenly gasped. She was attracted to Simon and that simple realization immediately filled her with guilt.

How could that be? Julia had loved Seth unreservedly and whole-heartedly, so how could she even look at his brother? Was it because he was identical in appearance to his brother even though the streak and scar gave him a much more roguish appearance? Or, was it because deep down inside Julia recognized Simon possessed the same undeniable dignity and integrity that had propelled Seth through his life? Seth had been the man of her dreams... so where did that place his highly attractive, but wilder twin? A treacherous desire stole into her heart, making her abruptly jump off the bed and begin cleaning up the cardboard boxes upon the table in a frenzied manner, her voice chanting frantically into the air.

256

Love Never Dies

"I'm sorry Seth, I'm sorry! It's just the anxiety and uncertainty of the moment. I'm really not attracted to your brother. I'm not!" Yet, in her heart, Julia knew she was as lost as that girl Marcie had been, and sinking down upon the bed burst into a traitorous flood of tears.

Adam Gable was livid. He cruised the streets of West Hollywood aimlessly searching for the elusive bronze Pajero, furious with himself for losing them in such a simple maneuver.

He quickly got on the line and dialed one of Alletti's cohorts in Los Angeles County. Adam reeled off the Pajero's license plate number and relayed to Joe Alletti's underling that Simon must be found. The opportunity had arisen to kill two birds with one stone and Adam felt exhilaration course through his entire body even though he wasn't exactly certain of the location of his prey. It was only a matter of time before they'd turn up and he was content to sit and wait until he heard from Alletti's men again.

He pulled into a sunny diner and ordered a big chiliburger smothered in onions, along with a strong cup of coffee. Adam chuckled as he waited for his burger and lit an unfiltered cigarette, wondering how long before Stan Garten's cohorts realized the police officer was locked in the trunk of his own car, unhurt but

257

certainly humiliated. And my, oh my, that woman had looked mighty fine in peach and Adam grinned once again to himself. Overall, it had been a very good day.

Simon, using two of the false ATM cards issued to him by Angus O'Leary, withdrew $500 on one and an additional $400 on the other. He needed the cash to secure another car, realizing it was just a matter of time before the Pajero was traced. Simon sauntered into an Internet café and paid for thirty minutes. Within twenty he'd sent off four e-mails; one to his cousin Lucas warning him to be on guard and not to trust his own safety to the police, and the others to Mandy, Angus O'Leary, and a contact he had within the Los Angeles Police Department. Hopefully, she would be able to locate Stan. Using a payphone just outside the café he rang up Paul Morris and was relieved to hear the recorded spiel of Paul's answering machine instead of a live voice. It was so much easier to lie to a machine.

"It seems that your sister, with the permission of her principal, has decided to remain in the area for a couple extra days. If you don't mind, I'm going to hang around as well and make sure she behaves herself." He kept it as light and airy as possible and signed off.

Simon then moved into a busy, but trendy clothing store and made a few purchases using a credit card stating the name Jeff Collins. He quickly acquired numerous packages and a canvas sports bag. Simon hoped he'd estimated Julia's size correctly since she'd lost so much weight. Seventy minutes after leaving the motor lodge, he once again opened the creaky door to the room. Julia was stretched out the queen-sized bed watching a Bette Midler movie. She leaped up, relief plastered across her face.

"I was getting so worried," she cried, as he crossed the room and dropped his packages onto the bed before embracing her.

"I told you I'd return as soon as I could. I'm sorry I didn't call but felt it was safer not to use the cell phone. I've become sort of a Santa Claus. Would you like to see what I've bought?"

"Sure, but why is your hand so muddy?"

Simon grinned mischievously. "I had to do a little work on the Pajero. I hope you don't mind."

"What do you mean?" she queried softly.

He walked into the bathroom and thrust his hands under a stream of warm water, energetically applying a liberal dose of the soap and rapidly scrubbing as the mud swirled down the drain.

"I didn't want anyone to decipher our license plates and since they're watering the flower bed next to the car I thought it might be good time to take a little mud and obscure some of the letters. Since I was having such a good time I thought I'd add a little mud along the runners and on the windshield as well. The 4x4 appears as if we've been off-roading somewhere."

Julia smiled. Simon definitely took care of the small details. "So what's in the packages?" she asked girlishly, her hands itching to open the parcels.

"Why don't you take a look," he said, as she dove right in, disgorging the contents of a bright red bag first.

"Oh Simon, this is just what I needed," she said enthusiastically, fingering a pair of blue jeans. "How'd you know I was size eight?"

"Previous girlfriend," he mumbled, hanging up his leather jacket.

Julia by now had discovered the long-sleeved red mock turtleneck and lavender t-top, as well as a light blue windbreaker jacket. She blushed at the two pairs of lacy underwear and a matching bra. She gulped as she examined the size. 34C? He observed a blush stealing down to her neck and grinned.

"Was I close?" he asked impishly, as Julia shoved the beige bra back into the bag.

"Close enough," she retorted.

"And I bought these as well." He tossed a pair of crew socks at her. "At least you'll have a nice change of clothes. I also thought you might need this. It's Laker town after all, so I hope you like the t-shirt." It was an oversized yellow shirt suitable for sleeping.

"And what's in the other package?"

260

Love Never Dies

"Just a pair of blue jeans and sweatpants for me with a couple tops, some clean underwear, socks, and... I thought this would come in handy." He pulled out two toothbrushes imprisoned inside their thick plastic packaging with a small tube of mint toothpaste. "Damn, I didn't think to buy you a hair brush."

"Not to worry," said Julia. "I have one in my bag."

"And, even though it's not my style, I thought I might try to disguise my face and head a bit." He pulled out a Dodger baseball hat and thrust it onto his head. Somehow, the image didn't fit.

"Hmm, well, it does change your persona all right. Maybe if you turn it around. What's in the smaller bag?"

"Something *really* handy."

Julia peered inside. A small sturdy cardboard box rested inside the bag and upon opening it she smiled. How very like Simon.

"I couldn't bear for you to be weaponless, even though you're equipped with that *deadly* can of mace. Look..." he pressed the button on the high-tech army knife and a huge corkscrew appeared.

"Well if he's a cork, we've got it made."

"Very funny, but check this out." Simon pressed the button again and out popped a one-and-a-half-inch blade. "It's amazing what one can do with a weapon like this, particularly if it's well-aimed, like in the vicinity of the eyes. I also thought this might come in handy." He squeezed again and a small ice pick appeared.

"You could kill a man with that," gulped Julia, recollecting a horrible scene from a recent action movie she'd viewed with her brother.

"If it comes to that point Julia, forget he's another human being. Aim for his eyes or the heart. Don't hesitate. Remember, this man has killed before." Julia gulped as an image of Seth's face floated before her and she resolutely took the knife from him, folding away its attachments and placing it in her purse.

"I won't ever forget."

"That's my girl. Once we leave here keep it in your pocket or purse at all times. I suggest you hold on to your mace as well. About three blocks down Altadena Boulevard is a place called Jiffy Car Rental. First thing in the morning we'll trot down there and rent ourselves a non-descript sedan."

"And then what?" asked Julia.

"I'm still thinking on it, but one thing's for certain. We can't take my Pajero. Adam Gable's probably already run the plates."

"My brother's going to be worried if I don't show up tomorrow," remembered Julia, retrieving the army knife and using the tiny scissors to snip the tags off their clothes.

"I left a message on his machine indicating you wanted a couple of extra days down here in the LA area. I need to take a shower. Why don't you see if there are any classic movies on TV?"

He swung his clothes bag off the bed and headed into the bathroom.

She found a movie all right, but it wasn't one she should have been viewing. A grief-stricken Meryl Streep stood on the edge of a battered pier gazing out to sea and wondering if her lover would ever return. Julia had always enjoyed this movie with Jeremy Irons, but tonight *The French Lieutenant's Woman* proved too much for her. The loss of Seth combined with the knowledge that Joe Alletti had sent Adam Gable to kill her, along with the fact that the brother of the man she loved now risked everything to protect her, proved to be her undoing. And... just how *did* she feel about Seth's twin?

Julia mutely watched the glowing images upon the small screen as tears coursed down her cheeks. Simon emerged from the bathroom a few minutes later, rubbing his dark hair energetically with a towel. He was startled to see her perched on the edge of the bed; her hands tightly clasped together, the knuckles stretched white as a dark gray sea crashed over the rocks upon the screen. Simon took one look at the TV and grabbing the remote, turned off *TCM*.

"Perhaps we should go in for a comedy tonight," he pronounced. "Please don't cry Julia," he begged, leaning over her and taking both of her hands, massaged the cold, damp fingers between his own. Simon's dark gray eyes searched her blurry ones. "It's just the strain of the moment. Don't worry sweet Julia. Everything will be alright."

Simon pulled her from the bed and enfolded her in his strong comforting arms. She could smell the clean fresh scent of soap about him mingled with the store-bought newness of the sweatshirt he'd donned. His dark hair glistened from his shower, the small hoop in his left ear glinting in the lamplight as he rubbed the small of her back comfortingly.

It was the strong beat of his heart that proved to be her undoing. Somehow, the warm glow always signaling Seth's presence intermingled with Simon's living essence. He gazed down at her before slowly lowering his lips, seeking the warmth and comfort of her kiss. That first kiss was not gentle, but desperate, as if a tormented being had been denied far too long. His lips were sweet and smelled of pizza and toothpaste and passion.

He strained against her until suddenly Julia remembered just who and what she was kissing and jerked away, appalled at her response to him. Her confused heart burned and ached as Simon stood for a long moment searching her eyes. He offered no apologies.

"I've lost everything in my life I love, except for my cousin whose whereabouts are unknown to me.

Love Never Dies

You were Seth's true love and I was Seth's brother. Somehow, I know that when I kiss you I feel complete. To remain separate from you would be a travesty of justice."

"I can't!" she cried, trying to pull away, but Simon held her fast.

"Please, please hear me out. Seth is never coming back Julia. So is your love to die with him; buried in that lonely churchyard in Santa Barbara you visit each Sunday? Yes, it's true; I admit I followed you there one weekend after I had stopped by your flat. You can't let yourself die with him Julia! Are you never to love again, keeping yourself isolated from the world like some sort of self-proclaimed nun? I swear to you that I'm as close to being my brother as you will ever meet again upon this earth and swear that the love he felt for you also flows through my heart and my veins.

And you my precious girl, were the love of his life and for good reason. There will never be another such as you and I somehow feel that if you cannot love me I'll simply perish. I promise to protect you and cherish you until the end of my days and pledge to take no other; this I swear on my brother's grave. Seth would approve Julia. I know he understands."

"Like he understood with Marcie, the girl you stole from him?"

"He was always a much better man than I, there's no denying it. I was the wild one, the one my mother worried about. I was the one the old women in our parish whispered about behind their hands as the poor priest shook his head. Yet, deep inside, I'm so much like him. For just like he did, I want someone to love me, to cherish me like you did Seth. And so, I offer myself to you completely; my body, my heart, *and* my soul. Please... please consider me."

Simon's lean cheeks flushed hotly as he awaited her answer. Suddenly Julia saw Simon as a man who'd always been overshadowed by his serious, and in many ways, more fortunate brother. Simon's eyes were so clear and loving, his lips warm and full, and suddenly her heart swelled, the warmth of Seth's soul urging her to love again. Julia wanted to reach out and touch him, to shove this nightmare surrounding Adam Gable, Joe Alletti, and Lou Tierney far, far away. She wanted to be held and cherished again, to be loved as fiercely as she had before. Her Seth was dead and now Simon stood in his stead, waiting and hoping.

They'd wrenched Seth's life from her, had stolen her love, and all Simon could do now was offer to fill that void. His eyes, so warm and understanding, pleaded for her love and suddenly Julia couldn't resist the sweetness that was Simon any longer. Julia reached up and cupped his warm agitated face before kissing him tenderly.

Simon swooped down, lifting her up in his arms and whispering her name over and over until finally settling her reverently upon the rust-colored bedspread. He swiftly moved to the lined curtains and drew them fully, switching off the lights in the bathroom and small bedroom. The room was plunged into shielding, beckoning darkness. He lay down beside her, kissing her softy upon the cheek, seeking to reassure her.

"The darkness will be our friend and our blanket," he whispered.

His lips trailed across her throat, still damp from her earlier tears, and then rose to nibble at her earlobe. His hair was long and brushed her face as she ran her fingers through its rich silk, enjoying the length and fullness of his ebony mane. The strange white streak spiraling upward from his crown glowed in the semi-darkness and she touched the patch, so much finer in texture than his other dark locks. Julia kissed the small puckered scar at the corner of his lip and ran her tongue over the fullness of his open mouth.

His body was leaner than Seth's and she noticed the raised protrusion of a large ragged scar upon his back as her fingers searched under the sweatshirt, but he didn't flinch as she ran her hands over the warm skin. He removed her peach top and fiddled with the front opening of her bra as her fingers danced across his upper torso. In the dim light Julia noted the serious intensity of his face. This was no late-afternoon fling or senseless act for Simon. Simon took his lovemaking as seriously as Seth, and Julia was vastly comforted by the passionate intensity flowing from his silvery eyes.

He slowly removed her pale orange trousers, kissing her knees and shins as he tossed the comfortable pants upon the thinly carpeted floor. The moment the soft cotton hit the ground Simon seemed to lose control of his previously restrained movements and began to kiss her wildly. He desperately begged her to love him as he moved his mouth frantically over her receptive body. It was easy to lose herself inside his eager arms as Simon kissed her deeply and passionately. His jeans joined hers upon the floor, and suddenly he was poised over her.

"Please Julia," he requested desperately.

"Don't stop," she urged, and he didn't.

It was a wild coupling, made desperate by circumstance and loss, yet so sweet and all-consuming that Julia forgot where she was and for one instant her heart burned as hotly as the rest of her body as she cried out his name.

"Seth!"

Simon froze momentarily, stunned by what he'd heard, yet unable and unwilling to stop the sweet madness between them. Julia hadn't realized she'd called out Seth's name and Simon vowed, as he passionately claimed the woman he loved, to never tell her. It was his deep, dark secret, yet as he cried out her name in that one final sweet spasm, a single tear slid down his beard-roughened cheek at all that had been lost.

Simon held her for a long time and finally, while she slept the sleep of the fulfilled, slipped on his jeans and opened the door of the bathroom. The light, issuing from the tiled room, illuminated the bed and fragile woman stretched out in exhausted repose upon the rust-colored spread. Many minutes later, with the door locked to that small bathroom, he scrubbed his tear-stained face and vowed that Julia Ann Morris would never again lose the man she loved.

When Julia awoke, Simon was seated in the wobbly chair from before, watching her unreservedly as she slept. She strangely felt no embarrassment as the fully clothed man stared at her so tenderly. On his right forefinger a blue-black revolver swung and it was the sight of that, not her state of undress that caused her to bolt upright.

"Don't be frightened," he said reassuringly, setting the handgun upon the narrow table that served as a desk and TV stand.

He joined her upon the bed, and settling her spoon-fashioned against him buried his face in the sweet fragrance of her neck.

"I didn't know you had another gun."

"I purchased it just this afternoon."

"I'm not sure that makes me feel any safer," but deep inside she knew it did. "Do you know how to use it?"

"I've been practicing at the range everyday."

His confidence was enough to end that line of conversation.

"So what do we do now?" Julia asked, wanting only to lie in his arms and sleep. Simon raised himself on one elbow and sighed as he studied her pale face.

"I can't get hold of Stan, so I'll try Angus and Mandy. Maybe they can find us a safe house."

"You trust them?"

"With our lives. Besides, I have no other choice. Stan has been watching over you for months now."

"Are you under Witness Protection?"

He gave a rueful grin. "I was, but violated the agreement by coming down to Santa Barbara. Angus said he would wash his hands of me if I did. He believed I endangered you unnecessarily. He was right of course."

"Curiosity did kill the cat."

"So that's what you are, sweet Julia? A curiosity?"

Julia lifted his hand to her face and kissed his palm. "I hope that's not all. It's strange, but for the first time in months, even in this situation and followed by a hired killer, I suddenly feel hope. And that hope is because of you Simon."

Love Never Dies

Simon turned his head away, distancing his suddenly numb body from her before lying face down upon the bed, not wanting those searching eyes upon his face. Somehow, he felt that if she analyzed him too much, he'd be found wanting.

His muffled voice came from the pillow. "Promise me something Julia."

"What Simon?"

"Promise not to compare me with him too much."

"I'll try."

His blurry eyes met hers.

"Thank you," he said quietly, and pulling up the bedspread, placed a strong arm over her bare body and willed himself to sleep.

Chapter 12

It was the sound of crows cawing the next morning that finally awakened Simon. He swung his legs over the side of the bed and heard the drizzle of the shower splashing inside the porcelain tub from the motel's small bathroom. Simon moved to the drawn curtains, and flicking them open, noted it must have been raining for a long time. Both he and Julia had slept deeply and all the painstaking work he'd taken with the disguising mud was for naught. His instincts told him he had to move quickly. Simon desperately wanted to join her in that shower and run his hands over her sleek soapy body, but realized that would be just too dangerous. He retrieved his leather jacket and hiding the Beretta inside the holster tapped upon the bathroom door.

"Julia, I need to check on the Pajero. I should be back in a couple of minutes. Is everything alright in there?"

Love Never Dies

Her lilting voice echoed through the closed door.

"Everything is fine. Why don't you come in and join me?"

"I would love to, but I believe one of us needs to be out in the front room at all times. I hope you understand. Can I take a rain check?"

"Of course," she laughed through the door. "Anytime."

Fortified by her words, Simon left the small motel room and checked on the 4x4. Sure enough the mud had dissolved and he moved to the back of the vehicle, opening the heavy rear door and removing the single umbrella he kept there for emergencies. He'd just returned to the room when Julia exited the steam-filled bathroom, a small white towel wrapped around her damp body. Simon quickly averted his eyes and took a deep steadying breath.

"If you'll wait just a moment Simon I'll get dressed and you can take your own shower."

I'd appreciate that," he mumbled, turning his head away, not realizing Julia observed him affectionately. She watched him battle his desire, mistakenly believing she understood why he couldn't lay with her that morning.

Fifteen minutes later Simon was showered and ready, Julia placing the soiled articles of clothing into the large plastic shopping bags and dropping the army knife into her purse.

"I added the Beretta to your handbag; it's loaded and ready. Don't think too much about how to use it Julia, simply aim at the largest part of his body and pull the trigger." Julia swallowed and nodded jerkily.

"I can do that," she whispered.

"Glad to hear it," replied Simon, and pulled her to him in a swift strong embrace. "Now I don't know about you, but I can't continue without having some food in my stomach. So let's head down to the Pancake Shack two blocks away and discuss our next move."

The cold rainy weather made Simon's leg ache even more than usual as he shook off the umbrella at the entrance of the very popular pancake house. The heady aroma of hotcakes, mingled with the strong odor of coffee and frying bacon, permeated the air.

Simon instructed the receptionist to take them to the rear of the restaurant if possible. Later, ensconced in a bright red vinyl booth, he ordered a tall stack of buckwheat pancakes, a rasher of bacon, and two sunny-side-up eggs. Julia eyed him quizzically.

"That's exactly what Seth would have ordered."

He cleared his throat. "I told you before we were similar in many ways and this is my mother's old standby. She made the best buckwheat pancakes in the world. I just hope these can live up to them." The busy waitress brought Julia tea and Simon coffee, and as he stirred in some sugar into the bitter liquid Julia tentatively asked.

Love Never Dies

"So what's the game plan for today?"

"The first thing we've got to do is hire ourselves another car. The second, I need to visit an Internet café to see if I got any replies to the e-mails I sent out yesterday. If I have, I hope we'll learn of a safe place to hide for a while. If not, I can't help but think the best bet is to head back to Santa Barbara, no matter how strange that seems. Seth had in his possession a disk, which both Joe Alletti and Angus O'Leary believe you've somehow inherited. I personally think Seth would have placed the disk in something he was certain you'd never part with."

"When you say a disk, you mean a computer floppy disk?"

"That's right, just a small black stiffy; the kind that goes into the A drive of your computer. What did you do with all of Seth's belongings?"

Julia shrugged sadly. "Paul and I went through his clothing and gave most of them, as well as his stereo and some of his furniture, to a local Catholic charity. Your family was Catholic I believe?"

"Yes, my mother was quite devout."

"All the furniture in the main part of the condo I asked my brother to keep. Seth had donated it originally to the condominium and I just felt he would have wanted my brother to keep it. Do you think Seth could have placed the disk inside the furniture?"

"No, he wouldn't have felt that attached to just furniture. Was there anything else?"

Julia thought for a long time. "Of course! There's at least one item I know he would never have parted with and after his death, I kept."

"Yes...?" Simon let the word dangle.

"I'd given him a sketch at Christmas taken from a photograph my brother snapped when we were decorating the house. A local artist made an ink sketch for Seth and I had it framed."

"And what happened to this sketch?"

"I couldn't bear to part with it so it's hanging above my bed."

"Do you believe there's any chance he may have somehow hidden the disk behind the picture?"

"Well..., it's certainly worth a try since the only other things I kept from Seth were a few books. I believe there was a *Lord of the Rings,* a copy of *The English Patient*, and some architectural books, but I've looked through them many times and there's definitely no disk in any of them."

"And his computer?"

"I donated it to the architectural firm because it contained most of his architectural programs. They seemed very happy about it."

"And his hard drive was compromised during the robbery," said Simon, snapping his fingers. "It isn't there. No—it's got to be hidden inside the painting. If we find it, we may have given Angus the ability to put Alletti away for years."

"And if it isn't there?"

"I can't believe that's a possibility," said Simon confidently, watching her brown-flecked eyes closely. "You know, they originally wanted to put you in Witness Protection even though you didn't have a clue you were in danger. Would you have considered it?"

The appalled expression clamping over her face was enough to tell Simon everything. Julia had her family, her friends, her job; she just wouldn't run and hide with her tail between her legs. That was not the life for her and he cringed inside. Their options were thus limited unless he could convince her otherwise, since Santa Barbara would likely no longer be a safe haven for the woman he loved.

The waitress interrupted his dark thoughts by delivering two overburdened plates housing huge stacks of buckwheat pancakes swimming in butter, as well as a generous helping of bacon and eggs. She also thumped down several kinds of syrup and the check.

"Whew," exclaimed Simon. "I do believe the service is a bit abrupt here."

"I wonder if I they have a meter running on this booth?"

Simon smiled back and reached for the maple syrup. It was good to laugh with her, to see the expression of pleasure flit across her face as they both tucked into their hotcakes with gusto. Forty-five minutes later they stood in front of the rental car counter.

"The only thing I have available is a Chrysler LeBaron; will that do?"

It was a bigger and flashier car than Simon would have preferred, but he nonchalantly signed the forms and gave the red-suited clerk his credit card. Julia's eyes widened, but she said nothing at the alias. Simon's false credit card was just one of his many surprises.

Whistling shakily under her breath, Julia strolled over and picked up an auto magazine, pretending to read the ratings for the upcoming year's SUV's. Later, seated behind the wheel of the black sedan, Simon retrieved his Dodger cap and tugged it low over his ears.

"How do I look?"

"Like an avid fan. I bet you can hardly wait until spring training." Simon frowned across at her.

"There's something I forgot to do this morning Julia; something I need to remember to do each and every morning when I wake up and find you near me." He reached an arm across the console and pulling her close kissed her soundly on the lips, snatching that brief moment to give her a heartfelt hug.

"I'm here with you sweetie," he promised, "and I'll protect you with my life."

278

Love Never Dies

"Because you owe it to Seth?" she asked shakily. Both Hayes boys were mighty fine kissers.

"No, because I *want* to. Yes, I owe Seth many things. I'm glad he found you, but from now on, it's not any obligation to Seth influencing my actions or feelings toward you. I just wanted you to understand that no matter what happens over the next few hours or days, I want you to trust me Julia, and if you can, grow to love me."

"I do trust you Simon," she said hastily, not willing to go any further than that. She pulled away from him, and clearing her throat, buckled her seat belt. "I'm ready I think," she said cheerily. "And if your last bout of driving was any example, I'd better remain buckled up."

The Internet café was amazingly crowded for a Sunday morning and Julia pulled up a chair behind Simon as he punched in his hotmail address and hoped for replies. There were none.

"Damn," he murmured under his breath. "Then there's no other choice, we have to head back to Santa Barbara tomorrow. I think this bodes ill for us Julia. God knows where Stan is and why our e-mails aren't being answered."

"Can we approach the local law enforcement agency?"

"That was the problem up in Toronto. Joe had too many of them in his pocket and it was impossible to know who to trust. The fact that he managed to get rid of Seth even while in prison doesn't sit well with me. I'd prefer to stick to Stan, Angus, and Mandy for now. I guess we're on our own until we hear from them, so that means we'll have to make another stop. It will just take a moment."

Julia waited in the black sedan as Simon slipped into a beauty supply shop. Upon his return he thrust a white plastic bag into her hands.

"I'm going to pull into the gas station over there and I want you to don that thing."

"What is it?"

"I've always wanted to make love to a brunette," chuckled Simon.

"There's no way!" she exclaimed at his outburst of laughter.

In the dingy bathroom Julia pulled and tugged at the oversized wig, the brunette curls tumbling around her face and over her shoulders. She studied her reflection in the warped gas station mirror. Simon had also purchased a pair of dark obscuring sunglasses, which she placed over her dark green eyes. She literally didn't recognize herself in wig, glasses, and blue windbreaker, and when she slipped into the passenger side of the LeBaron, Simon gave a low wolf whistle.

Love Never Dies

"Ow baby," he howled, as she punched him on the arm.

"It's too early to head back to Santa Barbara right now. I'd rather wait until dusk. Let's drive back to the motor lodge and I'll park the Pajero far away, maybe in Sierra Madre or something. You wait in the room until I come back. I paid for an extra day—so we can leave anytime we want this afternoon."

He parked the black sedan near the Pajero and nonchalantly got out, his gray eyes sweeping the parking lot.

"Let's go. I'll walk you to the door just to make sure we don't have any unexpected visitors."

The only person in sight was a blue-uniformed cleaning lady who hovered near the far end of the motor lodge, dumping used towels into her cart's laundry hamper. Simon nodded to Julia, who slipped the pass key into the lock and waited until the light turned green. Simon edged inside and checked out the room.

"All clear," he whispered. The maid has already made up the bed and straightened the bathroom. "You'll be alright?"

"Just fine Simon. Please... just hurry back."

"I will, my love, but it will take awhile since I'll probably have to walk a ways after I park the car. Maybe I'll get lucky and catch a bus." He leaned forward and gave her a gentle kiss. "Stay safe lady. I'll rap on the door five times, then pause and rap two more times. That way you'll know it's me." He gave her tense shoulders a strong squeeze and headed off as the rain continued its deluge.

Julia valiantly tried to amuse herself over the next hour as she waited impatiently for Simon to return. She flicked through late morning religious stations and finally settled upon a talk show about people who had left their vast fortunes to their pets. Ninety minutes later she was pacing the room impatiently. Julia had had a great deal of time to think and once again spoke to Seth.

"I think I love your brother," she whispered into the dancing TV screen. "I hope you don't mind so very much Seth, for I've been so lonely. Something about him seems so right." She tried to send out a message to her lost lover and as always, the moment she did, a fiery response slammed back. Her body tingled as her heart ignited and she could almost hear Seth's melodious voice.

"I want you to live and love, sweet lady. Love my brother- it's alright with me." The message resonated through the room and heated her heaving chest. Grateful tears streamed down her face as the soul housed within gave her permission to love someone he had once loved. She lay back upon the crumpled spread and cried, finally dozing off only to be awakened by several sharp raps upon the motel door.

Love Never Dies

Five taps, then two, and Julia flung open the door, throwing her anxious body into his arms, her chest burning in unrestrained response to his love. Simon was sodden but she didn't care, and finding his lips kissed their chilly firmness. He grinned down at her and she had to laugh at his disheveled state. His raven hair, plastered under the now dripping cap, spiked comically while raindrops slid off the tip of his straight nose. His pants were so damp they shone darkly and his black leather jacket was even shinier with damp, the rain puddling about his frozen feet.

"I think I'd better change," he suggested, giving an uncontrollable shiver.

"And take a hot shower." She helped him remove his soaked jacket and he left his Rockports right beside the door.

"I'll be out in just a few minutes. I'll hang my wet things on the wall heater and hopefully they'll be dry within a few hours." He swooped down, retrieving his only other clean outfit from the sports bag and hurried into the bathroom.

The rain continued to pour, punctuated by occasional flashes of lightning accompanied by thunder from the not-so-distant Sierra Madres. Within fifteen minutes Simon re-entered the main room, drying his hair with a small white towel.

"Are you better now?" Julia asked, noticing his cheeks were rosy from the hot shower.

Loren Lockner

"Much."

"The car?" she queried.

"I parked it in Sierra Madre, behind an apartment building. I chose the spot because I'd noticed a bus stop only a few blocks away and thought it would prove convenient. Unfortunately, the weather didn't cooperate and I was soaked by the time I made it to the bus stop. I stood there for at least fifteen minutes waiting for the pokey bus. Then, it dropped me two full blocks from here and I had to run in the pouring rain. I was never so happy to see the flashing lights of this motel in my whole life!"

Julia laughed. "Well, you're safe and warm now. "Why don't you come over here and I'll warm you up a bit more?"

Simon gulped, his eyes flitting to the burning lamps. Julia stretched out her arms to him and he melted into her embrace, kissing her long and hard.

"I want to see you," she whispered, her eager hands playing with the buttons of Simon's blue jeans. His hands stilled hers. "The accident...," he stammered. "It... it disfigured me horribly Julia. Not only was my leg mangled, but I suffered a severe injury to my back. You may have felt the scar?"

Julia had indeed sensed the raised scar tissue, but the glimpse of it held no fears for her. "I don't care what it looks like," she said truthfully. "I only care about you. Scars fade with time, but not how I feel about you."

284

Love Never Dies

"Or Seth?"

"Or your brother Seth." Her heart flared and burned as her brown-flecked eyes studied him, acknowledging his uncertainly. "I will love him always Simon, but there is room in my heart for another. Seth has allowed there to be room. His love burns through me as I touch you and I know I have his blessing. I will always love and miss him, but he will never supercede you."

The words were so sincere that Simon wanted to weep, but he had to stay focused in order to deny her what she requested.

"Please, at least for a while, let us love in the darkness. I need the darkness Julia, to hide my scars and my pain; pain I have not completely shared with you and am unready to do so as of yet. Please indulge me, love."

Julia hesitated and gazed up into his dark eyes for a long moment until finally reaching up to stroke the strange white streak dividing the crown of his head and moving to the scar near his mouth. "Alright, but only if you call me by that name again."

"My love?"

"That's it. Say it again Simon," and she kissed him full on the mouth.

"My sweet, sweet love," he repeated obediently, and pulled away from her for only an instant to switch off the table lamps, plunging the room into blessed darkness as the heavy lining of the curtains turned the room into night as the storm raged outside.

His hands sought her silky hair in the darkness as his nostrils inhaled her sweet clean scent. Her own hands played with the dampness of his hair and he lowered her upon the made-up bed, no longer able to hear the drone of thunder or pounding of the rain. Simon could only feel and hear Julia. He kissed her deeply, allowing her to remove his shirt and explore the warmth of his chest. Her hands stilled at the scar on his back, but he urged her on.

"It's an old wound my love. Never mind it." His lips lowered to her breast and he savored the feel and taste of her.

The thunder drowned out her cries as he loved her first with his mouth, kissing her so passionately and desperately that she thought her heart would burst from the very sweetness of it. Then his lips trailed downward, finding the sweet joining of her legs and teasing her with his tongue, causing her to cry out once, then twice as he brought her to fulfillment. Julia's hands desperately removed his restraining trousers and pulled him atop her and Simon moved slowly, almost languidly inside of her, enjoying the feel of her damp body and wanting to prolong the joy of the moment. Finally, he could hold back no longer and with a cry, collapsed above her, convinced she would forgive him for everything.

286

Love Never Dies

They slept long and deep into the afternoon, Simon eventually pulling the sheet and blankets over them to ward off the creeping chill. He nearly roused once to pull on his briefs and jeans, but sank back further into sleep before that important task was accomplished. And so the afternoon approached, as the rain slackened and the titter of the common sparrow could be heard outside their door followed by the barking of an impatient dog. Julia stretched and snuggled against Simon, the memory of his passion and fulfilling love causing her to lift her head and kiss the hard point where his shoulder jutted toward her. He slept deeply, his breathing even and relaxed, and Julia allowed him to continue his peaceful slumber, rising ever so quietly to retrieve her discarded clothes.

Julia headed into the bathroom, enjoying a long wash before returning to the dimly lit room to find the gym bag she'd hurriedly thrust clean clothes in the evening before. Simon shifted and pushed the restraining sheet away, sleeping half on his side to leave his bare chest completely exposed. The imp in her reared its mischievous head and stealthily she slowly slid the sheet away, wanting to revel in his beautiful male nakedness. He twitched, turning upon his back as the sheet lowered. Julia couldn't believe her eyes as the light from the open bathroom door poured into the room and over his still figure. She moved closer and actually reached out a finger toward the betraying mark, a cry involuntarily rising from her overwrought throat.

Simon bolted upright, one hand instinctively reaching for the covers, his other groping for the revolver he had laid upon the nightstand earlier. His eyes found her mortified face and started. She pointed shakily.

"Where did you get that... that tattoo?" her voice shrieked.

"Tattoo?" he repeated dumbly, following the accusatory path of her finger. There, nestled directly to the right of his left hipbone, and perfectly placed between it and his maleness were the delicate colors of a simple tattoo depicting two rose bushes, one pink, one crimson as they intertwined and trailed upward to become one. Upon the thorny base of the main stalk, the initials SMH rested above the letters JAM; the pair encased in the delicate outline of a heart. It was the same design found in the envelope behind Seth's chest of drawers over ten months prior.

Simon gulped as all color drained from his beloved's face.

"Seth drew that design," Julia gasped, trying to comprehend the implications of that artistic impression on Simon's abdomen, her chest burning painfully.

"I know," he said simply, not seeking to deny it.

288

Love Never Dies

"What's it doing there?"

"I had it done after... after I met you."

"After you met me? Isn't that taking your vow to protect Seth's lover a bit too far?"

Simon didn't reply, only pulling the sheet over his nakedness as he waited among the tumbled covers for her next assault.

"Those are Seth's initials."

"And mine as well," he said wearily.

"What?"

"His name was Seth Michael Hayes, mine is Simon Mitchell Hayes. We have the same initials."

"How convenient!"

"Yes," he said deliberately. "It was."

"Who are you?" she whispered, her heart suddenly constricting as she struggled for breath and control.

"The man who loves you."

"And which man is that?" she asked raggedly, the truth striking her like a bolt of lightning. There had been no twin of Seth. Simon was Seth and his guilty eyes didn't bother to deny it.

Julia screamed and tossed the nearest item she could find at his traitorous head, the remote hitting him squarely upon the nose, causing the blood to spurt into his suddenly attentive hand.

"Please Julia, calm down," he begged, trying to staunch the sudden flow of blood staining his fingers.

"Calm down? Calm down Simon, or is it Seth, or who is it exactly? You played me for a fool!"

He moved then, shooting off the bed, totally heedless of his nakedness or the dreadful scar that disfigured his once smooth back. Another thick cruel blemish ran the length of his thigh, showing the rough horizontal cross scars of desperate surgery. Simon hadn't underestimated the extent of his injuries. He grabbed her shoulders roughly and willed her to meet his eyes. Julia's head jerked in denial, her limbs frantically struggling like a trapped bird to escape his strong grasp as he clutched her shoulders and shook her fiercely, trying to make her understand and demanding she listen.

"It's true Julia. It's Seth. Please, please listen to me!"

She flung herself away from him and crawled across the expanse of the floor, desperate to shut out the image of her once dead lover. He let her escape to the corner, where Julia sat huddled, her knees clenched tightly in her arms as she cried tears of denial and agony. Simon methodically found his briefs and jeans, and once again decently clad, lowered himself by her trembling form. He reached out an arm and rested a hand upon her shaking shoulder, incapable of making her hysterical sobbing cease.

Julia never knew how much time elapsed before she was able to raise her blurry eyes to his adjacent form. He sat perfectly still and uncomfortable upon the thinly carpeted floor, crying soundlessly, the tears spilling over his lean cheeks as he struggled to control his own sobs.

"Simon?" she asked tentatively, her anger and grief suddenly dissipated. He was incapable of answering and she rounded her arms over his shaking torso and drew him to her. She sat that way for a long time, smoothing his hair and muttering incoherent endearments to her poor lost love. Her heart suddenly expanded, the burning soul swelling and bursting within, until the full force of his essence was once again inside of her. She gasped in amazement as Simon lifted his tear-stained face.

"Do you know me now love?" There was no question who now sat beside her. Only Seth's soul could burn and torture her heart as his did. Only Seth could fill her up, every fiber of her being resonating with his essence and love.

"Oh Seth!" Suddenly she was weeping again, only this time in joy.

She was violently hauled back onto the tumbled covers of their temporary bed where Seth cradled her as he swore explicitly under his breath. It was so very unlike him that she would have laughed if she could have possibly controlled her tears. She understood he was seeking to deny and retaliate against all the pain his passing had caused.

Finally, when they became calmer, he stroked her damp hair before sitting up and gazing down at her.

"It's high time for the truth," he announced, pulling her up beside him and propping some supportive pillows behind her weary back as she wilted against him.

"Yes," she agreed, waiting patiently, not getting enough of the lean lines of his face or the deep gray of his fatigued eyes. Deep lines furrowed his brow and the sides of his nostrils. They were lines she'd swear hadn't been there before this moment.

He swallowed deeply and began. "My real name is Steven Micah Hamilton and the details I gave you over a year ago regarding my background were pretty much true. I was an only child, having only my younger cousin Lucas as a companion while our parents pursued their mobile careers in civil engineering. It's true I lived on the east coast, in Britain and Canada, and did own a condominium on Lake Ontario which I sold recently. I had your brother Paul deposit half that money into the trust account set up by your grandfather."

She gasped but allowed him to continue.

"What I revealed about Joe Alletti, Mandy Gaskill, and Angus O'Leary was all true, except for one crucial fact. I'd discovered the money laundering myself, months before I infiltrated the firm. I took the assumed name of Seth Hayes and Angus suggested I create a back-up personality to revert to if something went wrong. I was vain enough to want to use my own initials. Basically a volunteer for the police, I was convinced I was doing my civil duty by aiding them, because you see, Taylor Reynolds, the witness Alletti killed was a good friend of mine. It was he, in fact, who stole Marcie from me and suggested the whole idea of having an evil twin as a backup. Somehow Tierney's group learned I was not only undercover, but discovered I had a cousin, who luckily Mandy had stashed away in the Yukon only a week previous. Both she and my identities were uncovered, but strangely enough, Joe Alletti accepted the story about identical twin brothers and sought to rub out the pair of us. This worked to my advantage in a sense. Only Angus and I knew about Steven Hamilton and a bizarre idea formulated between us. The original plan was to fake my death here in Santa Barbara, while I, using another assumed identity, hid out until the trial. I wasn't partial to the idea, since it meant leaving you, so Angus suggested we go into hiding as a couple. I was nearly convinced and about to reveal the true reason for my presence in Santa Barbara when Adam Gable struck. Stan was convinced Adam had returned to Stockton to get instructions from Alletti's gang. Instead, when we least expected it, he and a partner struck."

"The accident in January," Julia whispered, shivering as if cold.

"Yes, Stan had been tailing me as he always did, when an SUV swung out of its lane and pulled behind me, firing an AK-47 through my side window. I ducked, but not before the bullet entered my back through the driver's seat. I slammed on the brakes and the car careened and skid in the slick conditions caused by the heavy fog. The SUV continued down the road and I managed to drag myself from the Jeep Cherokee seconds before Adam's partner abandoned a semi-truck loaded with petroleum into my 4x4. I crawled off into the bushes, but not before exploding pieces of my car and the semi rained down upon me, impaling me and hurling a sharp piece of shrapnel into my scalp."

Julia winced and lightly touched the bleached lock of his hair. "And then," she urged.

"I don't remember much, but know I have to thank Stan for saving my life."

"Your back and leg," whispered Julia, finally understanding the true extent of his injuries. Simon leaned forward so she could examine his back and the horrible disfiguring scar. She ran her fingers lightly over the raised white tissue and fought back tears.

Simon eased back against the hard motel pillows and continued. "I was in a coma for three days, not realizing Angus had arranged for me to be whisked off to Las Vegas of all places. He stashed me in a clinic there under the name of Jeff Stone. To further protect me, he related to Stan, my contact in Santa Barbara, that I died in surgery since we'd never figured out where the leak originated. Stan was bitter since he took his job very seriously and volunteered to keep an eye on you. He wasn't the only one who felt guilty I guess. When I woke up, I was disoriented and in extreme pain. I remained numbed by painkillers for two weeks as they performed three surgeries on my leg and back. By the time I became coherent, I realized you believed I was dead and desperately sought to reassure you by sending out signals to you to hold fast."

"When my heart burned and felt you lacked all of your soul to travel to the hereafter?"

"I didn't know that's the message I sent, I just wanted you to hold on, not to..."

"Do what your father did?"

"Yes." He sighed deeply and took her slender hand. "Oh, the pain you must have felt, the agony. I never meant to hurt you so."

"I know. Once I dreamed you were locked in a sterile white building crying out to me. Could that have been the hospital?"

Seth looked strangely at her. "Maybe... could I have possibly sent you that image?" His beautiful gray eyes clouded and she touched his hand reassuringly.

"So then what happened?"

"With the testimony of a now present Simon Hayes, Joe Alletti was in big trouble even without the disk. I was shuffled off to another safe hiding place in

July until after the trial. I protested vehemently, because what kind of life was this anyway, with no work, no family, or woman I loved? Then Mandy let it slip that Joe Alletti had put out a contract on my life, as well as Seth's girlfriend who he believed held the disk the authorities needed to put him away for life. Only two days before my 'death' I stashed it in the back of your sketch, certain that was the only safe place for it. It behooved Joe to get rid of you, even though I was the only one who knew you were completely in the dark about the whole operation as well as my duplicity."

"You only wanted to keep me safe didn't you?"

"And a fine job I made of it!"

"Simon, I mean Seth. Actually it's Steven isn't it?"

"Yes, but I haven't gone by that name for so long you can call me what you please."

"My darling." The joy on his face was worth a hundred times the endearment. "So you had placed the disk in the sketch all along. Why didn't you just come and remove it?"

"That was the original plan. But when I saw your sad and forlorn face at the wedding..."

"The wedding!"

"I hid in the foyer to watch the ceremony. It was the least I could do for Paul, who'd been such a good friend to me."

Love Never Dies

"My heart burned so during the service. It was as if you were there with me. And you *were*!"

"I wished it were *my* wedding. Anyway, I couldn't leave you after that and told Angus I was going to enter into your life as my twin. He was livid, indicating that since I'd chosen not to adhere to the program I no longer could depend on his protection. He said I'd turned into a rogue, jeopardizing the mission and your life. Of course, Stan Garten, always a bit of a renegade, never halted his surveillance. And, for all his blustering, I knew I still had Angus and Mandy's support."

"I'd like to meet this Stan. Anyway, you could have taken the disk any time you know."

"Yes, but it was in your bedroom, and I knew I couldn't enter a room with you and a bed without being in *big* trouble. And, since I'd gotten the tattoo right before the accident, never realizing you'd actually seen the sketch, I was afraid you would doubt my motivations if you saw it too soon after we became lovers. Wouldn't it appear strange that Simon had an old tattoo with both our initials? I suspect Paul showed it to you?"

"He found it with the wedding set when he tried to move the furniture."

"My two big special secrets." His tone was self-mocking. "Here I was only worried you'd think I was infatuated with you way before the proper brother of

Seth should have been, but you already knew Seth had gotten the tattoo. How *did* you know that by the way?"

"Connie told me."

"What?"

"She observed you on the promenade the day of the accident entering a tattoo parlor. After I saw the sketch, I put two and two together and suspected you'd gotten a tattoo to show how much you loved me. And I was right."

"Yes," he whispered. "You *were* right." He leaned over to kiss her, but she pushed him away.

"You have to answer one other question before you touch me again, Mr. Seth Simon Steven Hamilton. How did you control the..." she hesitated, not sure how to put it into words.

"The burning that always accompanied our mingled souls?"

"Yes."

"I could barely do it. You indicated you felt my presence often, and many times I watched you touch that special spot over your heart where our two souls are entwined. I suspect you didn't even know how often you reached for the comfort of that spot. I had to clamp down hard upon all my emotions every time we met. When you came up with the idea of the twin brother's souls somehow being connected like yours was to Seth's, I could gradually release all those pent-up feelings, which caused your heart to burn, just like mine always did."

"That's why it felt so right between us?"

"That's why, sweet girl."

"I love you Steven."

"And I you," he answered, finally allowing himself to unleash the full power of his pent-up love with a single devastating kiss. Her body and heart burned and soared, the tension and agony of the past few months dissipating in the course of a single kiss. As his body joined hers, Julia wondered how she could have ever not known Simon was her soul mate. She would never be so blind again.

Chapter 12

It was 5:30 the next morning before Julia and Simon checked out of the hotel. They had planned to scoot right to Santa Barbara, but after their intense conversation and a wonderful session of lovemaking, the energy evaded them. Later that afternoon Julia made a phone call to Connie, indicating she needed a substitute for an indefinite period because of a family crisis, after which they'd both slipped into the sheltering cocoon of sleep, their high-strung nerves not allowing them to move further than the shelter of their bed. Simon awakened her at five a.m. to pack and shower.

The previous evening, in an effort to keep her sanity, Julia declared to her lover that she would refer to him as Simon for now; partly for his own protection but mostly because he as a person really existed for her. And, after all, it really didn't matter *what* she called him because she knew he was her one and only soul mate. Simon readily agreed to keep his alias for a while longer, just thankful she'd forgiven him his deception.

So, Julia solemnly donned the wig and obscuring sunglasses as Simon crammed the still-damp baseball cap over his dark strands. He'd dressed once more in the nearly dry clothes and now fiddled with the windshield wipers on the sporty LeBaron. Simon grinned at her wolfishly and openly leered as she dabbed some blush on her too-pale cheeks. His hand stole to her knee and gave it an erotic squeeze as he revved the engine and pulled out of the motor lodge's parking lot in the dim light of the encroaching morning, his fingers moving upward over the denim-covered leg.

"Just keep your eyes on the road bucko, and your hand where I can see it!" She laughed at being able to tease him once more, secretly delighting in his straying hand.

"Oh, alright," he growled good-naturedly. "Let's get back to Santa Barbara and finish this business then."

The 101 was extremely crowded as they headed toward Santa Barbara that early Monday morning, and often they idled at a complete standstill on the congested freeways leading into LA. At seven a.m. Simon stopped long enough to order coffee and egg burgers at a drive-through and they took fifteen minutes to eat and use the facilities before heading back upon the road. Simon clearly wanted to visit her apartment first, to retrieve the disk, but Julia felt more cautious, worried Adam might guess their plans.

Julia's small two bedroom flat was located near the Presidio in a modest middle-class neighborhood. She loved her apartment with its sunny kitchen, impressionistic prints, and cozy fireplace, and thoroughly enjoyed the year spent with Angie before her roommate had married her brother Paul. Strangely, it had been maintaining and imbuing the apartment with her own personal touches that had given Julia some sort of solace after Seth's apparent death. She stole a glance at him. Simon drove intently, his hands firmly gripping the wheel of the black LeBaron, and she wondered what he was thinking. In delightful response to her probing thoughts, she felt a warm tingle tease her heart as Simon cast a sideways glance at the woman he loved and smiled gently. His right hand left the steering wheel and grasped her hand, giving it a warm squeeze.

"How are you doing?"

"I'm frightened," she said honestly.

"Hopefully this will all be over soon. Promise me you'll hang tough girl."

"I will," she asserted, as the traffic slowed once again.

Over forty minutes had passed before Montecito emerged and Simon slowed as they headed toward

Love Never Dies

Santa Barbara proper. The huge city golf course appeared to her right; and on the left, the crashing waves of the ocean in the Santa Barbara channel dared any brave soul to venture into its gray waters as it thrashed the ragged shoreline. The early morning was foggy and countless times Simon checked his rearview mirror in an effort to convince himself they weren't being followed.

"So the disk was in the back of the sketch all this time," declared Julia as Simon changed lanes.

"It was the only safe place I knew of, believing my drawers would be searched. I also could rest assured that of all my possessions the sketch would be one you'd keep if anything happened to me. It killed me to pretend I didn't know where it was, but believe me when I say I always tried to protect you."

"I understand," said Julia softly, squeezing the hand that now rested on her knee. "You said you've been watching over me for while?"

"Yes. After my arrival, I took to following you even though I knew that it was driving Stan insane. I remember one Sunday in particular, you'd strayed to the cemetery and sat down at Seth's plot, replacing the old dried-up red roses from the week before with fresh ones. You spoke to him, I mean me, and I can't relay how much it tore me up Julia. I wanted to throw caution to the wind and march over that very minute and reassure you everything was alright. Your life had not disintegrated as you'd thought, but I couldn't do it. I stood there and cried Julia, hidden under a huge maple tree, watching you commune with me. I'd made a promise to Angus and Mandy to keep a low profile and I had to do as they asked. It was so hard to block my feelings and particularly my soul, which strove each time I glimpsed you, to reach out and gather you to me.

"So often, I felt you near," said Julia remembering. "Sometimes, during particularly bad nights, it seemed the very warmth of your soul spread over my entire body and soothed me just as a lullaby might."

"You didn't sleep for a long time," mourned Simon. "Even as I lay helplessly in my hospital bed, I realized you were in agony. I'm just so grateful you chose to go on. I tried in every way possible to let you know that love never dies; that you had to wait for me. And you did wait Julia; you didn't let me down."

"And now I know and will wait for you forever, no matter what happens." Her slender fingers tightened over his and they drove, fingers entwined, for a long time until the Presidio appeared upon their right-hand side.

They sat in the cloudy parking lot of a local fast-food restaurant not five minutes from her apartment sipping hot coffee and contemplating their next move.

"So what should we do now?" asked Julia, watching Simon keenly. "Once we have the disk it should be simple; all we have to do is forward it to Angus O'Leary."

"That's easier said than done," said Simon, searching the nearly vacant parking lot. "He's not answering his phone or his e-mails. Until we know the score with him we've got to find a place to camp out. I just wish I knew what happened to Stan."

"There's got to be a place to hide," murmured Julia, as Simon fretted over Stan's well-being. Suddenly she snapped her fingers. "That's it! We'll *camp* out! Adam will be searching for us everywhere else: at hotels, my brother's, and the apartment. We should head north to one of the campgrounds."

"You mean literally *camp out*?"

"That's right. When I was a kid, my parents used to take me to the Cachuma Lake recreation area. It's located about twenty miles north of the Highway 101 on Highway 154. If I can remember correctly, there's a huge RV park and campground situated among an amazing oak forest."

"We're not equipped to go anywhere like that," protested Simon, gazing at the cloudy sky. It had stopped drizzling, but the air felt damp and chilly.

"But we could be! All we need to do is head down the 101 into the center of town; there's a huge camping and sporting goods store on Chapman Street. It's probably open by now and we can pick up a couple of sleeping bags, a cheap tent, and a few cooking utensils.

Later we'll stop by my apartment, grab the disk, and hightail it up to Lake Cachuma. There's no way he's going to find us up there and it's only eighteen miles from the main highway so that we can easily venture back, find an Internet café, and keep trying to contact Angus. It's the perfect solution to our problems."

"You just may be right," said Simon, impressed by her ingenuity. "So direct me to the outfitter's store."

Ten minutes later at Sporting Quest, Simon adjusted his Dodger cap, pulling the brim down to fully cover his white streak and looped his arm through Julia's."

"Camping huh?" he said skeptically.

"That's right Smoky; it's the only way to go."

While they tried to go as inexpensive as possible, Simon still ended up spending over $500. They bought a small three-person tent, two down sleeping bags, a ground cloth, a strong flashlight, and basic cooking kit, as well as a hammer to facilitate pounding the tent spikes into the often hard ground.

"Now all we need is some food and gas and we're set," said Julia. "Just around the corner is a quick mart and gas station. While you fill up, I'll buy us a few basic supplies. Who knows Simon, it might prove quite romantic up at the lake."

One of the things Simon adored about Julia was her upbeat attitude and perky nature, and he responded to her enthusiasm.

Love Never Dies

"Yeah, maybe if you play your cards right Trixie, you might get lucky! Let's get those supplies and then head toward your place. Hopefully our luck will hold and we'll retrieve the disk before Gable even discovers we've left LA."

Simon eased onto State Street, realizing if he continued north they'd run right into the famous Santa Barbara Mission. Instead, after less than a quarter of a mile, he turned left into a pleasant residential neighborhood and parked his car nearly a block away from her apartment. The suburb was relatively quiet this Monday morning as Simon watched and waited in the shelter of a shady magnolia tree.

The paperboy whistled as he swung his bike into a driveway, stuffing eight to ten newspapers into waiting mailboxes before quickly peddling down the road. The front entryway to her security apartment opened and Ethel Meeker set down her beloved toy poodle, ushering the dog across the street for its early morning walk. A laughing couple strolled down the sidewalk in the opposite direction, arms around each other's waist and wrapped in scarves and jackets against the morning chill. So far, nothing seemed out of the ordinary. Simon scanned the neighborhood for the silver BMW until finally his shoulders relaxed.

"It seems safe. Let's go in."

"I don't think that would be a wise idea," countered Julia. "If I enter my apartment with you my neighbors will be instantly suspicious, especially decked out the way we are. Why don't you just wait in the car and let me go in alone. I'll retrieve the disk and be out in five minutes."

"I don't like that idea one bit," mouthed Simon, shaking his dark head grimly, the baseball cap causing him to resemble some die-hard Dodger fan. "Didn't I ever tell you that patience wasn't my best virtue?"

Julia smiled serenely and shouldered her beige purse. "I'll be perfectly fine Simon; I have the mace and army knife you gave me, plus the gun. The way I'm decked out, I'm practically a female Schwarzenegger; nothing can happen to me. I'll be back before you can recite the Gettysburg Address."

"Okay," said Simon reluctantly. "I'll give you exactly ten minutes before I come in to get you."

"The speech lasted only five, but I'll take the ten and retrieve some fresh clothes," laughed Julia, leaning over to give him a long hard kiss. "You're my true love you know," she whispered, "no matter *what* your name is." Her hand slid down to the hidden tattoo seated near his left hipbone. "You are branded as my man, branded forever and ever. After all this effort, do you really think I'm going to let something happen to me?"

She kissed him once more and gave the itchy wig a final tug before leaving him to watch helplessly as she trotted across the street. Julia disappeared under the shade of a drooping willow tree as a few large raindrops began to thud against the windshield. Damn, the rain would make it harder to keep an eye on her and Simon scooted over to the passenger side, cranking down the window a couple of inches so he could scan the empty street better.

The apartment building was quiet and Julia managed to climb the rear set of steps that led up to the landing outside of her apartment without being noticed. Her apartment, along with three others, was situated across the top floor of the rectangular apartment building. The security building was fronted by a large glass doorway and could only be opened with a passkey. Julia let herself in, never noticing the lanky man smoking in the shadows beyond the pool. He grinned evilly. She'd returned for the disk just as he knew she would.

Julia passed by the large turquoise pool situated in the center of the complex's quad and mounted the granite steps. A couple large round tables covered by huge green umbrellas hugged the pool's edge, and beautiful brick-edged planters filled with red and yellow hibiscus alternating with bottlebrush trees dotted the front entrance of the ground floor apartments. Her upstairs apartment was a modest two bedroom, though she possessed two separate patios; one each off the master bedroom and kitchen, plus her front entryway, which she'd adorned with healthy potted plants. A heavily scented jasmine sat directly to the left of her doorway while several hanging scarlet fuchsias in beautiful macramé pots dangled outside the patio.

Julia inserted her key inside the lock. So far so good. Luckily, she'd placed Mira in the kennel, so her overeager dog wouldn't announce her arrival to the neighbors. An apartment door opened down the hall and Fred Collins stepped out. A heavyset man close to retirement, he owned a successful insurance brokerage near Thornbury Park and had the luxury of setting his own working hours. He stopped abruptly upon observing Julia fiddling with the lock.

"Excuse me miss, that's Julia Morris' flat."

"Yes," answered Julia sweetly, trying to disguise her voice with a Texas accent. "My name is Barbara Woods and I'm a friend of hers. I actually teach at her school and she forgot some very important papers that have to be distributed to her students today and asked me to pick them up this morning because she's in LA and driving directly to work. She gave me a key." Julia jingled her noisy chain with the bright pink fuzz ball for him to see. "You're Mr. ...?"

"Collins, Fred Collins," he said suspiciously. Fred had combed the few remaining strands of his balding black hair over the huge shiny spot in the middle of his head. It made him look like a used car salesman which probably didn't hurt his image as an insurance broker one bit.

"I'll tell her you called," said Fred warningly, playing the good neighbor to the hilt as he pushed past her.

Julia watched as he placed a pudgy hand on the handrail and descended laboriously down the steep steps. Julia hurried quickly into her apartment and closed the door behind her, heart thudding. Before she'd always laughed off Fred's meddling, but it could have cost her dearly today. The apartment smelt musty and she didn't bother to turn on a light even though the drapes were pulled for the weekend. She moved unerringly down the hallway to her bedroom, flicking on the overhead light and standing for a moment staring at the beautiful sketch above her bed.

Julia telegraphed a message to Simon informing him she was inside her apartment, and kicking off her shoes, bounded upon the mattress and removed the sketch, placing it face down upon her bright blue bedspread. Thick brown paper surrounded by heavy duty packing tape covered the back of the sketch and without hesitation Julia dug into her purse, searching the cluttered contents as receipts, pencil, lipstick, and a nearly full packet of gum spilled onto her bedspread before she finally found the large Swiss army knife. She dumped the purse upon the floor and within seconds the small pair of scissors sliced along the paper backing, her heart thudding rapidly. She'd make a lousy James Bond.

Her instincts told her that the disk would probably have slipped down to the bottom of the painting and she felt about tentatively before giving a sharp cry of triumph as her fingers closed over the incriminating floppy. The otherwise plain label on the black surface stated only one word: Alletti.

Julia stashed the disk inside her huge handbag along with the knife as the rain started pounding loudly upon the roof and she knew she had to hurry. She smoothed the ruined backing of the picture, wondering if she had time to tape up the nasty looking tear. Deciding against it, she picked up the picture and was about to place it back on its hook above her bed when a low voice hissed from her doorway.

"I knew it was just a matter of time before you'd wander back." It was the man Julia only recognized before as Mike Cooper and now knew was Adam Gable. His hair, shiny from the downpour, could use a trim, and he wore a long black leather jacket over a stylish blue turtleneck and dress trousers. His expensive black patent leather shoes had left damp footprints upon her mauve carpet and his right hand remained menacingly in his coat pocket. Instinctively she knew he had a gun.

"Who, who are you?" she managed to blurt out, even though she knew full well his identity. Julia placed the sketch back down upon the bed and descended unsteadily to the floor beside the queen-sized bed.

"Just a friend of your deceased boyfriend, Seth Hayes. I hate to tell you this little lady, but he had something that belonged to me and I've been thinking for a long time that maybe you knew where it was." His faded blue eyes remained glued to the painting now resting upon the crumpled bedspread and Julia gulped. Mustering all her strength, she sent out a warning signal to Simon, praying their unusual telepathy would function at this crucial moment.

"You're that man," she stalled, "who asked me about his nephew at school. You said your name was Mike, Mike Cooper. Now you're telling me you're a friend of Seth's. That's certainly a lie for he'd never have hung around a lowlife like you."

The brave words got the desired result as Adam Gable moved closer, pulling his hand slowly out of his coat pocket. His long ugly fingers curving over the butt of the gun, he directed the barrel straight at her heart.

He snorted, "So where is your new boyfriend; the brother of your dear departed?"

"Boyfriend? I don't have any boyfriend; not since Seth died."

"Maybe that's what you want your brother and family to think, missy, but I know you've been spending a little extra time with your own personal bodyguard. I can't imagine what your dead lover would think if he knew you were banging his brother. So where is Simon? Isn't he around, or have you tired of him already?" Adam cocked an ear to listen. "I don't hear reinforcements and somehow can't believe he'd leave his own little lady alone. Nice disguise though, it would have fooled me at a distance, but never close up."

"Just what do you want?" Julia asked meekly. The image of the Swiss army knife and the gun secreted inside the dark confines of her bag motivated her and she edged closer to the purse resting upon the floor, hidden by the bed.

Adam moved to the bed and fingered the discarded contents of her purse, picking up the receipts and gum. He glanced at them a moment before pocketing them.

"Just the disk sweetheart. You see your boyfriend, the dear departed Seth, was into gambling and owed a whole lot of people mega money. His assets are listed on that disk and will placate those he owed. So where is it?"

Why he bothered to lie was beyond her. "I don't believe you. Seth would never have done anything illegal."

"That's what all the guys want you to think. If you'd known the kind the stuff he was involved in, you would have never looked at him twice. Hmm, nice painting, I saw it before when I checked out your apartment a few weeks ago."

"You've been inside my flat?" blurted out Julia, indignant that this skinny evil man had so violated her privacy.

"Yeah. I went through everything one day while you were at work. Had to muzzle your damn dog. Those are very pretty undies indeed, in your upper right-hand drawer. You must have really turned that Seth on, and you know it never occurred to me to check out that beautiful painting where he appears so moony about you. Now why have you come back here, taken it down, and destroyed the backing? One plus one is not three, little lady." He smirked as he moved to the painting, his pale blue eyes searching the ravaged binding of the sketch.

"It fell down, I was just replacing it."

"Now who lies, girlie? Give me the disk now. We both know you have it and if you do, I promise I won't hurt you."

Julia trembled in fear. "Alright, okay, it's in my bag, there on the floor."

Adam clearly didn't want to stoop over and retrieve the bag. "Pick it up real slowly," ordered Adam, the Glock handgun now focused upon the spot right between her eyes. Julia realized she only had one chance and bending over, slowly reached inside the bag.

"I put it in the zip pocket," she explained, fingers searching for the gun. It was too big and cumbersome for her trembling fingers to grasp and her hand moved to the Swiss army knife. She fumbled a bit, her fingers trying to work a miracle until the ice pick darted out, its sharp point pricking the tip of her forefinger.

"Put your hands where I can see them," shouted the suddenly nervous intruder.

"I'm bringing it out now," she said. "Please don't shoot!"

Adam Gable greedily moved forward, his menacing stare informing her that his promise of preserving her life was but another lie. Julia lunged forward, aiming the poker straight for his eyes, her right foot simultaneously kicking to make contact with his right shin. Adam must have been convinced she wouldn't fight back, for he wasn't prepared for the onslaught of rage propelling the miniature ice pick toward his eyes. He managed to fire that last second, missing Julia by a good two feet as the bullet embedded itself near the vanity backed against her far bedroom wall.

Adam's other hand flew up in a purely defensive movement and the poker, instead of stabbing his left eye tore into his earlobe. The assassin gave an unearthly howl as the sharp point of the tiny ice pick skewered the upper cartilage of his ear and rammed into his skull. He shrieked in agony as Julia kicked again, lifting her knee viciously into his groin and pushing her shoulder into the narrow expanse of his chest. Adam fell upon the bed, landing upon the painting, which shattered the glass into a hundred pieces as she dove for the bedroom door.

Unfortunately, he wasn't far behind her and as Julia glanced over shoulder, she saw him yank the army knife of his gushing ear and slam it onto the floor. Blood poured down his shirtfront as he aimed again, the shot reverberating throughout the small apartment. Julia recklessly careened through the lounge, heedless of her furniture as she sought the front exit. She nearly made it before Adam's skinny hand grabbed her arm like a vice and jerked her about just as she reached her doorway. Deciding she was not about to die without a fight, Julia flailed at him, her stinging hands inflicting harsh punishment upon his face and severely damaged ear. Her wildcat actions managed to keep the menacing gun away from her head.

Simon suddenly appeared through the doorway and giving an angry snarl, did something Julia thought strange at first. Instead of pushing Adam back into her apartment and pulling Julia out, Simon thrust her aside, his hand batting away Adam's gun as his fingers tightened around Adam's shirtfront. He pulled forcefully, thrusting himself backward through the door and dragging Adam with him. With one tremendous heave, he lifted the slighter man and hurled him over the balcony railing.

Julia had never witnessed anything like it before and it must have been the unrestrained hatred directed toward the man who'd nearly killed him the past winter that gave Simon superhero strength. One second Adam was stable upon the wide balcony and the next hurtled toward the low-lying bushes framing the pool. Adam must have had his own evil guardian angel, for instead of plunging to his death upon the concrete, he landed with a tremendous splash into the deep end of the chilly pool.

If Simon was disappointed, he didn't waste any time reflecting upon his foe's good luck.

"C'mon Julia!" he shouted, grabbing her by the arm and dragging her down the steps two at a time, the handbag slapping violently against her as she tried to keep her balance. By the time they'd reached the bottom steps, Adam had surfaced, sputtering and flailing; his ruined ear tingeing the pool pink, his gun lying useless upon the green outdoor carpet of the upstairs balcony where he'd dropped it during Simon's enraged attack.

For a man in such extreme pain, Adam had bolted out of the icy pool by the time Julia and Simon sprinted across the street to the Chrysler. Simon gunned the engine of the LeBaron and turned on the windshield wipers full blast as the rain pelted down. The road was slick and treacherous and the tires of the rental squealed as it sought traction on the wet road. Julia cast a glance over her shoulder to observe a drenched Adam Gable running after them for almost a hundred yards before raising a bloody fist and screeching obscenities at the top of his lungs. It was a long time before Julia's pounding heart returned to its normal rhythm.

Simon headed toward the mission, finally parking the powerful black car under the shelter of a beautiful oak tree in the historical site's parking lot as the rain hurled from the skies. He pulled the trembling Julia into his arms as she shivered violently.

"Everything's alright now... hush, sweet love," Simon soothed reassuringly. "Why don't you take off that wet jacket and wig and I'll turn the heater on full blast. It's okay, love."

He helped her remove the sodden wig and garments as the hot air from the engine's fan tried valiantly to warm them up. Simon threw his own wet jacket on the back seat and taking her hands once again, rubbed his fingers gently over their cold surface. They sat that way for a long while until Julia slowly calmed and they both warmed up. Julia finally opened her purse and pulled out the black floppy disk, flashing it victoriously at him. He smoothed back his long wet hair, and replacing the baseball cap grinned in relief.

"We need to get out of town Julia. He's seen the rental and will be calling in favors to find us. I should have known when he lost us in LA he'd head back to Santa Barbara."

"At least we have the disk."

"Thank God for that. So now you have to be my navigator once again." Simon started the engine and waited for her instructions.

The drive was one she'd always remember. Cautiously, they merged back onto the 101 and after a few miles turned onto Highway 154 and San Marco's Pass Road. For eighteen to twenty miles, Simon drove as fast as he dared, constantly glancing into his rearview mirror. The recent rain had made the road slippery and the mountainous grade turned incredibly twisty as they headed northwest toward the lake. Halfway up the road, heavy fog clamped down. While they knew it made travel safer in regards to Adam Gable, the road was highly treacherous.

"Can you remember if this road is a dead end Julia?"

"No, it isn't. There will soon be many turnoffs heading into various wilderness regions. The first will veer toward the Dick Smith Wilderness and later on to the San Raphael Wilderness area. We'll pass over an incredible bridge called the Cold Spring Canyon Arched Bridge, though I'm not sure we'll be able to appreciate it in this fog. This is a direct route to Los Olivos and later the 246 bisects it. Several roads run into the 166, which is on the west-hand side of the Calinte Range near the big valley, but we don't want to head that way because we need to stay west of the Sierra Madre Mountains."

"Do lots of people go to Lake Cachuma?"

"They do; it's a very popular spot to visit near the Chumash Painted Cave, but it's a Monday in November. I can't imagine there'd be whole lot of campers this time of year."

"The camp is open all year?"

"Yes, I believe so because the spot is famous for its largemouth bass and bird viewing. Lots of eagles and osprey call the man-made lake home."

"Let's hope the dreary weather proves to be a deterrent for nature lovers *and* fishermen. Even as he spoke, the fog lifted and pale sunlight illuminated the road as it curved and meandered through the beautiful lower range of the Sierra Madres in the Los Padres National Forest. A squirrel scampered across the road and Simon swerved, barely missing its long bushy gray tail. Simon glanced down at the odometer just as a sign stating *Cachuma Lake Recreation Area, 3 miles* came into view. Simon drove the LeBaron at a more leisurely pace as they pulled into the heavily wooded RV Park.

"It's more modern than I expected," said Simon, noting showers, public phones, and even a grocery store and gas station. The camp, for all of its size, was almost deserted and Julia replaced her wig and shouldered her handbag. The cloud cover had finally dissipated to reveal a bright blue sky and the tar road was now nearly dry.

"I'll get us as remote a site as possible. It seems to me that toward the northwest part of the camp there are lots of private tent sites. Hopefully we'll get lucky."

The female attendant chuckled when Julia asked if they had any tent openings.

"Are you kidding? It's too cold and damp this time of year. We have a few die-hard fishermen and their luxury RVs during the weekend, but you're my only customer this morning. You can have your choice honey." She pointed to a large wooden map behind her, indicating the location of all the different sites.

"My boyfriend and I would like to have some privacy and be away from any other campers that might arrive. Could you recommend a spot?"

"This is a nice one, right under a stand of oak trees. It is a little bit away from the lake and mighty quiet. As you can see I don't have any other campers."

"I'd really appreciate it if someone does want a tent site, you'd place then away from us."

The heavyset middle-aged woman gave her a wink. "I get the message dear. It's site forty-seven. Just follow the road to the right, then take the second left until it ends. There's a cozy little parking space right by the tent site. It's fairly flat and has a fire pit. Please be careful about putting out your fire and remember the store and gas station close at five."

Love Never Dies

"Is firewood provided?" asked Julia.

"Unfortunately not, but you can buy at couple of packs right here and I suggest you get some fire starters unless you're some kind of first-class Girl Scout."

Julia paid the woman a very reasonable fee and sticking the fire starters under her arm, grabbed the two bundles of wood, and hurried back to the waiting LeBaron.

They couldn't have asked for a more remote spot. Gray squirrels ran up the abundant pine and oak trees while a gentle breeze lifted its song through the brushy spikes of the pines. Tall brown grass edged the site and Julia could hear the screech of some water bird in the distance. The tent was relatively easily to erect after they had spread out the blue ground cloth and Julia began to stack the wood beside the round fire circle.

"You really held your own back there at the apartment," said Simon unexpectedly.

Julia grinned. "That will teach people to underestimate teachers with hidden weapons in their purses. He never knew what hit him."

Simon laughed. "I have to hand it to you, I never expected you to be so stalwart in the face of danger. You're an amazing woman Julia Ann Morris, and personally I'll never underestimate you again."

"I just wish we were here under better circumstances," she answered, basking in the warmth of his praise.

"Why don't you get a fire going while I scout around and make sure no one followed us into the camp? Since there's a grill, I'll buy some charcoal as well." Julia watched the tall denim-clad man limp quickly down the dirt path that led to the central section of the county park.

A gentle warmth tugged at her heart and Julia realized that Simon was reassuring her all was well. For a moment, overcome by the enormity of all that had transpired, she sank down upon the log bordering the fire pit and gazed at her trembling hands. While ecstatic Simon had revealed himself as Seth, she fretted she might once again lose the man she loved so dearly. She roused herself from her lugubrious thoughts and igniting one of the fire starters, soon had a roaring blaze.

Simon returned fifteen minutes later, lugging a heavy bag of briquettes upon his shoulder and carrying a bottle of red California wine.

"There's no one else in the camp except for an older couple in a huge Winnebago with a satellite dish on top. From the sounds of it, they're totally immersed in *One Life to Live.* So much for enjoying the peace and tranquility of nature."

Simon squatted before the fire and stretched out his hands. Even though midday, it was definitely chilly. He scanned the sky, relieved no storm clouds marred the beautiful clear sky. A white-breasted nuthatch descended a huge California sycamore, searching for insects; while a gray tree squirrel scurried up a huge canyon live oak in its endless quest for acorns.

"Let me get the briquettes going," he said, "while you open the bottle."

"Can't. I left my handy-dandy knife in Adam's earlobe."

Simon laughed loudly as he dumped half the bag of charcoal onto the round elevated grill. "Thank goodness I purchased a can opener and corkscrew in the store, since I don't think Mr. Gable is going to return your knife anytime soon."

She laughed as well and scurried about light-heartedly, uncorking the wine, dumping the chili into the cheap pot, and buttering some bread. Waiting until the coals were ready for the chili, she unpacked their sleeping bags and inflated the air mattress, adding two cheap pillows that lacked cases but hopefully would provide enough comfort. She had to admit the blue down sleeping bags looked mighty inviting.

Soon the smell of chili filled the air as Julia placed bread, meat, and cheese upon their plates while Simon spooned out the spicy beans as he sat upon the rough log.

"This smells great!"

Julia grinned, "Yes it's my gourmet chili, right out of the can. I can zest it up by adding a little cheese."

"Julia," he said quietly as she finished crumbling the cheese. "Can you ever forgive me?"

Her dark green eyes widened in surprise. "What do you mean?"

"I've put you through hell and back and here you nonchalantly make me lunch."

Julia dusted off her hands and knelt at his feet, placing her slender hands upon his knees.

"Seth Simon Steven Hayes Hamilton, it doesn't matter what name you go by, you've been and always will be my own true love; my soul mate. I'd rather remain on the run with you for the rest of my days than spend another minute bereft and lonely without you."

"I've always loved you," he admitted hoarsely, dropping his eyes as a sudden suspicious sheen covered his dark gray irises.

"I just wish you hadn't been so dreadfully hurt."

"Those were just physical wounds my sweet Julia; it was losing you that tore me apart."

"But you didn't lose me did you? I'm still here, half of your soul locked safely within my breast. It'll always be that way, no matter what your name is. I want to call you Steven but it sounds so foreign to me, and I can't call you Seth anymore."

"Pick a name then," he said hoarsely. "Any name you like; a name you feel comfortable with and that no one else would ever suspect. I can't be Seth or Simon anymore and you never really knew me as Steven Hamilton. Dub me, sweet lady."

Julia leaned back on her haunches and gazed into his dark gray orbs, mesmerized by the love emanating from them. "I've always been rather fond of the name Mark. I thought that if I ever had a son I'd name him that."

"Mark," he repeated. "It's sounds so nice on your lips." He leaned forward and pulled her into his arms.

"Is that tent ready?" he whispered, and Julia nodded mutely. He ignored the steaming chili and rose, pulling her to her feet and leading her into the tiny green tent where she'd spread out the two down sleeping bags and polyester pillows. Simon zipped up the opening to the tent and stood in its domed dimness for a full minute, just staring at her. Her heart began to burn and pulse as his hands slowly moved to his shirt, never removing his eyes from her face.

"I love you," he said softly. This time he didn't hide in the darkness, afraid to reveal his dreadful scars or the incriminating tattoo. His smooth torso was lean and well-sculpted, though still too thin for his frame. The raised golf-ball-sized scar hugged his right hipbone where the hot metal of the burning Jeep had passed through his abdomen to exit out his back. It was a most beautiful and terrible scar. Opposite it, as he slowly peeled down his denim trousers to reveal blue hip hugger briefs, the top of the entwined rose tattoo appeared, its pink and crimson flowers begging to be totally exposed. The tattoo glowed beckoningly, and even in the dimness she could make out the telltale initials proclaiming his commitment to her. Julia's eyes lowered to his ravaged leg and her heart jolted. Could she even imagine the horrible mangling pain he'd suffered nearly a year ago?

Julia hadn't meant to cry out in anticipation or lunge at him, but suddenly she was lying flat on her back, his kisses trailing over her body as her hands caressed his dear, dear flesh. It was fortunate their tent was located discreetly distant from the main camp and that only the noisy blue jays and busy squirrels heard their impassioned encounter, as their ragged breathing and occasional gasps penetrated the thin nylon of the small tent. They lost total knowledge of time or space, only intent on their love; a love that finally held no secrets.

"Seth!" she called out at first, and then later "Simon," as she passionately loved the man of her soul and her heart. "Sweet Steven," she finally gasped, never before having made love to the man using his real name.

"Julia!" he cried, and straightened against her, intense joy shining upon his damp face.

It was a long while before their furiously pounding hearts returned to their normal pace and they lay for a long while just savoring the feel of their relaxed bodies nestled against one another.

328

Love Never Dies

When he finally spoke, she felt an awesome burning in her heart at his quiet words.

"I swear to you now that I will never leave you again while I'm alive on this earth. Trust me my love, that all will work out for us, and remember that love never dies. Promise me you'll never forget that."

Julia could only nod mutely against his warm chest as the jays threw their raucous cries over the tent's domed top. Later, as she succumbed to sleep, Steven Hamilton; alias Seth and Simon Hayes, tried desperately to figure a way out of this mess.

Chapter 13

Adam Gable cursed up a blue streak as he jumped into his gray BMW. One of Julia's elderly neighbors screamed as he pulled away from the curb, and if he'd had time he'd have wasted that nosy old hag who was probably phoning the police right now, if only he'd had his gun. His delayed reaction to the fall suddenly hit him and he pulled over and spilled his guts onto the pristine flowerbed bordering an old Spanish style Mediterranean house covered in red adobe tiles. Adam reached inside his pocket for his handkerchief, forgetting everything he owned was soaked. His fingers tightened up on the limp gum packet and the dripping receipts. He squinted. These receipts were recent. One was from a mini-market for food, matches, and something else he couldn't decipher, so he checked out the other. Adam whistled; the water-soaked script barely revealed the words *Sporting Quest Adventures*. Well he'd be damned.

Love Never Dies

Stomach still rolling he flipped open his soaking cell phone, recognizing it was time to call Roy Geiger. Thank God it worked and he wasted no pleasantries upon the florid-faced man; giving his present location and asking for some advice.

"If you wanted to hide in the mountains so no one would find you but still be close to Santa Barbara, where would you go?"

For the next half-hour, with a map of the Santa Barbara region spread out over his knees and his ear glued to the cell phone, Roy and Adam finally came to the same conclusion; the fugitives would make for the Los Padres National Forest. Roy gave him several options; they could head back toward Los Angeles and drive up through Toro Canyon, or they could veer toward Cold Springs on East Mountain Drive, or lastly, venture north on Gibraltar Road.

He and Roy chatted for a few more minutes and then Adam sat for a long time parked next to the sunny curb and tried to dry out. He finally decided that since he wasn't familiar enough with the region to know where all the best hidey holes were located, he'd need some help; so Adam headed for the nearest book store.

"Do you have any campground guides for the area?"

"Yeah," yawned the skinny girl, barely out of high school. Her customer's wet, bedraggled appearance didn't seem to faze her. "They're in the travel section over there. I suggest you get a Woodall's." She turned back to her teen magazine as Adam headed for the travel section and picked up the large orange and blue book. Minutes later he sat in the comfortable seat of the BMW, after changing into set of dry clothes he'd retrieved from his trunk, and scanned the campground guide feeling thoroughly frustrated, his right hand straying to the ravaged ear, which still throbbed and ached. At least it had stopped bleeding.

There were so many campground sites in the Santa Barbara area, so how in the hell was he supposed to figure out where they'd bolted to? Adam forced himself to calm down; he'd learned a long time ago that the most important aspects of his job were to be, deliberate, methodical, and thorough. He finally determined they could easily have doubled back and headed toward Toro Canyon. So that was where he was going to start, and the best way to begin was to call all those campgrounds possessing phones and ask if his two cousins had shown up for some weekday camping. He turned his luxury vehicle south and headed toward Toro Canyon after swallowing a couple of aspirin and washing them down with a warm beer. Perhaps, he thought, the young lovers would try some of the more rustic and primitive campgrounds. One thing was for certain; no matter where they were he'd search each and every site until he found them.

Love Never Dies

When Julia awoke it was coming on dusk, and startled, she glanced at the luminous dial of her steel wristwatch. It was after 5 p.m. She heard the popping of the fire and the clink of metal against metal and slowly, after donning her clothes, unzipped the flap of the flimsy tent and peered out. Simon was in the process of cooking dinner. Without turning from his task at the grill, he threw over his shoulder.

"You might want to pull on a sweater; it's getting a bit nippy out here. I should have dinner ready within about ten minutes."

She darted out of the tent and hugging him from behind, folded her arms around his chest as she nuzzled his neck.

"Were you able to get some sleep?" she asked.

"A bit," he admitted, "but I've been trying to work out a plan I'll tell you about later." He hugged her encompassing arms. "Why don't you take a quick wash and by the time you get back I'll have dinner ready. The public washrooms are only a three-minute walk past the swimming pool if you head down that path."

Simon was true to his word and upon her return had whipped up a tasty omelet flavored with cheddar cheese and diced ham, and cut up some accompanying apples and oranges. The forgotten chili from earlier made a complimentary side dish and Julia ate hungrily. The simplistic dinner tasted amazingly good in the nippy evening air.

"I didn't think to ask," he said at dinner, leaning on his elbows and sipping a tin cup full of strong tea. "What name did you use to register us under?"

An impish grin spread over Julia's face. "Jon Lincoln and Jane Douglas. When she asked for names, all I could think of was Jane and John Doe and knew that wouldn't work, so my mind hit upon the Lincoln and Douglas debates we'd read about in one of our classroom magazines."

Simon chuckled and sipping on his tea, leaned back against the rough log. The bushes rustled and a covey of mountain quail, complete with black plumes, scurried past their campsite, seemingly oblivious to the close proximity of the campers.

"I could get used this," he said irrelevantly. "I've always loved the outdoors and it's amazing to me we're camping out here in November. In Toronto, we'd already be snowed in so I think there could be advantages to becoming a California boy, Julia."

Julia smiled happily. "So what's the plan for tomorrow?" she asked, setting down her empty plate and moving closer to him upon the log.

"I'm planning on getting up early and heading into town. I'll find a business center, make a copy of the disk, and mail it to Mandy. I'll also give those guys one more try via e-mail; maybe we'll get lucky."

"And after that?" asked Julia, lifting her eyebrows.

334

Love Never Dies

"I don't feel comfortable staying here for more than one night. I think we should head deeper into the Los Padres National Forest. Disappearing into the wilderness might be our best choice right now. I don't know about you, but I'm finding it hard to sleep knowing Adam's still out there."

"I'd have to agree," stated Julia, refusing to worry about it this evening. They finished the simple task of washing the dishes and threw breadcrumbs to a small Merriam's chipmunk who'd obviously received handouts before. Afterward, they sat and talked by the dancing fire as the stars came out one by one, holding hands and wishing this were a holiday retreat instead of a desperate attempt to escape a killer who simply refused to give up.

As the embers of the fire died down, Julia rose and stretched her arms above her head.

"I know something that just might help you sleep Mr. Hayes," she giggled, and dragged him into the welcoming confines of the small tent.

Adam Gable was used to staying up all night. Using a strong flashlight he always kept in the dash of his car, Adam methodically hit every campground in the guide, searching for the fugitive couple. Few campers inhabited the first campgrounds he checked, though once he beamed his light upon the scroungy countenance of a tattooed biker. When the man hurled expletives at him, Adam calmly removed his extra handgun from his belt and pointed it at the center of the drowsy man's forehead.

"You got other complaints?" he snarled, and the bushy haired biker shook his head violently.

Most of the campgrounds were easy to explore, clearly vacant on this Monday night during the first week of November, so he wound his way back toward Santa Barbara, wishing he instinctively knew where his prey might have hidden. It would have saved him a hell of a lot of footwork.

By the time he'd finished searching the southern campgrounds and headed toward Goleta, it was four in the morning. His eyes felt gritty and the country western station did little to stop the onslaught of yawns threatening to overwhelm him. As Adam turned up Highway 154 fatigue hit him in powerful waves and finally, after ten miles upon the incredibly twisty road, he pulled over under a stand of coastal live oak, and leaning his gray leather seat back, closed his eyes for a couple of hours. The fatigue and the cold caught up with him and he slept until after eight, never realizing a black Chrysler LeBaron slid down the highway past his idle car as he snored in the chilly interior of the luxury car.

By the time Adam reached Lake Cachuma, the car's heater had warmed him up, but he felt in dire need of a wash and good breakfast. A portly Hispanic woman greeted him in the front office.

"Camping?" she asked, noting he didn't have an RV.

"Nah," he drawled, giving his standard speech. "I was actually supposed to meet my two cousins at this campground last night, but I got a flat tire and ended up having to sleep off the road. I only repaired it this morning. I was wondering if my cousins made it. Simon's a tall man in his early thirties, with dark hair and gray eyes and my little cousin Sheila; well, I think this week she's a blonde, though sometimes she allows her mousy brown hair to grow out."

The dark-haired woman cocked her head, and noting his bloodshot eyes, smiled sympathetically. "I'm really not sure, I wasn't working yesterday, but I believe we had one couple staying here, though I'm not sure if they fit your description. However, I think I saw their black LeBaron leave this morning. I've always loved that car."

Adam wanted to curse under his breath. "So they left?"

"Yes, more than an hour ago I believe."

"If I pay you the camping fee, can I use your showers?"

"Absolutely," said the woman, glad to have a bit of business, and willingly rang up the total as he bought orange juice, a loaf of bread, and some lunch meat for his meager breakfast.

So Adam Gable took his time soaking in a long hot shower, never realizing Julia Ann Morris slept not five minutes away from him.

Simon finished his business relatively quickly, copying the disk twice, and as a safeguard mailing one to the architectural firm he'd worked for as his brother Seth. He express-mailed the other to Mandy Gaskill and placed the original in the dash of the LeBaron. One long e-mail awaited him and he gaped at the contents before letting out a shaky breath, realizing the instructions were for the best.

Simon then picked up a few additional supplies before heading back up the twisty road toward the lake and Julia. He'd been aware of when she'd awakened, feeling that insistent tug at his own heart urging him ever homeward, for he now viewed wherever she was as home. Simon wondered for the umpteenth time whether she would have glanced twice at him as Steven Hamilton, the cocky young architect from the upper class suburbs in Toronto, who, until now, had always loved them and left them.

As he negotiated the treacherous road, he pondered his dual identity. It was strange that as Seth, he had presented to Julia the man he had always wanted to be, though the wilder brother Simon was more his true nature. Perhaps, he could join the best traits of the two and become the real Steven Hamilton. If this whole terrible experience had a silver lining it was that he'd managed to meet her. He'd never have ventured down to the western United States except for the Witness Protection Program, and in his own strange way he thanked Joe Alletti for that.

He approached the camp cautiously, the LeBaron's sporty tires crunching upon the dirt road as his eyes scanned the surrounding campsites in search of a silver BMW. He relaxed, not realizing that very vehicle was parked behind the showers and the man he'd been trying to avoid sat munching a makeshift sandwich of processed ham and cheese, and sipping a beer even though it was not much past 9:30 in the morning.

Julia had made a fire, and much to his surprise, had apparently been collecting acorns because a large pile lay near the jumping fire. She bounded to him, the relief evident on her face, as he pulled her to him.

"I can see you have been making yourself useful," he joked, studying the pile of acorns littering the ground near the fire.

"Aren't they beautiful? There are three different kinds and I want to show them to my class." She pointed to a long narrow acorn. "That's from the coastal live oak and its acorns were the ones the

Chumash and Pomo Indians preferred. That fat one is from the canyon live oak; see the yellowish hairs covering the cup? And the last is the scrub oak acorn from that bush over there. I pricked my fingers on the spiny leaves getting those. Bet my students don't know there are so many varieties, Steven."

He smiled at the use of his real name.

"I've decided we need to head north toward Santa Maria and drop off the car there before moving to San Luis Obispo. We'll catch a train or bus or something to take us to Toronto."

"Toronto?" squeaked Julia. "You're taking me to Toronto?"

"There's no other choice Julia. I don't want to whisk you from the place you love or unduly worry your family or employer, but there's no way around it. The crime happened in Toronto and I have to return to Toronto. I could go alone, but simply can't bear to leave you behind. Will you come with me?"

She gulped. "Of course I'll go with you. You're absolutely right."

"Then let's take the tent down and get cracking."

Within twenty minutes, their meager possessions packed in the trunk of the car, Simon used an empty water bottle to douse the fire.

"Are you ready?" he asked as he positioned himself in front of the steering wheel, and Julia nodded.

Love Never Dies

"All we have to do is just tell the lady at reception we're leaving and then we can be on our way. I wish I could call my brother and let him know what's going on."

"I left him a message so he's not going to worry for a couple of days. When it's safer we'll give him a call."

Simon pulled up and idled the car at the reception as Julia got out to inform the attendant they were leaving the campground. It was a different woman from the previous afternoon and the heavyset Hispanic woman smiled broadly at her.

"Oh, I'm so happy you stopped by. A man came here this morning asking if a young woman fitting your description checked into the camp. He said he was your cousin."

"Cousin," repeated Julia startled. "Was he tall and dark-haired with very pale skin?"

"Yes, that would be him. He said he was looking for you and your cousin. Oh, there's his car just behind the showers. Why don't you stop by and see him."

"I'll do that," gasped Julia, backing away from the pleasant woman.

She lunged to the car, yanking open the stiff door. "Adam's behind the showers, Simon! Somehow he tracked us here."

Simon didn't waste time in responding, instead gunning the motor and kicking up gravel as the sedan's tires squealed. If Adam had lingered in the toilets for a bit longer they might have made a clean getaway, but as fate would have it he sauntered out of the bathroom just as the black LeBaron scooted around the corner and tore up the dirt road. Adam swore and dove into his BMW and grinding his gears, lurched after the recklessly driven LeBaron through a tunnel of brown dust.

The Chrysler was a powerful car, but unfortunately, the BMW was its match. Sometimes it seemed that Simon gained as he recklessly headed south down the 154, and once he was positive he'd lost the hit man, until the sun glinted off the sleek metal lines of the pursuing vehicle. Their frenzied driving continued for over twenty minutes, Simon never able to shake the persistent Beamer. As he maneuvered through the tricky San Marcos Pass, Simon shouted at Julia for guidance.

"A left Simon! Take the next left!"

Simon hung a violent left onto Camino Cielo Road. The twisty turns and hairpin corners made Julia nauseous as she was slapped against the car's interior with every turn. When Adams Gable's vehicle pulled only two hundred yards behind them, Simon tossed one of the two revolvers into her lap.

"If he gets any closer, lean out the back window and try to take out one of his tires. We've got to lose him Julia! Use my cell and punch in the speed dial for number four. You've got to answer me this time Stan!"

Love Never Dies

The line soon rang as Julia's sweaty hands clutched the Beretta. Certain the reception in the rugged mountainous area would have prohibited any contact using the satellite phone network; she was surprised when a deep voice answered tersely.

"Garten."

"Oh!" cried Julia. "This is Julia Morris and I'm with Simon Hayes and a man named Adam is following us and..."

Simon's wild turn momentarily knocked her against the door and the phone skidded onto the floorboard. Julia fumbled around and managed to locate the moving phone. She could hear Stan's voice shouting on the other end of the line.

"Sorry... sorry. I'm back. We're being followed!"

"Tell him our location Julia!"

"We're off the 154, north of Santa Barbara and heading southeast on the Camino Cielo Road."

"A sign's coming up Julia... The Arroyo Burro Road in five miles. Tell him we're going to take it and head deeper into the Los Padres National Forest. Tell him plan B!"

Julia breathlessly repeated the instructions adding, "We're in a black Chrysler LeBaron and he's in a silver BMW!"

"I'll..." the line echoed and went dead, Julia helplessly gazing at the useless phone in her hand.

"He was responding, but we got cut off."

"We'd better hope he can get us some help fast," cried Simon, turning the steering wheel sharply right as Julia hung onto the door and prayed.

The next four miles were excruciating. Simon drove faster than was safe, passing only one other ancient pick-up truck heading the opposite direction. Suddenly, the exit indicating Arroyo Burrow Road appeared. The turnoff was less than a half-mile away and the BMW suddenly accelerated and pulled within thirty feet of the car. Julia heard a sharp whining pop as Simon swerved. Adam was firing at them!

"We're going to take an abrupt left up here Julia," Simon hissed, his eyes glued to the dangerous road. "I want you to get into the back seat and roll down the window. Aim at his tires."

"Simon!" shrieked Julia, "I don't know how to shoot. And about the road, my family's driven it once before and it's very rough and twisty! If Adam catches up we'll be trapped!"

"Please Julia, just do as I ask. Get into the back seat and aim as best as you can!"

It was difficult hiking over the front seat as the car careened and lurched down the windy road, but finally Julia plopped in an ungraceful heap and rolled down the electric window. A vision of the car hitting a bump and her losing the gun and watching it bounce behind the car flashed in her brain, and Julia clutched the pistol until her knuckles turned white while desperately aiming it at the BMW that inched ever closer. The morning sun reflected off Adam's windshield and blinded her. She squinted desperately, trying to get a clear sight on the revolving rubber tires.

"Alright Julia, I'm going to make that turn now. As I do, aim at the car and fire!"

She began shooting as soon as Simon hit the corner, amazed at how simple it was. You just squinted, pulled the trigger, and tried like the blazes to hold on because of the responding kick.

Adam Gable swerved his vehicle immediately at the sight of her drawn gun, but not before Julia, who'd been aiming at a tire, broke the passenger window directly behind him. Adam swore viciously and lifted his own gun, firing with one hand while keeping the other upon the steering wheel. Julia shot again, one of her bullets ricocheting off his bumper. Unfortunately, none of her shots found their mark and suddenly, with an incredible burst of speed, the BMW pulled up directly beside her, the barrel of his gun staring her directly in the face. Julia gasped hysterically and pulled the trigger. The driver's window burst into a thousand splinters of glass.

"For God's sake get down!" screamed Simon, and Julia ducked just as Adam twisted his steering wheel and slammed his car into the side of the black Chrysler!

"We're not going to make it!" she screamed, as Simon fought the wheel.

Julia peered up over the opposite side of the car. They slid along a narrow section of the highway where the embankment plunged down a good hundred feet on each side of the road, protected only by a feeble aluminum guardrail. The Beamer smashed into them again, shattering the passenger window, which rained glass upon Julia's Levi-clad legs. She didn't need Simon's frenzied urging to lift the gun again, and shot blindly. It was a fluke shot, passing through the destroyed passenger window of the BMW to strike the rearview mirror, the bullet ricocheting downward and reverberating against Adam's firmly grasped steering wheel. The leather-bound steering mechanism sparked dangerously and exploded, the bullet severing the steering wheel column right in half, leaving the useless wheel in Adam's terrified hands.

Simon slammed his foot upon the brake, the LeBaron screeching and swerving, spinning two full times before stopping, smoke pouring from its rear tires. Adam screamed as the car plunged forward, its momentum causing the BMW to sail over the railing. The British car looked almost as if it could take flight, gliding a full forty feet outward, until slowing and plunging headfirst into the waiting pines of the Los Padres National Forest.

Simon's car had miraculously stopped two inches away from the twisted remainder of the metal guardrail, the foul stench of its burning tires filling the midday air. Simon was out of the car in an instant, running toward the edge of the embankment, his eyes straining for a glimpse of the hurdling silver BMV. The vehicle turned end over end through the manzanita, oaks, and pines, before finally bursting into a fiery inferno. Julia halted shakily beside Simon, his arm reaching out to steady her as she watched in horrified fascination as the flames from the blackened car began to ignite some of the knobcone pine trees it had finally lodged against.

"Wow," said Simon, "that was some mighty fine shooting."

"I killed him," exclaimed Julia, suddenly shaking uncontrollably.

"No, no you didn't," said Simon, pulling her close. "Your bullet only hit the interior of his car, causing him to lose control. It was him or us." Simon paused, keeping a firm arm around her trembling shoulders as they gazed over the embankment at the smoke drifting upward, a single turkey vulture circling high overhead.

Simon hauled her away from the rising smoke and gazed steadily into her blurry green eyes. "Look Julia, I'm sure we don't have very much time since the authorities should be here in a matter of minutes. I didn't tell you this, but this morning I finally managed to get hold of Stan. An associate of Adam Gable's waylaid him at UCLA and stuffed him into the trunk of his own car. I'd asked him to drive up to the camp and meet us, so that's why you were able to connect with him on my cell. I want you to sit down right here on that rock and keep an eye on the burning vehicle while I make a call."

He distanced himself from her and dialed the number. The surrounding hills made the line echo but because Stan was relatively close he was able to relay a brief but insistent message. Julia didn't pay attention to the stilted conversation, instead folding her arms across her chest as she peered at the black clouds pouring over the embankment.

She roused to observe Simon feverishly going through the trunk. The blue sports bag where they'd stuffed their clothing and few belonging sat upon the gray pavement and Simon was going through it, removing and stuffing her articles of clothing into a large plastic bag.

"What are you doing?" she asked, her throat suddenly dry.

"Stan Garten, the police officer assigned to this case and trying to protect you for a long time, should arrive within ten minutes, hopefully before any other authorities arrive. You're going to get into his vehicle and head in the opposite direction."

"But what about you?" she squeaked.

"I'm not going with you. From what Stan related to me this morning it's not going to end here with

Love Never Dies

Adam Gable. He might be dead, but someone else will take his place until Alletti's certain I'm history. Most likely, as long as I'm alive, they'll try to take you out as well. But I think Stan and I have figured out a way to ensure your safety and provide you with a normal future, so you'll have to trust me Julia and listen well. Can you feel it?"

He tapped his chest with a long, tapered finger and suddenly the warm glow indicating his undying love and devotion began to swell through her chest, easing the pain and guilt and fear caused by the bellowing smoke. Julia gazed up into the gray eyes of the man she loved and listened intently.

"I want you to do everything I tell you. When Stan arrives, get into his car. He'll drive you back to LA where you'll pick up your Taurus. He moved it near the university in an effort to make it appear you left the hotel. Adam Gable already told his cohorts I have the disk, so Alletti will know you no longer have it in your possession. I want you to think about what you might have done this weekend if I hadn't been along and none of this had happened."

"What?" she cried, suddenly aware of the significance of his simple words.

"When you get back to Santa Barbara," he continued, ignoring the desperate plea in her eyes, "you'll tell your brother you haven't seen me since Saturday. That I turned out just like Seth said; a womanizer and cad who took off with some woman you didn't even know after making a pass to you which you stoutly rejected."

"No," she exclaimed, her hands reaching up to grab at his arms; but he remained steadfast.

"You haven't seen me since Saturday, do you understand? You didn't have anything to do with me after I offended and insulted you. Say it."

"Offended," was all she could manage.

"That's right, I insulted you and offended you and was nothing like Seth. You fell in love with the better twin; do you understand me?"

"Yes," she affirmed.

"Then, upon your arrival home, you relate to your brother that the weekend was a real eye-opener. You finally realized that life goes on and that maybe someday, in some way, there might be room for another man."

"No," she moaned, "you can't be saying this."

"Look into my eyes now. Do you see their color? Forget that color. Observe my hair and streak one last time and forget about it. These cheekbones, this mouth, the strange upturned scar; none of them matter Julia. They're only identifiers to the others in the world, but we will have our own private identifiers to indicate how much we love one another won't we?"

His soul seared hers, and Julia gasped in pain as a lean hand slid down from her arms and touched the tattoo where it lay hidden under the denim of his pants. "Here," he tapped and lifted his hand to his chest, "and here. This is how we know love never dies. Say it Julia; repeat the words."

"Love never dies, it never dies," she cried, as the approaching whine of rubber ground against the tire-marked pavement. Stan Garten arrived much too quickly.

"When you get into that car I don't want you to look back. Promise me that Julia, and remember that time is of no relevance. You know what to say to your brother, parents, to everyone, so tell me now. What was Simon?"

"A womanizer and a cad."

"And about our love?"

"It never dies."

"Don't ever forget it and brace yourself for whatever you might see or hear over the next few days."

Steven Hamilton, alias Seth and Simon Hayes, leaned down and kissed her as tenderly and sweetly as he'd ever done before. It was a lingering goodbye kiss, yet somehow held promise and her heart glowed with the unrestrained love he poured into her.

A tan Chevy pulled up abruptly behind them and a tall, mustached man with a terrible bruise on his cheek and traces of blood on his temple opened the car door.

"It has to be now, Stan," said Simon shortly, and shoved the woman he loved into the passenger seat. He picked up the plastic bag and dumped it onto the seat behind her.

"You remember what I said Stan; not a word, do you hear, not a word to anyone." Stan nodded an affirmative while Julia numbly buckled her seatbelt. She waited as Stan reversed the car and heard Simon's beautiful voice wash over her one last time.

"Don't look back Julia. I love you forever and always." The last words faded as Stan gunned the engine and shot down the highway, driving faster than safe.

They'd progressed no more than a half-mile down the road when a massive explosion tore the late morning air, searing the sky in one bright burst. A tremendous jolt of excitement ripped through her heart, but the continuing glow of his soul never altered, only sparked intensely as a prudent reminder before retreating once more into its banked state. Stan Garten drove for another five minutes before turning onto the main highway. Within ten minutes screaming red-lighted vehicles tore past, heading toward the mountain explosion and subsequent brush fire.

"You okay?" he asked, his voice deep and gravelly.

"Yes. Everything's going to be fine," she replied, and he nodded. She noted he was a handsome man except for the incredible lines of fatigue and the bloody battle wounds Adam's cohorts had given him.

Love Never Dies

He turned south on Highway 154 and then left on Highway 101, slowly heading back toward UCLA where he'd left her Ford.

"You need to see a doctor," she said, noting his pallid face and clenched teeth.

He grimaced. "I don't deserve to see a doctor after falling for a trick like that. I spent the last eighteen hours locked in the trunk of my car until a little old lady with a bright yellow parasol opened my trunk. I was so happy I kissed her."

Julia was able to laugh. "Did she faint dead away?"

"Nah, just gave me her phone number." He continued to chat to her pleasantly, allowing her to relax, while she in turn kept him awake and alert until finally he pulled into the UCLA Medical Center's parking structure. Near a wide pillar sat her dark blue Taurus, just as if nothing had happened.

As he pulled up beside her Ford and she shakily departed the big car, Stan watched her with dark brown eyes before reaching into his wallet and pulling out a business card.

She stared at the police insignia and his name in bold print. "*Stanley L. Garten*. You've been watching me for months haven't you?"

"I'm not sure I made much of a guardian angel, but I did the best I could. At least you're still alive." His words mocked himself and Julia almost wished she could tell him the truth about Seth. He continued. "I checked you out of the hotel and your bags are in the trunk of your car, compliments of LAPD. Drive home. You never met me, you never knew me. You don't know a damn thing about what happened on that mountain road this morning, do you Julia Morris?"

"I don't know anything," said Julia obediently. "Nothing at all."

Stan raised a hand and pulled the heavy car away while she tucked his card inside her purse and swung the plastic bag onto the passenger seat.

Three hours later, after practicing her alibi at least twenty times, she numbly punched the numbers of her brother's cell phone and listened to his chipper welcome.

"Tell me all about your trip," he said.

"I will," answered Julia. "Maybe I can come over to dinner tonight and tell you all about it."

"Did Simon come back with you?"

"Simon," repeated Julia. "Was he supposed to? I haven't seen him since Saturday and that's a tale in itself. I'll fill you all in on the details tonight if you and Angie are game. I know it's rude to invite myself over, but I'm tired and don't feel like cooking tonight."

She listened to his response for a moment and rubbed her burning chest before agreeing on a time to arrive for dinner.

———————

Love Never Dies

Angie had made a delicious beef stew for dinner and by the time that Julia arrived at 6:30 she had recited her modified weekend story to herself another dozen times. When her brother asked once again about Simon she managed to shake her head scornfully and snort out,

"He's as bad as Seth said he was. Not only did he make several undignified passes at me, but as soon as this busty redhead walked into the room he was buzzing about her like a bee to honey. I was fortunate to be rid of him. Besides, I needed some time to myself and really didn't relish his face constantly reminding me of Seth."

"I'm sorry," grimaced Paul. "I was kinda hoping that maybe you and Simon would hit it off."

"No," lied Julia. "We didn't hit it off at all, but don't fret about it Paul. This weekend has given me space to reflect on how it's time to start moving on with my life. I understand that my beloved Seth will never be replaced and will remain one of the most important parts of my life. Yet, I'm positive he wouldn't want me to sit here and waste away. I'm only twenty-nine years old and maybe someday..." her eyes flickered hopefully at her brother and sister-in-law, "he'll send someone to me to take his place."

Angie gave her an impulsive hug. "I'm so glad to hear you say that."

"But you've got to promise me," stated Julia determinedly, "that you won't match me up with any of those young doctors at your hospital. Let me muddle through this at my own pace and in my own way. Please Angie?"

Her dark-eyed sister-in-law grinned at her husband. "Okay, it's a deal. Besides," she said slyly, "you'll have a lot of other things to think about since you are going to be an aunt."

"An aunt," gasped Julia, "but you've only been married for two months!"

"Shoot," said Paul, "you ought to know by now that it only takes a minute."

"I going to be an aunt," said Julia delightedly, relieved and thankful there was now something to take her mind off what had happened this past weekend. They chatted quietly and affectionately for the next hour until her brother flicked on the local news. There had been a blaze in the Los Padres Mountains above Santa Barbara that very afternoon.

The perfectly made-up female newscaster for the local station reported from the scene.

"The police are trying to piece together what happened in what seems to be a bizarre incident.

All authorities can surmise is that a silver BMW and black Chrysler LeBaron were racing recklessly along this twisty dangerous road before colliding and plummeting over the cliff. The police have recovered two bodies and have identified the

Love Never Dies

first as a mechanic from Stockton by the name of Adam Gable and the second as a Canadian national, Simon Hayes, who appears to have been visiting southern California as a tourist.

"Oh my God," shrieked Angie. Her brother tried to calm down his hysterical wife as Julia listened numbly to the newscaster's final statement.

"I knew he was reckless," croaked her brother, who was beside himself in a mixture of rage, confusion, and indignation.

As Julia watched the firefighters douse the remains of the brush fire, her heart swelled and called the newscaster an unknowledgeable liar. The glow intensified as the camera revealed a close up of the mangled remains of the blackened BMW and Chrysler LeBaron, and she turned her attention to comforting her distraught sister-in-law. By the end of the newscast, Julia Ann Morris was firmly in control of her emotions and prepared herself to wait for whatever the future chose to bring.

Chapter 14

It was the Tuesday after the long Labor Day weekend, a full ten months after Simon Hayes and Adam Gable had plunged their cars to their death upon that twisty mountain road, when something strange happened. The fervor regarding the accident had died down within a couple months and Julia rarely spoke of it. She'd even gone against her own better judgment and ventured out on a couple of double dates with her well-meaning brother to prove that she was healing. Her brother and parents had taken her vow to start anew way too seriously, and it was often with barely bridled impatience that she brushed off their well-meaning attempts at matchmaking.

Now, she examined the nineteen bright new faces of her eager second grade students and grinned. They'd just placed their brand new backpacks into newly white-washed cubbies and sat down at their tables, hands folded primly in front of them.

Love Never Dies

She'd just introduced herself, taken roll, and discovered one student was missing, when her principal, the irrepressible Connie Fernandez, knocked on the door jam and ushered in a tiny little girl with reddish-brown hair and bright hazel eyes.

"We have a new student for you Ms. Morris. Her name is Gertrude Johnson, but she likes to go by Gertie." The little girl smiled unreservedly up at Julia as she politely shook the hand of her new teacher.

"This makes things just perfect," said Julia. "Now I have an even amount of boys and girls. I was wondering when my twentieth student would show up and here you are. Why don't you sit at that table right over there Gertie?"

The petite girl sat down beside two other second grade girls and placed a bright red pencil case upon her desk. Gertie wore a pretty red-checked dress with matching bobby socks and black patent leather shoes and carried the fresh-scrubbed face of a first day student. Gertie listened intently to Julia's instructions and began writing immediately about her summer, working quietly and diligently until the recess bell rang. She then traipsed up to Julia's desk, her black shiny shoes gleaming upon the gray carpet. She hadn't spoken since the first few minutes of class and now laid a white envelope on her new teacher's desk.

"My grandma and uncle said that I should give you this." It was common that nervous parents gave

359

their children letters for the teacher on the first day, and Julia smiled back.

"Are you new in town Gertie? I don't recall you being at this school last year."

"Yes I am," she said, revealing a missing front tooth. "My grandma and mom moved down with my uncle to Santa Barbara just last week. They say this is where we are going to live for a long time."

"And your daddy?" asked Julia gently.

"My mom and dad are divorced but my uncle stays with us and he's a lot of fun. He's an 'ivil' engineer."

Julia thought hard. "You mean a *civil* engineer?"

"Yeah that's it," lisped the little girl, breaking into a huge smile. "Anyway, he made me promise to give you this letter. I'll see you later Ms. Morris; Katie and Juanita are waiting for me." And with that the little girl skipped off, her braids bouncing against the geometric pattern of her new first-day dress.

But Julia didn't open up the letter immediately, instead spending the short recess period reading the files regarding her new students. Within twenty minutes her sweaty class returned from their energetic recess and she walked them to their music class, spending the next fifteen minutes grading a pre-spelling test she'd given the children to determine their grade level. Finally, she remembered the bulging letter housed within the plain white envelope with her name

360

written on it. She thought it was a bit odd that the girl's uncle would already know her first name.

Julia opened the envelope but no piece of paper rested inside. Instead, two delicate rosebuds tumbled onto the table, one the deepest purest red, the other, the palest pink. Their thorns had been carefully broken off, leaving the stems and petals perfectly unblemished and beautiful. Julia sat for a full three minutes staring at the two rosebuds, her heart quickening; and when she closed her eyes and reached out with her soul, an answer floated back. It started out as a slight tingling, spreading from her heart down to her fingertips until finally erupting into flame. She lifted the two rosebuds to her lips and kissed them tenderly.

Later, when she was calmer, and after placing the two rosebuds in a tiny glass of water, she approached little Gertie. She and her partner Juanita were reading the first chapter of *Charlotte's Web* to each other.

Julia pulled the small child away and spoke quietly, her heart pounding in excitement. "Thank you for the letter from your uncle. What did you say his name was?"

"His name is Mark. Mark Sebastian." Her hazel eyes were guileless and Julia's heart quickened.

The rest of the day passed too slowly, until finally the end of the day bell rang at 2:20. Eager parents and siblings showed up at her classroom door to help their sisters, brothers, and friends pack up after the first day.

Gertie carefully and methodically placed her polka-dotted lunch box inside of her Barbie bag, as well as the first day information normally distributed to students at the start of each school year.

A plump woman in her mid-fifties materialized beside Gertie and gave her a swift hug and kiss.

"How was your first day sweetie?"

"It was wonderful," breathed the tiny girl, gazing up into her grandmother's eyes. She dragged at her grandmother's hand. "Come meet my new teacher. She's over here!"

Julia straightened her shoulders and gazed steadfastly at the middle-aged woman approaching her. The woman was of average height, her short brown hair shot through with gray. She possessed shrewd blue eyes underneath gold wire-rimmed glasses and her beige pants suit was tailored and stylish. She stuck out an unhesitant hand to Julia.

"I'm Meredith Johnson, Gertie's grandmother."

"And I'm Julia Ann Morris," said Julia carefully, watching the older woman intently for her reaction.

Gertie's grandmother gave her a thorough once-over before proceeding. "I just wanted to let you know that Gertie was originally meant to be in first grade, but because of her academic performance and the fact that her birthday is in January we decided to move her up. If there are any problems at all, could you please let me, her mother, or her uncle know, and we'd be happy to meet with you. Gertie will normally catch the bus home, but today I decided to take an hour off from work and make sure everything turned out alright for her."

"I believe Gertie had a very good first day and she reads so well!" The little girl beamed up at her, the gap in her front teeth immensely appealing.

"I work for the county offices as a postal investigator. Gertie's mother Elizabeth is a library assistant down at the Santa Barbara Public Library."

"And Gertie's uncle?" managed Julia.

"He's a civil engineer working for the City of Santa Barbara. We're all in our first week of new jobs and he couldn't break away today to come and pick up Gertie himself, though Mark said maybe he'll be able to make it on Friday. He says he'd really like to meet you. Anyway, I need to get Gertie home and have a snack. We're still unpacking boxes and everything's in an uproar."

"You promised you would pick me out some blue butterfly curtains today Grandma," blurted Gertie, tugging at her grandmother's sleeve.

"I did indeed; how could I have forgotten? Anyway, it was very nice meeting you Ms. Morris, and I'm sure we'll be in contact."

Julia gulped as the stout middle-aged woman pulled her granddaughter's hand as they headed down the hall, the pink of the girl's bright backpack glowing in the mid afternoon sun.

A wave of confusion settled down over Julia and her eyes flitted back to the small cup where the two rosebuds nestled against one another as they floated in the small container of water. Julia shuffled papers aimlessly on her desk for a full twenty minutes before finally giving up and heading home, thoroughly unsettled by the whole situation.

That evening at the dinner table, her entire family quizzed Gertie. Her mother Elizabeth was most concerned about whether or not Gertie had finished her lunch, since the girl was a bit underweight.

"I did mommy! I ate all my peanut butter and jelly sandwich just like you said." Liz Johnson smiled at her daughter, and reaching forward tousled her hair.

"I'm proud of you Gertie and hope you made a good impression on your teacher."

Gertie chirped up excitedly. "Ms. Morris is the nicest teacher and the prettiest in the whole school. She had her hair done in this interesting braid. I wish you could do my hair like that grandma! And how was your day mommy?" she added politely.

"Very good, I'm enjoying working at the library; it has just the right amount of peace and quiet for this world-weary woman." Liz raised her blue eyes to her mother, who gave her a reassuring pat upon her too-thin hand.

Love Never Dies

"And your day Mark?"

Mark Sebastian leaned back in the oak dining room chair and surveyed Meredith Johnson with warm brown eyes. "Just what I expected. I'm getting into the routine and can stumble through my day without too many major fiascos. And so you met her teacher?"

"Yes, she is a lovely young woman and I think Gertrude is going to have a fine year. More pork chops Mark?" Her blue eyes met his and nodded slightly. Their unspoken communication was unrecognized by the excited Gertie, who jabbered to her mother about her busy day and all the new friends she'd met.

Meredith Johnson leaned forward and placed a hand over his. "Remember that patience is a virtue my boy. Slow and steady is our motto, at least for now. You've got to hold fast for all our sakes."

Mark's teeth clenched and he set down his fork, his brown eyes meeting hers over the table.

"Patience *has* become my best virtue. I won't let you or the girls down." The tall man with the barely noticeable limp left the table, followed by the sympathetic eyes of the woman he'd come to know and love dearly and now referred to as mother. She only wished she could ease his pain and return his life to normal, and she quickly sent a message up to the heavens to make everything work to plan.

The roses faded and the banked coal nestled inside of Julia's heart still glowed in peaceful slumber as September stretched to an end. Julia stopped waiting in anticipation for a meeting with Mark Sebastian who never arrived to pick up his niece, though she found it difficult to shove her hopes aside. That final Sunday in September Julia made a belated visit to Seth's grave. She didn't know what motivated her to visit the empty grave, since he wasn't really buried underneath the marble headstone, but somehow it comforted her to see his name engraved upon the white rock and remember his passionate hands upon her willing body.

Julia sat back and talked to him, her fingers playing with little stubbles of freshly mown grass as she related to him all the tidbits regarding her week and new students. She even mentioned Gertie to him and how she'd hoped the envelope from the child's uncle had really been from him. A shadow passed over the gravestone and Julia glanced up, the sun casting the stranger's entire body into shadow. The glow surrounding his silhouette appeared like an aura and suddenly her heart began to glow and expand.

Julia reached her hand up to try to shade her eyes as he moved, and a tall man in a leather jacket and blue jeans stood quietly before her. His face was one she did not recognize; the hair a golden brown crown over eyes of milk chocolate set above a straight and slightly arrogant nose. His full lips were pursed below high cheekbones as his searching eyes peered at her from behind wire-rimmed glasses. He remained motionless for the longest moment, simply gazing down at her before he spoke. His voice was rich and deep, and irrelevantly she wondered if he was a singer.

"Do you come here often?" he asked, the glow within her spreading until her very fingertips tingled with it.

"No," she managed to croak out, "not often. But today I felt like I needed to talk to a friend."

"It's strange," he observed, peering across the wide expanse of well-manicured lawn with its pristine row of white headstones, "but this place holds no trepidation or fear for me. It's instead peaceful and welcoming." His eyes cast downward to the tombstone and he read the words engraved there aloud. "*Seth Hayes, 1970-2004. Love Never Dies*. Was he your husband?"

"No, my fiancé; well almost."

"It's hard to say goodbye to those who meant so much to us. But you know, I have come to the conclusion after all these years that things always work out for the best." His dark eyes scanned the quiet graveyard. "I also realize that sometimes things are not what they seem. A person dies and moves on to another place, but they leave so much of themselves behind that their life was not futile or lived in vain. I just hope whoever I've loved will never forget me."

"That's exactly what Seth hoped."

He smiled down at her. "Perhaps I'd better introduce myself. My name is Mark Sebastian and I'm Gertie Johnson's uncle."

The glow enveloped her completely as she peered up into his gentle brown eyes. "My fiancé here said that love never dies and I believe him. I still feel him around me and near me, enveloping my very being because I shared his soul. So how did you know I was here Mr. Sebastian?"

"A good friend told me," he said, extending a hand to help haul her to her feet. Julia brushed the grass off her beige trousers. "I would have liked to have known your fiancé. He must have been a very fortunate man."

"I was the fortunate one," said Julia joyfully, "and I have a feeling that little Gertie is as well."

"Would you care to go for a walk, madam?" he asked, presenting an arm. She hesitated only a moment before looping hers in his and they walked in the bright sunshine as the sparrows chattered and the marble on Seth's tombstone glowed in contentment.

Epilogue

It was a simple ceremony that flower-filled June, at the very same Congregational Church where Seth's empty casket lay buried behind the sanctuary. Julia's brother, sister-in-law, and parents beamed, and in Angie's arms bounced a round-eyed cherub of a toddler who miraculously kept quiet during the entire service, content to play with his father's often-lost car keys. Gertie was present as well, feeling proud and grown up and ecstatically delighted her teacher was now marrying her uncle.

Mark Sebastian looked magnificent in his somber black tux and smiled at Gertie's grandmother and mother, who sat with their hands clasped together, certain happy endings truly did happen. The church was not packed by any means. Connie Fernandez and her irrepressible secretary, Kerry, were present; along with a subdued Alvaro who wondered if his girlfriend just might be getting the wrong idea. A few teaching friends and new acquaintances Mark had made at the county offices also attended, but overall it was a quiet wedding.

As the bride kissed her new husband, she smiled into his kind, brown eyes, eager to start a new life, and turned toward the applauding audience before giving a graceful curtsey, her green eyes shining with joy. The reception was a dinner at a local Mexican restaurant and everyone sat and drank and toasted, and until quite late did all those wonderful things everyone does on their wedding day. Finally, Mark rose to set off with his bride to the island paradise of Maui for a full week-long honeymoon.

Meredith sidled up to him for one last hug.

"I'm so happy for you," she whispered. "Did you see him?"

Mark nodded and swallowed heavily. If only he could have spoken to Lucas, but regrettably the man had remained in the foyer during the entire wedding ceremony, trying to blend into the shadows. He'd worn dark, obscuring sunglasses and a long brown trench coat even on this warm June morning, his unruly long hair falling over the collar. He'd given a brief thumb's up to Mark before disappearing out of the arched doorway, his golden blonde hair glinting in the sunlight for a brief second before the sunny day swallowed up the refugee. Mark felt warm contentment steal over him. At least he knew that Lucas was safe and he sent out a small prayer to protect that fine man.

370

Love Never Dies

Meredith leaned forward and placed her arms around his neck. "You know," she said. "If I could have picked you for a relative I would have." And with that lovely statement, Mandy Gaskill kissed him soundly upon the cheek. It had been easier for all of them to disappear together to form a new family unit, and now their family had grown, encompassing the entire Morris clan and the lovely serene Julia. "Take care of her Mark," she whispered, and he promised her with a squeeze of his hand.

Their honeymoon condominium faced the ocean as unruly white waves curled and crashed against the sandy shoreline. The newlyweds felt no hurry that morning to venture to the sea and bake in the sun. Tide pools lined a small inlet and a placid seawater lagoon beckoned the snorkeler, but they made no move to rise. All that would come later. Instead, Mark Sebastian reached for his bride and cradled her within the circle of his strong arms. He looked different this morning, the brown contact lenses for once missing and allowing his eyes to reveal their true silver-gray. His new wife's hand strayed down toward his abdomen, touching briefly the intricate tattoo located there. They lingered over the entwined roses and Seth smiled as a tear of pure joy slipped from her eye. He kissed it away, savoring its saltiness.

"It's true you know; everything I said," he whispered.

"I know," she sighed. "I just wish... I wish that you could be who you really are."

"And who is that really, except your husband? Seth, Simon, Steven, they're all men of the past and you must let them hide in your memory; it's safest that way. You promised me, Julia, that you would only call me Mark, and even here in this private quiet place you must refer to me by the name you dubbed me so many months ago. Your brother, parents, sister-in-law, and later on, whatever children we parent need never know."

"And Lucas?"

"Maybe there will be a time when he can come out of the cold himself. Wouldn't it be lovely if the day arrived when Mandy could state her real name aloud? But until that day, my love, we have to remain strong and cautious for each other and them. Our secret is safe here," and with that Seth tapped his heart, where the banked fire of their combined souls burned and comforted, soothing any doubts she may ever have had. "Because I was right, you know."

"Yes" she said softly, repeating the words she knew he was thinking. "Because love never dies."

"No," he agreed, "it never does."

The End

Printed in the United States
58086LVS00001B/8

9 781589 399051